Droplets

a short story collection

by Scott A. Johnson

A CLB Publication

Published by arrangement with the author.

Droplets
A Short Story Collection

by Scott A. Johnson

ISBN-10: 0615620965
ISBN-13: 978-0615620961

Cover Art by Scott A. Johnson
Interior Layout and Kindle formatting by Owen CLB

For Tabby, Anna and Zoe, my reasons for writing.
Thanks for encouraging my behavior.

Table of Contents

Foreword

I'm not entirely sure where I'm going with this, so bear with me. Gary Braunbeck, a writer of some note and a person I'm proud to count as a friend, once wrote of me in his introduction to my novel, *City of Demons*, "This is a man who does not see the same world the rest of us do. I do not mean that he sees the world differently than us - he sees a completely different world..."

Fair enough.

I suppose it's true that my perception is skewed a little in odd places. I've been called many things...Disturbed, twisted, hilariously bent. All of it comes down to one thing: Horror. I make no apologies for the world I see, because it is the world as I truly see it. I see the fantastic in the ordinary, the bizarre in the mundane. And, I suppose, all us writers do. We must. We cultivate that sense of make-believe that many lose at the waning edge of childhood, because the world needs those crazy moments of *what if* and *why not*. Without them, the world is a boring mess of monotony. Without the glorious mayhem of make-believe, our shine tarnishes, and we become less remarkable.

What you hold in your hands is not intended for the faint of heart. It has no central theme, no through-string that binds the stories together. They are just as I imagined them, random and odd.

Chained to the Pell

Smoke from a column of ash, a long forgotten cigarette, lazily climbed past the glowing computer screen in the dim light of the living room. The cursor blinked, obnoxiously cheerful, at the disheveled figure whose hands were poised over the keyboard, a blank look on his face. Gabriel's hair stood almost on end from his constantly wringing and clutching at it, as if by pulling hard enough he could extract an idea by its roots. His bloodshot eyes showed no emotion, save that of the happy cursor reflected back upon itself.

It seemed like a good idea at the time. But then, all his ideas seemed brilliant on conception. It was never until Gabriel sat in front of his keyboard that he realized that the phantoms whirling around in his head were either shadowy memories of movies he'd seen or just so inanely stupid that to put them to paper would have been to risk being laughed out of the Department of English. He pulled at his hair again and wiped his stubbled face.

It was too quiet. Music. Music would help. It always worked in the past. His joints cracked as he pulled himself upright and stalked over to the small CD player and the pile of disks that promised release and to herald the muse. As he flipped irritably though the titles, he glanced over to the corner where his wife sat quietly reading. She had it so easy, reading her paperback trash-novels, other peoples fantasies. It took nerve to write one of your own, he thought as the jewel-boxes clacked softly together. Grease, Blues Traveler, Led Zeppelin...no, nothing with words. Words would only distract him. Something instrumental. Mozart? No, too cheerful. Gabriel was trying to write a seriously frightening piece of horror fiction. He needed something ominous, foreboding. Something light yet ballsy.

He selected a title from the pile and placed it in the player. He closed his eyes as he heard the disc begin to spin and the hauntingly lilting melody of "Tubular Bells" began to play. He strode purposefully back to his chair and sat staring into the screen. The music would speak to him. It had to. It was the theme from "The Exorcist," one of his favorite chillers. If anything could inspire his mind to formulate terror, this piece could.

He sat drinking in the music, his fingers poised at the keyboard, ready to write whatever demented little thought popped into his head. But the ideas would not come. He sat staring at the screen, the cursor blinking at him defiantly.

Gabriel thrust his chair backward and marched to the CD player, jabbing a thumb at the stop button.

"Not working tonight, Hon?"

His head snapped toward his wife, her nose still buried in the trash romance that was her favorite.

"What?" he asked, his voice a little too tight for such an innocent question.

She lifted her head slightly, her eyes meeting his. She looked so smug, he thought. She was gloating.

"Just relax," she said sweetly. "It'll come."

"Sure," he mumbled and threw himself back down in his chair.

Now it was too quiet again. The music proved to be a distraction, but the absence of sound was even more so. It seemed to him that the world had come to a standstill while waiting for him to write that all-too-important first word. He took a deep breath and stopped in mid-exhale. He'd had a thought. Not a large idea, just a faint glimmer of brilliance at the edge of consciousness. He began to type the words that were leaking from his mind.

It was then that he became aware of the sound. Like sandpaper on metal, or fingernails against glass, but rhythmic. It was driving the thought away from his fingers. He whirled around, attempting to find the noise's source, his desperate hope to silence it before the idea retreated into darkness, but he could see nothing in the room that could produce such a din. His eyes moved from one object to another until finally resting on his wife's body, still but for the rising and falling of her breast.

"Will you stop making that noise?" he shouted.

His wife looked startled.

"What noise?" As if she didn't know.

"That horrible rasping sound! It's breaking my concentration!"

"I'm only breathing."

Sure she was. That's what she always said. He took another deep breath as if in example. She didn't have to wheeze so loudly, but he'd never get her to concede, and the time wasted on the argument would take precious hours away from his writing. It wasn't worth pursuing. She'd never admit to the sound. She never did, no matter how convincing his argument. He turned his chair back toward the computer.

"Damn," he said.

"What?"

He turned to her, his irritation evident.

"I had an idea, but now I've lost it."

"Well what was it?"

The incredulity of the question struck him as surely as if someone had slapped him with a large fish, a herring perhaps, or a trout. No, nothing so high on the food chain. A bottom dweller. She was verbally abusing him with a flounder.

"If I knew what it was," he said, his anger growing, "I'd have written it down, now wouldn't I?"

She blinked and shook her head and planted her nose back in her book. He could feel the muscles in his neck grow wooden. How he would love to slam the book on her nose, but that would take time away from his quest. The perfect story was in his head somewhere, all he had to do was find it. He began to feel a bit like Ahab searching out the great whale. Now, staring at his own reflection on the blank page, he understood what it was that drove a hunter to find an elusive prey.

"I grin at thee, thou grinning monitor!" he cried.

"What?"

"Nothing," he said, suddenly aware that he'd given the thought voice.

He ran his fingers through his hair again. It was still too quiet. Perhaps some background noise would help. He pushed his chair away from the desk and reached for the remote control. As the television screen jumped to life, he pulled a cigarette from his pack and lit it. He took a long pull and held it for a moment, then let the smoke go in a small cloud that hung over the glowing computer monitor. Now the ideas would come. He set his cigarette in the ashtray and pulled his chair around.

He began typing immediately after he sat back down. The words were coming easier now, as though dictated to him. He smiled, pleased with himself for having found the right combination to appease his muse.

The telephone rang, jangling his nerves and making his knuckles cramp as his hands tightened. He attempted to keep typing as his wife casually got up and sauntered over to his desk and picked up the telephone.

"Hello? Oh, hi, Shayla. I taped Buffy for you. Hmm? Sure. Okay, I'll have it here tomorrow."

He attempted to ignore the banal conversation by typing, even mouthing the words as he set them to the screen, but the harder he tried, he more it invaded his consciousness. His fingers gave up trying to type. He turned slowly and stared, grinning and wide-eyed, at his spouse.

"Okay. I'll see you later. Bye." She cradled the receiver and turned, noticing for the first time Gabe was staring at her.

"What?"

"Why didn't you take that call in the other room?" he asked with forced patience.

"I thought it would only take a minute."

"It didn't."

"Sorry," she said, obviously annoyed at the rebuke. She went back to her chair and planted her nose in her book again.

Gabriel turned back to his monitor. All was not lost. Maybe if he read over what he had just written. His smile faded. It *was* being dictated to him. He'd just written the dialogue that had been spoken on the remarkably bad sitcom that played on the television and added the telephone prattling that had so distracted him. He let out a low groan as he selected the text and hit the delete key.

He picked up the remote control and hit the off button with force, as if he could hit it hard enough to make the television collapse under the weight of his thumb. When it didn't explode, he threw the small plastic piece to the ground and set his head in his hands.

"Having trouble, hon?"

Her voice was like nails raking across his scalp. *Having trouble, hon?* as if she didn't know. As if she couldn't recognize the signs of despair he sank into. *Having trouble, hon,* like she didn't have a care in the world.

"Yes," he said, venom dripping off the final sound.

"Well," she said, her nose never leaving her book, "Why don't you take a break?"

A break? Now? Not bloody likely. He knew what would happen if he took a break. The muse would light on his chair and, finding him absent, leave without so much as a short story, a paragraph, a word, or even a drop of muse shit. Taking a break now would be literary suicide. He glared at his wife.

"I don't think so," he said with quiet intensity.

She let out a long sigh. And what was that supposed to mean? Was it one of those *Gabe's-not-listening-to-me-again* sighs, or perhaps a *I-should-just-shut-up-and-let-him-brood* sighs? Either way, it made him bristle.

He turned his chair around to face her, a maniacal grin on his face.

"What's that supposed to mean?"

She looked up.

"What?"

"You know. That sigh. Obviously, you've got something to say."

"Well, I know what your problem is."

How could she possibly know what his problem was?

"You're trying too hard, " she said matter-of-factly. "Just write what you know. From experience, I mean."

His head reeled from the statement. His past stories had not been from experience, and they had met with some success. His heroes Clive Barker, Stephen King and Dean Koontz did not write from personal experience. At least he hoped it was not personal experience from which they wrote.

She glanced at the clock.

"It's late," she said. "I'm going to bed. Are you coming?"

"When I'm finished," he said, turning his hunched shoulders back toward the monitor.

He listened to her pad across the living room and close the door to their bedroom. Now alone, he stared again into the computer screen, her words echoing in his ears. *Just write what you know.* His first story had been about a man who butchered his family. That, lucky for her, was not based on his experience. It would be fitting if he did something like that, telling the judge afterward that he had just been following her smug advice. But no. That would take time away from his quest for a story.

Just write what you know. And what did he know, he asked himself. What experience did he have that others could relate to, yet was not so trite that it had been done a thousand times over. What was it that struck terror into his heart? At present he could only think of one thing.

It was then that he experienced a moment of clarity. Why not, he asked himself. He couldn't think of another story about the subject that so deliciously tempted him, so why couldn't his be the first? He thought of his wife sleeping and silently thanked her for her inspiration.

He almost leaped from his chair and quietly scurried into his room. She was already asleep, snoring softly, her book across her chest. He crept beside her inert form and kissed his muse gently on the forehead, then he silently rushed back to the happily blinking cursor .

His fingers began an intricate ballet upon the keys as his story began to unfold, his smile growing wider as the worried lines in his brow smoothed. This would not be what they expected of him, but they could all relate to it. It would reach them.

He pushed his chair away from the desk and read his opening line aloud.

"Smoke from a column of ash, a long forgotten cigarette, lazily climbed past the glowing computer screen in the dim light of the living room..."

Droplets

Childhood Fears

"...and God bless Mommy and Daddy and Grammie and Grampa. Amen."

Martin kissed his son on the head.

"Amen," he said. "Lights out now. Time for sleep."

Andy wriggled his ten-year-old frame into bed and pulled the blanket up to his neck.

"Daddy," said the child. "Are monsters real?"

"Of course not," he said as he stood. "Why?"

"I keep hearing stuff. At night. When it's dark."

"Like what, buddy?"

"Scary stuff."

His son looked so small to Martin, even though his age now ran in double-digits. The toddler bed was long gone, replaced by a twin mattress and a "big boy" headboard. Every day brought a new discovery, a new assertion of independence. But with the blankets pulled up just beneath his chin, his eyes wide in fear, Martin could not see him as anything other than his baby boy.

"Well," he said as he sat on the bed. "This is an old house. It's bound to make some weird noises, don't you think?"

Andy looked up at his father through brown curls.

_____

"I guess so."

"There's nothing to be afraid of," said Martin. "Your mom and I are just down the hall, and we'd never let anything hurt you. You know that, right?"

Andy nodded.

"Good," he said. "Now get some sleep. You have school in the morning. I love you."

"Love you too, Dad. G'night."

The child meant the world to Martin. What Andy lacked in size, he made up for in pure precocious zeal. On every subject, Andy had an opinion. Every question, a theory. And he was only too happy to explain his wondrous view of the world with anyone who happened near. To some people, he was obnoxious. To Martin, he was everything a son was supposed to be.

He smiled as he closed the door to Andy's room and made his way down the hall. Every kid went through the fear of the dark at one point or another. Andy's imagination was so vivid, it was little wonder that every sound made him jump. The sooner he confronted his fears, the better.

"How's he doing?" asked Sarah as he closed the door to their room. She sat on the bed, reading with her ankles crossed.

"He's fine," said Martin. "Just scared of the dark. Said he heard noises."

She looked up over her book and between strands of her dark hair.

"Again? He's been having nightmares all week."

"Yeah," said Martin. "I went through the same thing when I was about his age. It's normal."

"Maybe." She seemed unconvinced. "But he was so sure there was something in his room."

"Like what? A _monster_?" he laughed. "I'm telling you, the sooner he gets over this fear, the better. You don't want him still sleeping with us, do you?"

_____

"Well," she cocked an eyebrow and grinned. "No. I can think of other things I'd like to do in our bed."

"Good," he said as he flopped onto the bed next to her. "Because we haven't had any adult snuggle time since he started this."

"What makes you think you're getting any, mister?" she giggled.

He pressed his lips to hers. She faked fighting against him for just a second, then wrapped her arms around his body and dragged him down on top of her. His hands roved her body, and found her soft in all the places he remembered and cherished.

"How fast can you get out of those clothes?" she purred into his ear.

One hand fumbled with his pants while the other found the soft warmth of her breast and his mouth found hers again. He tasted her lips and moved his zipper down.

"Daddy!"

They froze. The sound echoed from down the hall. At least he hadn't left his room this time, but damn the kid had bad timing.

"He sounds scared," she said, worry in her voice.

"Probably heard a noise again," said Martin as he zipped up and headed to the door.

"Be nice," she called after him.

"I always am."

It would be easier to do as his father had, told the kid to suck it up and be a man. He remembered countless nights laying in the dark, tears dampening his pillow as he was sure some toothy beast crept ever-closer in the darkness. He hated his father for it, and promised himself he'd never be the same. But still, at least now he understood *why* his father handled his childhood fears the way he did.

"What's up, sport?" he asked as he opened Andy's door. The boy looked so small, huddled against his headboard with his sheets pulled up close to his chin.

"I heard something."

"Like what?"

"Breathing. From over there." He pointed to the closet.

The old *Monster in the Closet* routine. The dark, cavernous confines of the closet always held something. He smiled to himself as he crossed the room.

"In here?" he whispered. Andy nodded.

Martin flattened himself against the wall like a television cop and slunk to the door. He held up three fingers to Andy, who gripped his blanket tighter.

"Three," he mouthed. "Two...*ONE!*"

Martin sprang to the closet door and threw it open.

"Whoever's in there, come on out!" he bellowed. "Monsters aren't welcome here!"

The closet looked as he knew it would, wrecked from having a ten-year-old owner. But there were not drooling monsters, no slithering snakes, no creatures with eyes that burned like fiery coals. Still, better to finish out the game. He rifled through the closet until he was sure Andy would be satisfied, then he backed out, turned out the light, and shut the door until it clicked.

"Okay, buddy," he said. "No monsters in there. Satisfied?"

Andy grinned and nodded. Martin leaned down and kissed his son's head.

"I love you. Now get some sleep, okay? No more monsters."

He shut the door behind him and made his way back to his own room.

"How is he?"

"He's fine," said Martin as he pulled his shirt over his head. "Monsters in the closet."

"I remember those," said Sarah. "Was the closet door open or closed?"

"Mostly closed. Opened maybe a crack."

"That's what did it," she said as she reached for her husband. "I could never sleep with the closet door even a little open. Still can't."

He pulled her close and kissed the curve of her neck.

"Not even with me here to protect you?"

"Nope," she giggled. "Closet monster beats big strong he-men like you."

"Closet monster's no match for me."

He slid his hand beneath her waist-band and along the smooth skin of her hip. She sighed as she wrapped her legs around his waist and pulled him close to her.

"You gonna sleep with those pants on?" she teased.

"Daddy!"

"Oh for crying out loud..."

"He-man has to go protect and serve," she giggled.

"This isn't over," he huffed. "He's got to get over this."

Martin tried to calm himself as he stormed down the hall. Two months without sex would make any man grumpy, and to be jerked out of it when he was so close was infuriating. Still, he reminded himself, Andy was just a kid. Yelling at him wouldn't do any good and would probably piss Sarah off. Deep breaths. Deep breaths.

"You okay, sport?" he said as he opened the door. Andy hadn't moved since the last time he came in.

"I heard it again," he said. "Louder."

He was scared, that was plain to see. He wasn't just calling out in the night to be a pain. Something really scared the kid. Martin looked toward the closet. The door was open, maybe an inch or two.

"I closed that, didn't I?" he said.

Andy nodded.

"It opened by itself," he said.

Bullshit. Doors didn't open by themselves. Faulty latches, maybe, but they didn't open themselves.

"Oh, I don't think so," said Martin. "Let me see."

He marched to the closet and slammed the door, then pulled without turning the knob. It pulled free without much effort.

"Aha! The doorknob doesn't work right." He pushed against the closet door until he heard a click, then tried the knob again. When the door didn't come free, the turned triumphantly to his son.

"There," he said. "It won't come open by itself again."

"Are you sure?" said Andy.

"Look," said Martin as he sat on the bed. "What probably happened was the air conditioner clicked on. It blew the door open, and the breathing sound you heard was air rushing out the door."

He didn't look convinced.

"There's nothing in the closet. And I'm right down the hall. I promise you, I wouldn't let anything get you."

"Thanks Dad," said Andy.

"Now get some sleep," he said. "And let Mommy and Daddy get some sleep too, how 'bout?"

"Sorry."

"Don't be sorry," he said. "Look, I used to be afraid of the dark. But whenever I heard something strange, I had to tell myself that it wasn't real. Just keep telling yourself that it's not real and you might be able to figure out what the sounds really are."

"Okay," said Andy.

"Sleep," said Martin. "We'll fix that door in the morning."

He closed the door and made his way back down the hall. When he opened the door to his room, Sarah lay naked on her stomach with her head propped in her hands.

"If you're done protecting him, maybe you could serve me?" she teased.

Martin didn't waste time with a reply, but instead peeled his pants off and left them where they lay by the door.

"Very nice," she said of his nude body. "Now come over here."

She was soft, warm. He ached to touch her bare skin. For two months, she wore t-shirts and sweat-pants to bed and they slept with Andy between them. For a few nights, it was fine, but he missed the warmth of her butt curved against him, the smell of her hair. He loved his son, but between his fear of the dark and Sarah's body, he'd choose his wife in a hot second.

Their bodies slid together like puzzle pieces, each meant to lock around the other in perfect symmetry. She felt so good.

"Daddy!"

Their eyes snapped open and locked with each other's.

"You're fucking kidding me," he said.

"Martin..."

"No way this happens." He withdrew and climbed off the bed, stormed to the door and snatched his pants up.

"Be gentle," she said.

"Sarah, he has to get over this. I'm not going to go for the next six months without having sex with my wife!"

"I don't like it either," she said. "But he's really scared."

"He's got to get over this."

Martin zipped his pants and stormed down the hall. Bad enough to be stopped before he started, but in the middle? Not like the kid knew, or would even understand what he was interrupting for a few more years, but still, in the middle? Three times in one night? It was too much.

"What?" he said, louder than he'd intended, as he opened Andy's bedroom door.

"I heard..."

"From the closet again?"

"No," said Andy. "It moved. I heard it move under my bed."

"What did it sound like?"

"Claws," said the child. "On the wood floor. I heard them go under

———————————

my bed."

"Andy," he said with forced patience. "Your mom and I are trying to get some sleep. We can't do that with you calling us every five minutes."

"But it went under my bed," protested the child.

"Oh for Pete's sake..." he groaned as he squatted and threw up the bedskirt. "There's nothing under here."

"But I heard it..."

"There's nothing under there," said Martin. "Now, son, this is ridiculous. You've got to stop. Now go to sleep, and don't call me in here again."

"But..."

"I mean it. If I get called in here again for nothing, there's going to be trouble."

"Okay."

He was crestfallen, and the little boy's expression made his father's heart ache, but it had to be done. Not just because if he didn't, he'd never have a moment's peace with his wife again, but because Andy needed to confront his fears. Ten years old was old enough to start acting like a young man.

"I love you," he said.

"Love you too," pouted Andy.

"Goodnight." He pulled the door closed behind him.

* * *

But it was real. He heard it. Whatever it was, he heard it. It was in the closet. How Daddy'd missed it, he didn't know. It must've hidden from him. When the closet door opened, blazing orange eyes peered out of the darkness. He almost felt its wet rasps as it growled in the closet. But Daddy came the first time and it shrank back.

The second time, it must've snuck out. It must've hidden somewhere else. When Daddy pushed the door all the way closed, Andy dared to hope. Maybe it was trapped. Maybe he could sleep in his room, by himself,

———————————

without Mommy and Daddy's protection. But when Daddy left, he heard it again. He heard long claws click together in the pitch black of his room, and he knew. It wasn't trapped. It was out.

In the pool of light from the window, hadn't he seen a fleeting shadow, serpentine and scaly as it darted back into he darkness? Didn't its claws click against the floor as it scuttled about? The sounds came closer. He didn't want to call for his father, but they were closer, right at the foot of his bed. If he hadn't called, the thing might have climbed up and gotten him. But when Daddy came in, it darted under the bed. Daddy looked, but he couldn't see it. It hid from him.

Daddy was mad. Andy knew why too. They weren't sleeping. They were trying to do what Daddy called "Grown-up Time," whatever that meant. He knew it involved them both being without their clothes and lots of noise, but it didn't sound like much fun to him. Daddy didn't want him to call again, but he was scared. Daddy said monsters didn't exist, but Daddy was wrong.

He listened as his father's heavy footsteps faded down the hall. The door closed down the hall. It would wait until it heard the sounds of "Grown-up Time."

He clutched the comforter tight and pulled it up to just under his nose. A few moments later, he heard his mother giggle. Whatever "Grown-up Time" was, it sounded gross.

From beneath his bed, he heard a click, a ping against the metal bedframe. Then another. Then another. Then a long, low breath let out in a growl.

"Not there," whispered Andy. "Not real."

The pings beneath his bed increased as what sounded like a thousand claws tapped against his bedframe. It was moving.

"You're not real." His voice caught in his throat so the words came out in a half-hearted croak. "You're not real."

The tapping moved to the foot of his bed, then he felt something

_____

pull his blanket. He stared as a large black shape rose up from beneath. A needle-sharp foot glistened black in the darkness, and another, and another. The front of the shape shone with huge black pincers that dripped. Its breath was foul.

"You're not real!" he shouted. "You're not real!"

Let Daddy hear. Let him interrupt "Grown-up Time." He'd take the spanking, and the grounding, and whatever else Daddy gave him if he just made the thing go away.

Its legs rippled as it moved forward, silent on the blanket. He felt them through the fabric as they pricked his legs.

Don't scream. Don't call Daddy. It's not there. It's not real. Monsters aren't real it's not real don't scream don't scream...

"DADDY!"

He heard the door down the hall fly open, heard his fathers footsteps as they ran down the hall. Heard his mother's softer footsteps as she called out to him. But the thing was on top of him. The needle-sharp feet punctured his blanket and his chest. The sharp pincers closed against the sides of his face. He couldn't scream any longer, he couldn't cry out. He couldn't move to fight or to run to his mother's side. He saw. He felt. He smelled its horrible breath like rotting garbage. He heard his parents scream as they threw open the door, felt his body thud to the floor as the monster dragged him away, to the open window, and out into the damp night.

He was awake when it started to eat him. And all he could think was of his father's words. *Monsters aren't real.*

_____

Closet Boy

Another well-meaning neighbor tipped off the authorities, which led several large men to break down the door and drag Mary out of the house while they searched. She screamed, hysterical over what they were sure to find, begged them not to release him from his cage. They didn't understand, she wailed. It wasn't child abuse.

She heard the sickening sound of twisting wood inside, sending her into a greater frenzy than before, as the men used pry-bars to pull the latch and lock from the closet. Shouts of discovery from inside the house seemed to paralyze her, the look on her face a mixture of rage and terror. As the social workers stepped out of the house, she went limp in her captors' arms, sobbing uncontrollably at the sight of the seven-year old towheaded boy between them. His large dark eyes seemed to bore through her as he stared intently at the object of his anger.

"The tip was right on," said the man closest to him to the woman who put a blanket around the boy's shoulders. "Sick bitch locked him in the closet. Looks like she's been feeding him under the door."

The woman turned toward the limp figure in the officer's arms with disgust in her eyes.

"You're entitled to representation," she said, her voice full of venom. "But you're going to prison for this. I'll see to it." She nodded her head

---

toward the officers and kept her eyes fixed on the glazed stare of the woman as they put her in the back seat of the cruiser. What could make a woman do such a thing to her own child, she wondered as the police car rolled away, the terrified face of the woman still staring unblinking at the child on the lawn.

"We're ready for you," said a voice behind her.

She crossed the lawn, doing her best to replace the anger at the boy's mother on her face with kind sympathy. The situation was, sadly routine for her. Parents who, for one reason or another, thought it was perfectly acceptable to starve their children, or beat them, or lock them in closets. Mary Carter was of the worst sort, claiming that her son deserved to be mistreated in some way. As she was drug away, Linda felt cold toward her, ignoring the look of fear on her face. In her mind, she imagined the boy, Eon, with the same look when she threw him into that closet.

Eon stood between to officers with a blanket wrapped around his shoulders to protect him from the cold night air and cover his dirty pajamas. He watched as the taillights of the police car disappeared into the darkness, ignoring the approach of the social worker. She wouldn't be gone long enough, Linda told himself. They never were. In the meantime, he was free of the closet, of her.

"Hi," said the social worker, squatting in front of him. "My name is Linda. I'm here to help you." Establish trust, she thought, then see to his health. The warrant gave her the ability to place Eon in a Foster home right away, but she wanted to be certain that there were no hidden injuries. Too many times the bruises and dirt hid the worst of the pain. She'd already put in a call to a psychologist she trusted, but the hospital would be his first stop.

"Mommy says I'm bad," said Eon without looking up. "She's the only one who really loves me."

His words gripped her heart like an iron hand, squeezing so that she had to fight back the tears that came every time a tiny voice equated abuse with love.

"Your mom's not feeling well, honey," she said in her best soothing voice. "She needs help. In the meantime, we're going to take you someplace safe."

"We found this on him too," said a deep voice behind her. She turned to see a large man, his face etched in remorse for the boy, holding out several lengths of hemp rope. "She'd tied him up."

"No one will ever do this to you again," said Linda as she hugged him. She hoped he would not notice her trembling hands, but she could not help the rage she felt toward the woman who dared call herself a mother.

After a brief, but thorough, examination, the boy was given a clean bill of health from the physician on call. The rope burns on his wrists were treated with antiseptic and the dirt was washed from his face. Eon was a little undernourished, and was obviously in need of a good night's sleep in a real bed, but was otherwise in good shape. Linda took him to the home of a trusted foster family, who welcomed him warmly, despite the late hour, with hot coca and a clean change of clothes. Mrs. Johnson smiled brightly with grandmotherly countenance on the boy before shooing Linda out the door with assurances that everything would be all right. No matter how many children Linda had brought to Mrs. Johnson over the years, she always doted on them until they were placed in a permanent home, and always kept in contact with them when they left. Linda left Eon that evening feeling better about his welfare.

The drive home was uncharacteristically silent that night. Normally, Linda would roar down I-35 toward Austin with her radio blaring, singing half-remembered lyrics at the top of her lungs. Tonight, however, Mary Carter was on her mind. Pop music just seemed to grate on her nerves tonight in a way it didn't usually. Only the rushing air of the wind outside the car and rhythmic bump of the highway seemed appropriate as she rehearsed what she would say to Mary in the morning. Her job dictated that she could not be overly nasty to her, only inform her of her crimes and the punishment they entailed. But the things she would like to say, however...

Droplets

She fumed as she drove, not really paying attention to where she was going or who else was traveling at this ungodly hour. Occasionally the air was split by Linda spewing venomous oaths and angry gibes toward the woman who was not even there.

It was nearly three in the morning when she finally put the key in the lock and stepped inside her apartment. She skipped her usual routine of a hot bath and a beer, as she had to be up in less than five hours, and went straight to bed, where she lay sleepless until the sun rose. Why had she become a social worker, she wondered. It certainly wasn't the pay. No matter how much money she made, it couldn't buy back the memories of battered bodies and tear-stained cheeks that were now hers forever. Was it because she enjoyed feeling that she was fighting the good fight, righting wrongs and all the rest of the super hero bullshit? More than likely, it was because she knew she could never have children of her own. Cancer had seen to that. Now, every child was hers to protect.

As the sun peeked through her window, she got up, frustrated and exhausted. No sense staying in bed, she thought. Might as well get up and get on with it. She showered and dressed, making sure to conceal the bags beneath her eyes with makeup, then ate a light breakfast before heading to the hays county lock-up. The thought of seeing Mary Carter again so soon after her incarceration was distasteful to her, especially without the tempering effects of a full night's sleep. She wondered if she would be able to keep her temper in check long enough to say what was necessary.

As she passed through the checkpoints, she nodded and smiled pleasantly to the guards. Though she'd been here dozens of times, and most of them knew her on sight, there were still rules that had to be followed. Every entrant into the holding areas must be searched for weapons, drugs, or anything else that wasn't allowed. Credentials had to be checked and rechecked, then, finally, she would be allowed in to the interview room.

She could see Mary sitting behind the table through the large window of the room. She looked different to Linda somehow, calmer, more refreshed. How that woman could sleep after putting that child through what she did only served to stir a coal of anger in her stomach. She passed through the doorway and slammed the steel door behind her.

"Good morning, Ms. Carter," she said tersely. "My name is Linda Green. I'm with Child Protective Services."

"I know what you think of me," said Mary with a weak smile. "I'm a monster, right? A disgrace to motherhood?"

"That's not for me to decide," she replied sharply. "That's for the courts." She looked around, as if realizing for the first time that something was missing.

"Ms. Carter, where is your attorney?"

"Don't want one," replied Mary casually.

"Why not?"

"What's the maximum penalty for child abuse and neglect?"

"It's a federal offense. You could get life."

"Good," she said flatly. "Last night was the first good night's sleep I've had in three years. Eon's your problem now. You deal with him. I want to be in here where it's safe."

"He's a seven-year old boy, for Christ's sake," said Linda, her voice choked with anger and wonderment. "You're his mother."

"I been his mother for seven years, and I'm telling you, I can't do it no more." She sat back in her chair, no trace of emotion showing on her face.

"You make me sick," said Linda as she spun back toward the door.

"Be careful where you put him," called Mary after her.

Linda's hands shook with rage. That woman dared call herself a mother. In a perfect world, women like her would not be allowed to have children. And what did she mean, "where it's safe?" It was as if...

Her cellular telephone interrupted her mental rant.

"This is Linda," she spat into the phone.

"It's Marcus," came the voice from the other side. There was something in it that told her he was shaken. "You have to get over to Mrs. Johnson's place."

"Why?" she asked, her coworker's obvious state giving rise to panic in her voice.

"Not over the phone," he said. "Just get over here now. It's bad."

She pressed the button releasing the call and walked briskly to her car, her mind reeling with every different reason that a seasoned social worker like Marcus Trudot would be so rattled. He'd seen it all, or so she thought until now. As she sped down I-35, the words of Mary Carter seemed to float wraithlike through her mind. *Be careful where you put him.*

As she pulled around the corner of Mrs. Johnson's street, she felt the bottom of her stomach drop out at the number of police cars parked in her yard. The uniforms with lost expressions stood behind the barrier tape, moving with learned motions instead of any real desire. Something had shaken them all, destroyed a small part of their sense of reason.

Her car jostled to a halt and she half-ran up the lawn, identification in hand, as Marcus stepped out of the front door. His normally dark skin had a pale caste to it and great tears welled in his eyes. Though she was no more than a few feet from him, he seemed not to see Linda's approach.

"Marcus," she said. "What the hell is going on?"

"It's horrible," he said without looking up. "I'd have never thought..."

She felt her stomach clench as he walked out into the yard. What had Mrs. Johnson done, she wondered. After so many years of trust, had it all been misplaced? What had she done to the boy? *Be careful where you put him,* that's what Mary Carter had said, as if she cared for Eon.

She stepped into the house and followed the trail of lost looking officers to the kitchen, where Mrs. Johnson lay cooling in a pool of sticky crimson. The butcher knife that was used for her dissection jutted menacingly from the vinyl flooring.

Linda felt her stomach revolt against such an improbable sight.

The old woman was nothing but kindness toward anyone, and Linda felt ashamed for having so quickly suspected her of wrongdoing.

"Where's Eon," she asked an officer. His eyes widened as he pointed to a bedroom deeper into the house. There was true horror in his eyes at the mention of the boy, though he said nothing before turning back toward his work.

Time seemed to slow for her as she passed through the house, beyond the crime scene to the room where the officer had indicated the boy was. Whether dead or alive, the cop had not said, and Linda wondered which was more merciful. Had he been murdered like his caretaker? Or had he seen it happen? She approached the two uniforms that surrounded the door to the room and flashed her identification. They opened the door to reveal Eon, very much alive. His face betrayed no emotion as his large eyes scanned her up and down, recognizing the revulsion on her face at the blood on his clothes and hands. The blood on his face, so obviously not his own, seemed to cause Linda some concern, as did the shining handcuffs that kept his wrists together.

"Eon," she said, disbelief thick in her voice. "What happened?"

"I been bad," he said with a grin. "Mommy says I'm bad."

"Eon," she said again, her voice trembling in disbelief. "What happened?"

"She didn't want to play. But I played with her anyway."

His dark eyes glinted with malevolence that she had not seen before, and suddenly Linda was taken with realization. His face no longer held a child's innocence and joy, but twisted into a mask of hatred, of pure darkness. Evil was no longer the sole propriety of the adult.

She slowly backed out of the room as the boy's lilting giggles echoed in her ears. In a daze, she went to the front lawn where she found Marcus sitting on the hood of a police cruiser, trying to make sense of the boy. She sat beside him, saying nothing. There was not anything she could say that would have eased their minds or answered the myriad of questions they had.

Droplets

When at last the silence was broken, it was Marcus that turned to her, eyes still haunted by the giggling cherub.

"I quit," he said softly. "I can't do this anymore."

Death Around
the Corner

The first thing Jason noticed about the old man was that he was out of place. People dressed like him just didn't mix with the refuse and college students that made up Austin's Sixth-Street district. More so than place, he seemed out of time, a walking throw-back to a day when people did not leave the darkened rooms of their own homes without wearing a tie and jacket. He had to be part of an act or maybe part of a performance troupe. From the top of his bowler hat to his dark blazer over a pale gray vest, pinstriped slacks, it was like a character from an old Marx Brothers movie just stepped into the street. He even wore spats - Spats, for crying out loud! - to cover the tops of his shoes. It wasn't the old man's clothes that held his attention, however, but the glittering gold chain and pocketwatch. Costume or no, Jason knew something worth stealing when he saw it. But as the old man ambled along the street, his cane swinging to and fro, the passers-by seemed either blind or too jaded to see him. Save for Jason, the old man might have been invisible.

He was a target, an opportunity, too tempting for Jason pass up. Seldom did anyone so overtly rich venture to his part of town. Most of them found the loud music and drunken debauchery of Sixth Street distasteful, and preferred to stay in their plush restaurants to sip champagne from flutes instead of beer from bottles. To Jason, however, Sixth Street was home, and a good place for a thief. His nimble fingers could pull a wallet from any drunkard's pocket without worry of getting caught, and his smile was witty, his eyes bright, enough to steal something even more precious than money from the women who seemed to find him irresistible.

It was a good life, most nights. He pulled enough money from his exploits to pay his rent, although he seldom needed an apartment due to the open invitations and beds from so many women. But, as always, his restless nature crept up behind him. No one stayed lucky forever. A thief was only good if he could blend in with the crowd, if he wasn't recognized wherever he went. He'd been on Sixth Street too long, he knew, when bartenders greeting by name and with a smile. He grew wary of the same faces and music, sure that he'd be caught soon and put back in jail. It was time to move on.

But then the curious old man walked by, whistling of all things, and distracted him. Jason found himself following him just to see if it was some sort of costume, if the man was part of a comedy troupe that played in one of the bars. He would've fit right in, the way the outsider twirled his moustache and smiled broadly, a living caricature of an old-world dandy. It was as if he thought that predators such as Jason did not even exist, or that he was so above them that they wouldn't dare. It would be too easy.

Jason followed the old man for nearly a half hour, fascinated by his jaunty walk and strange appearance. He stalked him as he chose the perfect moment to relieve the old man of the weight of the inviting bulge in his jacket pocket. The man continued walking, oblivious to his shadow until he came to an abrupt stop on a corner.

His heart pounded as he ducked back into a shaded doorway. Maybe the old man saw him. He watched as the old man checked his pocket watch, then smiled and snapped it closed. As if on cue, a car came careening around the corner, squealing its tires as it pitched from side to side.

From his vantage point, Jason could see that the man did not move, even as the car zipped dangerously past him. He could also see the bicyclist as he came from around the other way. He wanted to cry out, to warn the cyclist, but it happened too fast. He could only watch in horror as the car struck the front tire of the bike, bending it awkwardly inward, sending the rider over the handlebars and into the windshield, his head erupting in a burst of crimson. The car screeched to a halt, throwing the rider more than a dozen feet from its final resting place, his body at impossible angles, leaking life onto the pavement.

A crowd gathered, full of horrified gasps and screams to call the police and an ambulance. They surged forward, equal parts pinning the grief-stricken driver in his car, and attending the already cooling body that lay on the ground. It seemed surreal to Jason, strange that even amid all the chaos, the people pushed right past the old man as though he didn't even exist.

The old man moved purposefully toward the body, and crouched by what was left of its head. He seemed to be whispering to the cyclist. Now was Jason's chance, he realized as the other side of his mind jarred into motion. He darted forward, through the crowd, and gave the man's jacket a light brush, then he sprinted away, clutching his prize tightly in his hand. He'd be far away long before the old man knew his pocket had been picked.

When he finally stopped, behind an Italian restaurant's dumpster, his hands shook badly from the scene he'd left. It wasn't like he never saw an accident before. He'd seen several, some involving a particularly bloody fatality. What made his limbs tremble, however, was neither the blood nor carnage, but the old man. There was something odd about the way he coldly stood, as if he knew what was about to happen. He could have stopped it, but did nothing but stand placidly by and let the drama unfold.

Jason looked around, making sure that no one had followed nor seen him. Escaping at night was one thing. There were scores of shadows in

---

which he could hide. Broad daylight, however, was a trick for only the most skilled of his kind. Care had to be taken.

He looked down into his still-trembling hand to see his prize. His expression of fearful glee melted to disappointment. It was not a wallet, but an address book that he held. There was no money, no credit cards, not even a driver's license. All it had in it were names and addresses.

"Excuse me," said a voice barely above a whisper. Jason looked up to see the cyclist, what was left of him, standing directly in front of him. "What do I do now?"

His legs kicked of their own accord, sending Jason backward into the street, his eyes still riveted to the gruesome apparition. It stood there with a puzzled look on its face, as though it were completely natural for it to be here, conversing with the living. He tore his eyes away just in time to see a large white car screech to a halt in front of him, the angry driver shouting to get out of the way.

Without knowing where he was going, Jason broke into a dead run, putting as much distance between him and the specter as he could. He dodged between buildings and back alleys until he could no longer run, his lungs threatening to explode with every breath. He stopped in front of an old movie house and crouched, panting and sweating, beneath the awning.

"Um..." he heard again. He lifted his eyes to see the dead cyclist standing before him again. "I really could use some direction here."

"Go away," he croaked. His mouth went dry as the cyclist took a step toward him. "Get away from me!"

"But where do I go?" begged the wraith.

"Go to hell!" screamed Jason, cowering in a corner and closing his eyes against the vision. After a few moment's silence, he opened his eyes again to find the sidewalk full of only normal people, staring at him. He pushed himself to his feet and ran down the sidewalk, frantically searching for the way to his apartment.

He didn't stop running until his own door was safely locked behind

---

him. He pulled the blinds down and crawled onto his couch, watching every shadow carefully. The specter still loomed heavily in his thoughts, beckoning him with his plaintive questions. He went to his refrigerator and pulled a beer, wrenching the top off and downing the entirety of the bottle in no time. Better, he thought. That was better. He threw the bottle in the sink with the other empty bottles and retrieved another from the refrigerator. As the second beer disappeared down his gullet, he felt better still, telling himself that it was just trauma. There was no specter, no apparition. He saw the wreck, saw the rider die. His mind was playing tricks on him.

Another bottle in the sink and a third in his hand and he'd managed to convince himself that there was nothing more to it. Just his imagination. He sat down on the couch and gingerly picked the address book off the coffee table. It was old and worn, probably from years of use. Its black leather cover creaked as he opened it, revealing the first few yellowed pages beneath. Strange, he thought, as he looked from name to name. Every entry on the first dozen or so pages were crossed out, some in blue, some in red. As the pages grew more white, he almost lost interest. Page after page of crossed through names was not enough to keep his interest. Halfway through the address book, however, he found names not yet crossed, and though that alone would not have stopped him, two things in particular made the hairs on the nape of his neck prickle. Beside one name was the address of the corner where the cyclist died. Beside it, in a separate column was a time, which happened to be around the time of the accident.

The second thing that gave him pause, and truly made his skin creep, was several names down on the page. There, next to an address he'd never been to, was his own name.

He stared for a few moments, unable to comprehend. How did the old man know his name? And what was this address? And the time, 10:30 a.m. What did it mean? He took another long gulp from his bottle. Someone else, he thought. Someone else must live there. His was not an uncommon name, first nor last. So what if the old man had another acquaintance named

Jason Keller? It was just a strange coincidence. And the time, probably an appointment, was not so strange. An old man like that probably had to write things down, lest he forget them.

It was getting late, his usual time to head back out to the streets to ply his trade, but the day had been too strange. He could tell himself, and maybe even believe, anything he wanted. But there was still an uneasy feeling that he just couldn't shake. He finished his beer and tossed the bottle into the sink, reminding himself to take out the garbage in the morning, then he slumped down on the couch and drifted into a dreamless sleep.

When he awoke the next morning, his burning eyes and pounding head drew his attention away from any thought of ghosts and address books. The best thing for him, he decided as he rolled off the couch, was a shower.

Once in the bathroom, the water rained down on him like a baptism, cleaning away the pain in his skull and memories of the day before. He lost track of how much time he'd spent in the shower, reveling in the warmth of the water. By the time he emerged, steam hung heavy in the air of the bathroom, fogging the mirror. He toweled off his head and wiped his hand across the mirror's surface. When he looked at the space he'd cleared, his blood froze in his veins.

"Can you help me?" said the girl.

It wasn't that she was unattractive. Quite the opposite, in fact, but her sallow face, the way she moved, quivering as though unable to keep still, set his nerves on edge.

He spun around to face her but found himself in front of only a blank wall.

"Please?" said her voice.

He slowly turned back toward the mirror, finding that she'd moved since he looked away. She now was standing closer, enough so that he thought he could smell her acrid breath.

"What...Who are you?"

"I'm Andie," she said, as if he should know her. "Andie Plummer?"

The name struck a chord in his memory. Where had he heard it before? No, he realized. Not heard, but seen. It was only four names above his in the address book.

"I don't know what to do now," she said plaintively.

He turned his back on the mirror and walked quickly to his closet. He dressed in the fastest way possible and ran out the door to the apartment, trying to find any place where he could escape the girl. She couldn't be real, could she? There were explanations aplenty for the cyclist, but he'd never seen her before. Why would he just make her up?

He happened to glance up as he left the building, catching his reflection in a large window across the street. There, following him closely, was the girl.

Jason didn't bother looking behind him, as somehow he knew she wouldn't be there. He began to walk briskly down the street, consciously looking away from any reflection, but feeling her presence heavier with each step. When he couldn't help himself anymore, he glanced up toward another window, finding her hot on his heels.

He quickened his pace, hoping he could outrun her. As he rounded the next corner, he nearly fell over himself as a young boy stepped out in front of him. The boy wore pajamas and had red marks around his throat, his bluish skin evidence that he should not be here.

"Where do I go now, mister?" asked the boy.

Jason gaped like a fish, his jaws flapping with words that he didn't know and wouldn't form.

"What about me? I was here first," he heard the girl say.

"No!" he cried, running headlong across the street. For the second time in as many days, he had no idea where he was going, only that he had to get away from them.

Around another corner came two, each impossibly wounded with large holes in their heads. It seemed to them to be perfectly normal, to walk about with their brains leaking from their skulls, but Jason felt the last of his sanity slip from his mind as he screamed, throwing himself backward into the street. He turned and saw the reflection of the girl coming fast, realizing too late that she was trapped in the reflection of the bumper of an oncoming car.

An instant of pain, indescribable in its intensity, and he found himself on his back on the pavement, staring at a skyline he didn't recognize. It was a part of town he'd never been to, but in his futile attempt to get away had wound up here. His head lolled from side to side on the pavement as he lay in a spreading pool of blood. He let his head fall toward a nearby corner, and was not at all surprised to see the old man walking his way.

"I believe you have something of mine," he said, reaching into Jason's pocket. He pulled the address book out, though Jason did not seem to recall taking it with him. "Made a mess of things, didn't you? It'll take me a while to get that business with the cyclist sorted out. Hell, indeed," he smiled.

"What do I do now?" whispered Jason.

"Simple, my boy," said the old man. "You die."

Jason smiled as the light faded from his eyes.

The Dinner Party

"Don't worry Lacy," said Gwen with a sly grin. "Believe me, after tonight, you won't have to worry about another man breaking your heart."

Lacy gave a weak smile. She doubted anything that Gwen, or her friends, could do would cheer her up. It couldn't. Dennis was her first real boyfriend. Sure, she'd dated through high school and her freshman year of college, but never seriously. A kiss here and there, but no boy was ever allowed to break her underwear rule. Dennis was the only man she thought about growing old with. He made her feel alive, beautiful. She gave him her virginity after dating for over a month, and the next morning, he was gone. She found him later, his arm around another girl's waist, and he acted like he'd never seen her before. Worse, when she tried to talk to him, he laughed at her. Like anyone would believe a stud like him would go out with, let alone bed, someone as dowdy and plain as she. It was the single most crushing blow she had suffered in her life.

Gwen listened to her cry, hugged her tight when Lacy asked why he would leave her. Together, they laughed over imagined revenge schemes, each one more ridiculous than the last. Gwen was her truest friend. But despite everything, she still felt hollow inside. She ached for him in a way she was sure no one could ever understand.

Now, as they walked up the path toward the stately mansion, she couldn't help but wonder whom these friends of Gwen's were.

"It's just a dinner," she said, and "you'll never see men the same way again."

It was a sisterhood, Gwen explained, a support group. But more than that, it was a way for jilted girls to gain strength from one another, and never be manipulated by sex-crazed apes again.

Gwen rang the doorbell and smiled mischievously to her friend. Lacy had no illusions. If this group consisted of women like Gwen, all of them slender with full hair and perfect skin, all of them brimming with confidence, it would only serve to remind her of her own imperfections. Her hair, though blonde, was straight and wispy around the edges. She was not obese, but could no way pass for thin. It was no wonder that she gave in to Dennis so easily. In truth, he made her feel beautiful and she craved him. And it was no wonder that he left her for the cutesy cheerleader-type. Compared to her, Lacy was hideous.

Lacy raised her eyes when she heard the door open, only to be pleasantly surprised by the girl who answered. She was roughly the same build as Lacy, every bit as average, down to her mouse-brown hair. There was, however, something about her that Lacy envied. It was the confident air that radiated from her, the way she held her head and the ease of her smile.

"You must be Lacy," said the girl as she took Lacy's hand. "I'm Rhonda. Don't worry honey, we take care of our own."

"But I'm not one of your own..."

"Yet," said Gwen with a wink. "You will be soon enough."

The main hallway was lavish in its decor, with heavy velvet drapes lining the walls and candles providing the only light. Rhonda closed the door behind them and took their coats. Another woman, closer in beauty to Gwen than either she or Lacy, emerged through a doorway at the far end.

"Gwen!" she squealed as they hugged and kissed each other on both cheeks. "This is Lacy? Hi. I'm Terry." She hugged her warmly.

"Is everything ready?" asked Rhonda with a raised eyebrow and a sideways grin. Terry nodded.

"Come to the parlor," said Rhonda. "We have a few things to discuss before we get on with the evening."

The parlor was cozy, smaller than she would have expected. Gwen and Terry sat in two brocade chairs while Rhonda took Lacy's hand and sat next to her on a matching loveseat.

"Lacy," she began. "You know why you're here? It's because of a man. A boy hurt you, made you feel less than your worth. He treated you like shit. Right?"

Lacy nodded. It was true, what she said, but it ran so much deeper than that. Inside, she felt empty thanks to Dennis. There was a feeling that she would never be whole again, as if her virginity and dignity were organs he'd pulled out and put on display. She would always be that stupid slut that gave it up for Dennis. He used her. She could have handled it if he'd at least had the decency to call, to break up with her, to string her along for a few days anyway. Something. But he used her. Deposited his seed and left her before she even awoke the next day. Angry was too slight a word, as was hurt. She wanted to cause him pain. She wanted him to suffer for his callousness.

"Go on," said Gwen. "You can tell her. We've all been through it."

"He..." A dam burst inside her chest, pouring out through her eyes. "He called me a stupid cunt," she sobbed. "I wasn't good enough in bed to keep him. He said I should be grateful I ever got laid."

Rage blazed in the eyes of the other three girls.

Rhonda pulled an ornate box from the shelf behind her and lifted the lid. Inside, nestled on a bed of white satin, was an onyx spider with a blood ruby inlay on its belly. A black widow. She glanced up to find that Terry and Gwen wore identical pins, though how she had not noticed them before she could not guess.

"That son of a bitch..." muttered Terry.

"What we're offering depends on silence," said Rhonda. "You can never tell what happens in this house. The pin you should always wear, but never ostentatiously. What we're offering is freedom from men's control over you."

Lacy listened eagerly. She wanted to be free, to walk with the same confidence that the other three so easily commanded. She wanted to fill the yawning emptiness he'd left in her belly. Moreover, she wanted Dennis to suffer. She wanted to know that the power was hers, not his.

"Please," she said quietly. "I want to belong."

The three smiled as Rhonda removed the spider from its cage and pinned it to her lapel.

"You're one of us now," she said brightly. "You're a sister to us. Let men everywhere be afraid."

"Good," blurted Terry. "Now can we eat? I'm starving!"

Food? Was this how they coped with rejection and loss? She found it hard to believe that any of the three could be emotional binge-eaters. They were too thin and beautiful. Unless they were bulimic as well. Eating and vomiting up food wasn't a habit she wanted to build.

Rhonda giggled and took Lacy by the hand and led the group back through the main hall toward the back of the mansion. They passed through several sets of doors until they stopped outside a room that lay deep within the core of the house.

"Remember," said Gwen. "The power is yours. Not his."

Lacy looked confused. Before she could ask what was meant, Rhonda threw the doors open into a room in which there was only one pool of light. In it, there was a table. Strapped to it, lay the naked and struggling form of Dennis, his mouth covered in duct tape.

Beside the table was a preparation area, consisting of a griddle and condiments, knives and oils, the likes of which Lacy had only seen in the elaborate kitchens of television chefs. She looked down at Dennis. The whole scene was too surreal. Here he was, naked, bound with his arms and legs apart, vulnerable to her will. Only moments ago, he'd held her in some kind of power, diseased and crushing. Now, his whimpering form drew neither longing nor pity. He simply was there, nude and ridiculous on a table, watching as Terry hummed and selected a meat cleaver from the butcher's block.

"First," she said gaily. "We'll start off with appetizers." She advanced on the table, approaching between Dennis' legs and gestured for Lacy to do the same. She brought a length of line from her apron pocket and looped it around the struggling man's scrotum and pulled hard, stretching the skin tight and pulling his balls downward. She handed Lacy the cleaver.

"The first stroke is yours," she purred into Lacy's ear. "How bad did he hurt you? Go on. No one here will tell. He deserves it, doesn't he? Before he does to some other girl what he did to you?"

Lacy looked down on the stretched flesh, his bulging testicles and felt disgusted. It wasn't what Terry wanted her to do, it was that, only days before, she'd allowed him to touch her with those things. She'd kissed them, licked them, and their adjoining parts. She slowly raised the cleaver high above her head, making sure that his eyes followed, then brought it down with one strong stroke. The resulting stream of blood was more than she expected, as was his reaction. She thought he would scream, maybe cry out. Instead, he made a choking sound, as though trying to inhale and exhale at the same instant. His stomach spasmed, his body to bucked wildly against the restraints, then he collapsed. His body simply shut down, and he fell into deep unconsciousness.

"Bravo!" cried Rhonda, clapping. Gwen also applauded while Terri held up the string with the ruined prize still tightly bound in it. "Now sit," she said, gesturing to a chair and table. "You've rid yourself of his influence. Now it's time for us to celebrate."

Lacy watched as Terri, with great skill, separated the testicles on a cutting board and rolled them in a bowl of a yellow powder.

"Parmesan and bread crumbs," she said with a smile.

When they were covered to Terry's satisfaction, she placed them on the grill and hummed to herself while the smell of cooking flesh filtered through the room. It was not as Lacy imagined it would be, acrid and foul, but sweet, like fine steak. It made her hungry. A moment later, Terry plucked the sizzling morsels up with a pair of tongs and put them on a bed of lettuce.

"Cheese balls?" asked Terry with a grin.

Lacy took one gingerly from the serving dish. It was smaller than it had seemed when he was forcing them into her mouth. The heat from the grill shriveled them a bit until they were just bite-sized. She glanced around to see the other three, eagerly awaiting her reaction. She took a deep breath, as she always did when trying new things, and popped it into her mouth.

As the nugget burst between her teeth, the juices from within mingled with the parmesan in a singularly wonderful taste. It was unlike anything she'd had before, but it made her ravenous for more.

"Well?" said Rhonda, who was busying herself with stemming the bloodflow from Dennis' groin with clamps. "What do you think?"

"My God!" said Lacy, the juices from the tasty morsels dripping from her lips. "It's fantastic!"

Terry beamed. "It's an old family recipe," she said as she deftly severed and diced his penis. After a few deft strokes with her knife, she heaped the pieces onto the grill. "Wait'll you taste the rest. This just has to cook for a few minutes."

"Now," said Gwen. "What part of him were you most attracted to?"

"What do you mean?"

"When you first saw him, what made you want him?"

Lacy blushed, unsure if she could even admit to such a thing. It seemed so juvenile, but what did she have to hide from these, her newfound sisters?

"His ass," she giggled. "It just looked so perky and round..."

"The ass!" cried the others in unison, letting her know that they'd been through the same thing themselves.

"I was hoping you'd say that!" squealed Terry. "I have a great recipe for that! Gwen, wake him up. He has to feel this!"

Gwen nodded and went to Dennis' head, producing a large syringe from beneath the table. "Adrenaline," she said, reading Lacy's eyes. "It'll wake him up and keep him awake so he feels everything for a while."

She jammed the needle into his jugular and pressed the plunger. Dennis drew sharp breath as his eyes snapped open and he struggled to sit up.

"Shhhh," said Gwen in his ear. "We didn't want you to miss this."

His head lolled from side to side as he fought to free himself. His struggling only paused momentarily as his eyes widened with recognition when Tracy and Rhonda pulled a long serrated blade from beneath the cook station and slid it under his legs. His face contorted into a mask of agony as one pushed and the other pulled, sawing through the tender meat of his backside. Ragged noises came from his throat as he tried to cry out. When at last his buttocks were separated from his body, he went limp again.

"He's no fun," said Gwen as she slapped his face irritably. "He passes right out."

"It doesn't matter," said Terry. "We're almost past reviving him. One more time should do it." She turned to Lacy. "See, I need to cook some of the intestines along with the rump roast. It really brings the flavor out."

Lacy was enthralled by the display of such skill. Clearly they'd cooked such meals before, and many times, but as certain as she was that only days ago she'd be appalled, now she found the whole display fascinating. It was empowering, intoxicating even, the way they reduced the bastard to the animal he was. He treated her like a cow, now it was his turn.

His body jerked again as Gwen hit him with a second adrenaline dose. He gagged and rasped. He struggled so hard one of his own shoulders dislocated while trying to pull himself free from his bonds.

"Last round," said Gwen sweetly. "Say goodnight. Burn in hell."

His body tightened as the massive hook entered his body just above his pelvic bone. Terry pulled hard against it. She strained as it cut through the flesh up to the base of his sternum. When it punctured his diaphragm, Lacy smiled as he struggled to breathe. His face changed to a bluish tint and his eyes bulged even as Terry and Rhonda pulled at his intestines, cutting them free with poultry scissors, and placed the sticky mess into a foil roasting pan around the now skinned pieces of his own butt.

"You deserve this," said Lacy into his ear. "You know that."

When he finally stopped struggling, his eyes stayed open and glassy, staring at Lacy in a way that made her feel warm and powerful.

"Roast will be ready in about an hour," said Tracy between seasonings. Why don't you start on the dip? Anyone want this last cheese ball?"

"Ummm, I do," said Lacy shyly. "Unless someone else does. "I don't want to be greedy..."

"Nonsense," said Rhonda. "You earned it!"

Lacy took the other cheese ball and savored it in her mouth, letting the juices run down her throat as before, but being careful not to let any dribble down her chin. It was just too good to waste.

"Mmmm," she purred as Gwen brought over a tray with crackers and a bowl containing the minced penis. "That has to be the best thing I've ever tasted."

"Wait'll you try the cock-dip," said Gwen with a smile. "It's kind of like pâté, but better. Less salty. The slow roasting really brings out the flavor."

"And while we wait," boomed Rhonda, bringing over goblets which she'd been filling from the crimson river that flowed from Dennis' mangled body. "A toast!"

"A toast!" they cheered.

"To our new sister!"

"To never being powerless again!" called Lacy.

"To the sisterhood of the Black Widow!" giggled Gwen.

They raised their glasses and drank deeply, as Lacy realized that now, finally, she was in control. The fresh coppery taste on her tongue flooded her with warmth, the kind she wanted, and finally got, from her man.

Droplets

_____

The Drowning Pool

I saw her fall, slipping gently downward as though swallowed whole, down the gullet of some great watery beast. She'd been standing at the edge of the pier, playing and laughing, with a daisy in one hand and a bag of breadcrumbs in the other. She loved to feed the ducks.

As I watched, time slowed. It must have happened quickly, because the smile never left her face, but from my perception, it took a lifetime for her to completely disappear beneath the dull green water. I felt my heart stop as the viscous green closed in around the hem of her cotton dress and hugged her ankle. And then she was gone, beneath the glassy water to the wavering reeds below.

I don't know how long I stood watching, too stunned to pray, to stupid to beg God. I do remember running headlong toward the water and leaping. I remember the slap of the water against my face, the cold sting against my cheek as the murky green closed in around me. It seemed as though the pond didn't want me, wanted to throw me back to the pier, but I couldn't leave without her, she who'd smiled and talked to me, who had not played the silly games that girls do.

My eyes stung with algae and scum, my vision blurred. I could still see her, falling backward through the waving reeds that jutted from the bottom of the pond. I never consciously took a breath, but the stale air in my lungs pounded against my chest in a way to let me know I'd taken air in.

She drifted backward, just out of my reach, as the cold of the slimy water began to sink into my skin. I could finally feel it weighing down my blue jeans and sneakers, making them feel as if they were made of lead. The lilies and water plants reached for me, tendrils, as I saw them grasp at her arms and legs and hug her in closer, eclipsing her still-smiling face within their weedy bed until all that remained of her was the billowing dress that was only barely visible above the sickening green and the strands of hair that became as plant life themselves in their rhythmically swaying movements.

I tore at the plants with my hands, pulling them away from her face, but for each one I pulled away, one seemed to grab at me, holding me tighter, pulling me downward toward her bed. They ensnared my legs, encircling my ankles in steely bands that slowed my thrashing to nearly nothing, but still I pulled with my hands, trying to free the girl from their cold and slimy embrace.

My lungs seemed to want to burst with stale air, and I could feel my heart pounding in my ears when at last I uncovered her face and saw that her eyes were still open, her lips still smiling. She put her arms around my neck and hugged me tightly as I struggled to free her, my only thought to keep this girl, whom I had only just met, from becoming one with the sludge at the bottom of the pond. But as I thrashed at the weeds, I could feel her arms tightening, squeezing the rotten air from my lungs. I pulled away hard, and saw her smile still, but the kindness in her eyes was gone, the smile twisted somehow.

She rolled me over into the clutching weeds and kissed me with her cold lips. I could see her now, the real her, translucent in the water with groping tentacles for hair and burning embers for eyes. I fought against the bonds at my ankles and arms, my head lolling from side to side as if I'd find some pocket of air for my seizing lungs, but I saw only bones among the weeds. In my panic I screamed, letting free great bubbles of poisonous air into the water in a curtain of expended life. Then came the pain of my lungs filling with slimy filth as they drank in the water, sending me into spasms.

At last it was over, and I gently drifted deeper into my weedy bed, joining my brothers' perpetually smiling faces as we watched her gain substance and climb from the water, in search of a new friend.

Droplets

Dunawali?

In their travels as missionaries for the Baptist academy of New Jersey, Ben and Elsa believed that they were doing the Lord's work. Elsa, a licensed dentist, felt that it was her calling, as did her husband, to travel the world to impoverished and underprivileged peoples and spread the word of God and gospel of good oral hygiene. Ben would play his Backpacker guitar and sing of the glories of God to the heathen masses around forced worship services in the evening while, during the day, Elsa would poke and prod at the teeth of those who, until they arrived, believed they needed no such treatment. Where ever they were placed, they left behind stacks of the King James Bible and whiter teeth.

It was in the summer months that word reached them that they'd be traveling to the central mountain region of Paupa, New Guinea to share their love and wisdom, as well as toothbrushes, with the Huli people. It was a plumb assignment, as every missionary wanted to be the first to convert an aboriginal people to the proper religion. So what if they'd existed for thousands of years unchanged and were perfectly happy? Did it matter that their religions may have been, in fact, older than the whole of Christianity? Certainly not, for, after all, it was their immortal souls that Ben and Elsa were trying to save, whether they wanted salvation or not.

They made arrangements and left New Jersey on the earliest

flight they could get, neither of them able to contain their excitement. An untouched people, they marveled. How good to them the Lord was!

When they arrived in New Guinea, they were taken by overcrowded bus, which they rather enjoyed, to the edge of the great mountain range of Paupa. They got off the bus, oblivious to the confused expressions on the faces of their fellow passengers, none of whom spoke English, feeling as if they'd already done a fair share of the Lord's work. Though the other riders didn't know what on earth they were to do with the Bibles the two strangers left behind, nor did they really like singing the chorus to "Michael Row Your Boat Ashore" for the entire trip, they smiled and waved, more out of happiness that the two strangers had gone than politeness.

At the designated meeting place, Ben and Elsa found their guide, a small and rugged man who looked as though he was not far removed from a heathen himself. He smiled broadly, showing the whiteness of his teeth to Elsa, and spoke to them in broken English about the journey they were about to undertake.

"Three days journey," he said, nodding vigorously. "We hike through mountains to grass in heart. There, we find Huli."

Ben and Elsa were thrilled, feeling that the time in nature would bring them closer to God and more at one with their mission. They set off on their journey without delay, slinging their rucksacks over their shoulders and following the little man into the tree line with Ben playing his guitar and Elsa singing along.

When they emerged into a clearing just outside the Huli village three days later, Elsa never wanted to hear "Michael Row Your Boat Ashore" again. Her husbands incessant playing of the song over and over again gave her reason to think that maybe that was the only song he really knew how to play. Ben was sullen due to the blisters on his feet from his new hiking boots that were now broken in, and the guide seemed to have shrunk, giving him the wide-eyed appearance of a gnome. He bid them a hasty goodbye and disappeared back the way they came, happy to be away from them.

Ben and Elsa sat and rested for a few minutes, silently forgiving each other for their trespasses.

"We're finally here," said Ben with renewed enthusiasm.

"Yes," said Elsa. "Praise God!"

"I know the last three days have been rough, but..."

"God tests those he loves the most," replied Elsa with a smile. "We'll be stronger for this. I know it."

"And we'll be closer to the Lord!" added Ben, hugging his wife fiercely. He took her hand and together they made their way into the village, heralded by children who stopped their playing to run and tell everyone of the fair-skinned strangers that were approaching.

The Huli people proved to be hospitable, more curious about the strangers' blond hair and khaki shorts than afraid of what they might bring with them. They were welcomed by the head of the village, who, they discovered, spoke some English. When they explained that they were missionaries, his eyes brightened and he ushered them in as honored guests. A great feast followed honoring the missionaries and their noble work.

That night, with the sounds of tribal drumming in the air and a fire roaring to keep the cold mountain air at bay, Ben and Elsa felt they belonged. The Huli welcomed them with open arms, eager to learn all that the outsiders had to teach, and presented them each with gifts of the tribe. Ben received a traditional string apron, called a dambale, decorated with something called nogo-erene, which he immediately put on despite Elsa's protestations of his backside being exposed. When he later found out that the curly decorations were, in fact, severed pigs tails, he folded it neatly and resolved never to let the grotesque thing touch his body again. Elsa was presented with a beautiful necklace with white beads on either side and an iridescent center plate that she found enchanting. It wasn't until she had the chief translate for her that she truly appreciated that the plate, called a halepage, was in fact mother of pearl. The beads on the side, however, she became immediately less fond of as their name, dange, gave insight as to what they really were:

dog's teeth.The feast went well, each of the succulent dishes strange and wonderful to their city palates. There was a sweetness to one dish that both recognized, but could not identify right away, and so they ate their fill until the night hours and sleep made their eyelids heavy, then they retired to their hut, giving thanks to the Lord for all he had given them.

The next morning, Ben was immediately aware that something was amiss. Perhaps it was the fetid stale scent that seemed oppressively thick in their hut, or it could have been that he was covered in insect bites. More than likely, it was the deathly pale face of Elsa, who rolled onto the side away from him and retched onto the dirt floor. It was only then that Ben was able to place the strange taste in the food from last night. Sweet potatoes. As a mainstay of the Huli people's diet, a fact that neither of them knew until it was explained later by the village chief, nearly every dish last night contained sweet potatoes in some fashion or another. All well and good, save that Elsa was allergic to the orange roots.

The effects of having ingested such things were evident, as she writhed with stomach cramps and released such noxious smells that Ben had to seek refuge outside the hut. Combined with the unfiltered water of the Huli people, the effects were indeed frightening.

Ben went to the village chief, asking if there were anything that passed for medicine in the village. After a few moments of misunderstandings, the chief nodded in recognition. As the shaman approached, Ben tried to prevent such an ungodly creature from entering the hut, but, after much persuading from the chief, finally allowed him in.

The hut was dim as the shaman entered, his mordu decorated with beautiful feathers and hair, giving him the appearance of more a man of wicker than a man of medicine. Elsa took one look at his clay-encrusted face and let out a yelp. The exertion of shouting seemed to aggravate her condition, for she immediately was doubled over with intestinal cramping. The shaman watched with wide eyes as the woman, who only the night before had been so kind and gentle, lay writhing and moaning on the dirt floor. He crept closer, hoping to glean some cause of her malady. As he neared her, she sat abruptly up, her ashen face glistening with sweat.

"Get away from me!" she bellowed, further aggravating her condition. Her face contorted in a most unnatural way as she strained and released a loud and foul burst from deep within. Whether it was the noise, Elsa's yelling at him, or even the stench that made his eyes sting that drove him from the hut, Ben could not say. All he saw was the shaman burst forth screaming.

"Dunwalli!" he cried, bringing worried looks and fearful whispers from the Huli.

From the chief, Ben got only the most cursory of explanations. Dunwalli, as best as he could understand, was an evil goddess, the very idea of which repulsed him. This false deity supposedly lodged itself into the internal organs of an unfortunate woman and made her the unwilling vessel for its evil powers.

He tried to explain to the chief that no such creature existed, and that hers was a condition of biology rather than faith, but since there were no words in the Huli language for "allergy," there was no convincing the chief nor his tribe.

The gathered tribe gasped in unison as Elsa emerged from their hut wearing a plastic smile on her sweating face. In one hand was her bag containing all her tools of dentistry. In the other, a small worn bible.

"Let's get started," she said with just a bit too much enthusiasm. She explained to the chief what she wanted to do and asked him to translate to the rest of the tribe. She brushed the idea of her having an evil goddess in her belly as ridiculous and went back into their hut to prepare for examinations.

Ben began to worry. If these poor backward people, who still believed in such things as goddesses rather than the one true God, got it into their simple minds that his wife was somehow possessed, it would end their mission work to this village quickly. Best, he thought, to try to put their minds at ease. And what better way to soothe their worried mind that with the heavenly gift of song?

He smiled broadly as he stepped back into the hut, turning to find Elsa, still sweating and cramping from the sweet potato-water combination, glaring at him from behind a makeshift examination chair composed of two boxes and several shirts for padding.

"They think you're possessed," he said quietly, hoping not to ignite her fury.

"Oh?" she said, cocking an eyebrow. There was an edge to her voice that he was not at all comfortable with.

"You know...the cramping, the moodiness...They think you have something called a Dunwalli."

"I see," she said, her voice trembling with forced patience. "I have gas, so I'm possessed, is that it? What, does no one here ever have to fart?" Her voice became louder the longer she spoke. "I mean, possessed? Maybe I have dysentery, but I am a woman of God! I'm here to save their souls! And I'm not going to let a little thing like a stomach cramp keep me from bringing these unwashed heathens to glory!"

Her tirade excited her so, that she began dry-heaving into a corner.

"Now send the first one in so we can get on with this!" she said as she slowly raised her head.

Ben reached for his guitar, only to be stopped by Elsa's piercing stare.

"What are you planning on doing with that?" she asked pointedly.

"Well," he said, hoping not to rouse her ire. "I was going to play for them and maybe, you know, soothe the savage beasts? They're a little jumpy."

"Fine," she replied. "Just not that song."

"What song?" he asked, pretending he knew nothing of what she was speaking.

"You know very well what song," she growled. "You play it, I'll wrap your guitar around your head."

"That's not very Christian..." he mumbled as he went out the door.

The other members of the tribe, he could see as he emerged, heard her shouting and were quite fearful. They stood, hushed whispers rushing between them, tightly packed in front of the hut. Ben smiled again, a little less broad this time, strummed a chord on his guitar. It seemed to immediately brighten the mood around, and the natives stared in wonder at such an instrument. He continued in an easy chord progression, taking special care not to play the forbidden song, as he approached the chief. He explained what they wanted to do, prompting a quizzical look from the village's leader, but agreeing nonetheless. He raised his hands and informed the gathered Huli of the intention, assuring them that all would be well and that Elsa was not possessed by the Dunwali. When he asked for volunteers, he was met with a silent sea of fearful faces, after which, he volunteered to go first. As he disappeared into the hut, a fearful silence settled over the villagers, which Ben attempted to quell with his trusty guitar.

"Does anyone know "Michael Row Your Boat Ashore?" he asked in his overly cheerful way.

Before he could strum a single note, a blood-curdling scream erupted from the hut. All eyes, including Ben's, looked fearfully at the door, certain in their own way that no good was in that dwelling.

Another scream, followed by the sounds of a struggle, sounded, after which the chief emerged, his mouth bloody, from the hut, followed closely by Elsa, who was holding a shining dentistry hook in her hand.

"Get back here!" she growled.

The chief wanted nothing of it and ran to his people, his eyes wide with terror and pain.

"Dunwali!" he cried.

"Before Ben could attempt to smooth the relationship over, the village shaman appeared, flanked by two muscular Huli men. Their faces were painted in yellow clay and their bodies glistened with tree oil as one held his axe and the other a knife of bone. The shaman pointed at Elsa, who shrieked and ran back into the hut, baring the door behind herself, as the chief made his way over to Ben.

"What's going on?" demanded Ben.

"Dunwali," said the chief as he wiped the crimson stains off his face. "They fix."

"What do you mean. 'fix.'"

"Only one way fix Dunwali," said the chief. "Cut it out. Come...We smoke mundu while..."

"Cut it out?!?" cried Ben. "Are you people crazy? She just has gas!"

"Dunwalli," said the chief, shaking his head. "Come. Over soon."

"No!" he cried, rushing to the entrance of the hut. He burst through the door to see the shaman dancing around his wife, who was pinned to the floor by the two glistening men. Her shirt had been ripped open to expose her belly giving a better target for the heathens. One had his knife out and looked as though he were going to lay Elsa's belly open.

"Get off her!" he screamed, rushing the two men and knocking them off Elsa. He took her hand and hauled her to her feet and pulled her through the doorway. In the open air, he realized that their situation had not improved. Inside the hut there were only three godless heathens to contend with. Now, in the open, there looked to be more than twenty.

The chant began low, only by one or two people, but by the time they could understand what was being said, as well as just how much danger they were really in, the entirety of the village had joined in.

"Dunwali! Dunwali! Dunwali!"

They began to advance on them, bone blades appearing from beneath dambale or from out of the string purses that they all seemed to carry. Ben held fast to Elsa's arm, pulling her violently away from the advancing crowd and ran as fast she was able to keep up into the woods. They didn't know for certain if they'd be able to make it back, but anywhere was better than the village.

As they disappeared into the foliage, the chant died down, and the villagers all turned to their chief, whose bleeding mouth he was still holding. After a few moments, he began to laugh. Before long the entire village had joined him.

"Can you believe those shmucks?" he said to whomever would listen. "I hate missionaries!"

Droplets

———————————

Epiphany

We used to joke about it. We'd laugh at all the brainless people in the malls and offices, at their mindless obedience and their blank stares as they made their way to and from jobs that sucked the life out of them. We called them zombies because, really, what frame of reference did we have? My friends and I watched all the horror movies, saw slow shambling masses, and never understood why people didn't just run away, or do away with them, or something other than panic and board themselves up in a house while they gathered outside. We never understood. We thought we knew everything there was to know about the walking dead. We were wrong. So wrong.

When they first began appearing, we thought it was a joke and we laughed. The newspapers and television reports showed sobbing faces and corpse-littered streets, and we laughed. We knew better, we told each other. It had to be a joke, some Orson-Wells prank played by the networks to boost ratings and scare the hell out of gullible, television-saturated America who believed everything they saw on the news. They were the same people who believed that Iraq had something to do with the 9-11 attacks and that they too could be slimmer and more people would find them sexy if they just bought the right product from some hyper-active pitchman on an infomercial. They were sheep, unable to cope with the harsh reality of existence because all they'd ever known was the "normal" world. Go to work. Get your paycheck. Spend your paycheck. Lather, rinse, repeat. We thought we were smarter. They tried to tell us, but we didn't listen, so proud, so arrogant in our teenaged minds. It didn't matter that no one knew who or what made them. We watched and laughed, even reveled, in the supposed fall of civilization because, after all, it couldn't be real, could it? Monsters weren't real, and we, my teenaged friends and I, knew how things really worked.

I saw my first one at my mother's house. I came home late, drunk, stoned, surly. I came in through the basement door and listened for the sounds of my mother pacing the floor, waiting for me to come home. I didn't hear it. I thought she'd finally given up and given me some freedom. Good. I didn't need to hear her crap anyway. I was seventeen years old, dammit, and I could do as I pleased. I remember latching the door and falling straight into bed without undressing. I don't remember when I fell asleep, but my head swam in inky blackness until I was one with it.

The next thing I remember, there was light coming through the window and the door at the top of my stairs opened. I heard heavy steps on the stairs and I knew the routine by heart. If it was Mom, she'd fret and cry about why I smelled of pot and why couldn't I just finish high school. Dad usually called me lazy and worthless and threatened to kick me out or kick my ass. Either one was a hollow threat. I knew I could take the old man.

I rolled over and opened one eye to see my mom's housecoat coming down the stairs. Guilt for breakfast this morning. I lay there waiting for the babble to start. But she didn't say anything. She didn't call my name or cry. She came down the stairs and stood in a shadow, staring at me. Then she stepped into a sunbeam.

My mom was a pretty woman back in the day, I guess. Marriage and children put a few pounds on her, and I guess that some of the wrinkles on her face are my fault. She stopped really taking care of herself a couple of years ago, when I got into high school. But I remembered her from when I was little as having a kind, carefree face, with jet black hair that hung down past her shoulders. She always had the kindest eyes. When she stepped into the sunlight, though, her eyes were milky white, her pink skin sallow. Her beautiful cheek was torn, smeared with blood, and hanging in chunks from her jaw. I felt an arc of fear rip through me.

Surely I was wrong. It was a trick of the light. It had to be. Mom came toward me, hands out, like she wanted a hug. Mom was fine, and all she wanted to do was hug me, her first born, because she loved me. Mom would never hurt me. She cared too much about me to willingly let me stay out all night, and that was proof, right? What I saw must not have been blood, but lipstick, or ketchup, or something else. Her eyes weren't milky, they couldn't be, but the light from the window made them seem that way. I just sat there, knowing what she was but unable to reconcile it in my mind. The closer she got, the more I wanted nothing more than to hug her and make the nightmare go away, like I was a kid again. Mommy always chased nightmares away, looked under my bed, always told me that monsters weren't real. She told me that she'd never let anything hurt me.

When she reached my bed, she let out a moan. It wasn't the same lyrical voice that my mother used even when she cried. This sound came from deeper, pushed through purpling bones in her neck and choked on the way. It snapped me out of whatever fantasy world I was in. I rolled off the other side of the bed as she lunged at me and scrambled to my feet. I took my old pee-wee baseball bat from beside the headboard and pulled back like I was going to score a home run with her head. But I couldn't. I couldn't hit her. Not my mom.

She looked almost comical, her slow body trying to wriggle over my bed to get to me. I stepped back and felt my throat squeeze with sobs. It couldn't be happening. Not to me. Not to my family. I was smarter, charmed. It was never supposed to happen this way, to us. Stuff like this happened to other people, movie characters. Not us.

She tottered and righted herself, still trying to reach me. I warned her to stay back, though the words hung on tears in my throat. But she wouldn't stop coming. She kept reaching for me no matter how many times

Droplets

I pushed her back. I gave her one last shove onto my bed and made for the stairs before she could right herself.

We used to make fun of people in horror movies for staying in a house, for not leaving and not adopting the "every man for himself" philosophy. But I couldn't leave. I had to make sure that the rest of my family was alright. My dad. My sister.

I ran to the top of the stairs, into the kitchen, and slammed the door behind me, my heart hammering against my ribs. Dad would help. He had to. Dad was the one in charge of the family, even if I didn't want to admit it. No matter what happened, Dad always had the answer.

I made my way through the kitchen and into the living room, holding the bat tight so as to stop my hands from shaking. The living room looked just as it should've, old furniture facing an even older television, it's screen tuned to another report, now terrifying, of the walking dead.

I looked over to the couch, my Dad's usual resting place, only to find puddles of wet crimson and small chunks of flesh where his body usually lay. Mom must've gotten him. Her cheek was torn, no doubt from struggling with Dad. But he was so much bigger than her. I turned to go up the stairs and saw him stand. Dad was always a big man, but now, covered in his own blood and my mother's bites, he seemed larger than life, the type of thing I'd see in nightmares or enough to scare the hell out of a movie audience. Except this was no movie, and he wasn't a man under latex and red-colored syrup. This was my father, his face and neck torn out, his shirt soaked in blood, and his milky-white eyes locked on me.

I drew the bat back over my shoulder. Mom I couldn't hit, but Dad I'd been wanting to take a swing at for years. I waited until he got within arms reach of me and got ready to swing the bat as hard as I could. But I couldn't. I'd imagined the scene so many times in my head, whenever he pissed me off or tried to impose some stupid rule, but when it came down to it, I couldn't. He was my dad, the same guy who helped me through boy scouts and taught me how to ride a bike. As much as I wanted to, as much as he made me feel like doing it sometimes, I couldn't hurt him. His lips curled back revealing broken teeth and swollen gums. I tried to push him with the bat, but he was too close. The bat came loose from my hands and clattered to the floor, and he was on me. His teeth snapped near my face and I could smell rot on his breath. I wriggled and squirmed and managed to fight my way out from under his weight.

I scrambled to my feet and ran up the stairs to my sister's room. Holly stood beside her bed, still dressed in her pajamas from the night before, a teddy bear clutched loose in her hand,. My baby sister was nine years younger than me, always craving attention and always a pain in my neck. But now, despite how I'd treated her in the past, all I wanted to do was hold her close to me and keep her safe, to act the way big brothers are supposed to. But I was too late. She stared up at me, her blue eyes gone pale, red dripping from her lips proof that she'd been the one to turn my parents. Both of them with bites on their cheeks, both turned. In my mind, I could see her reaching for them, hugging them, and tearing into them. She was only eight years old, my baby sister. She loved to laugh and sing and play with her dolls. She always wanted to be with me and hug me, and all I'd done in the past couple of years was push her away. She'd never given up though. Looking at her pig-tailed, twitching form, I felt a lump in my throat. Somewhere inside, I knew she wasn't my sister anymore, but it didn't matter. Maybe if I'd come home last night, I could've protected her. Maybe I could've stopped my family from dying. Maybe I could've done something, anything.

Behind me I heard my father's slow heavy steps coming up the stairs, and it occurred to me why people were afraid of zombies. It wasn't because they were walking corpses or because they craved human flesh. It was more simple than that. It was because they were my family, my loved ones, the people I cared for and who cared for me, and now they were coming to kill me.

My sister tottered and stumbled toward me, arms up as if she were asking for a hug, her expression the same as the ones she wore when she didn't feel good. It made my heart ache to see and to realize there was nothing I could do. I couldn't hurt her, even if it wasn't her anymore. I couldn't hurt any of them. But I couldn't let them hurt me either.

She hissed as I grabbed her arms and shoved her away. Dad growled from the doorway and I could hear Mom groaning from the stairs behind him. I tore the curtains and blinds off the window and slid it open, kicking the screen away. The roof was a full story off the ground, but I'd rather risk jumping than have to face them. If I turned to fight, I'd lose. They'd kill me, and I'd let them rather than hurt them.

Once out on the roof, I could see other families running out of their houses. One neighbor lay facedown on the ground while his screaming wife held her son with one hand and a smoking pistol in the other. The guy across the street had managed to get his snarling, infected wife tied up and was stuffing her in the car when his neighbor came from behind him and started tearing into his flesh. It was all happening, just like in the movies. No one knew what to do. My friends would, though.

How many times had we talked about what we'd do if we were ever in a horror-movie situation? How many zombie flicks had we watched and talked about all the mistakes the characters made? How many times had we told each other that, if the zombie-apocalypse ever came, we'd be the only ones to survive? And how many of our "rules" had I already broken?

I moved to the lowest point on the roof, said a silent prayer, and jumped. I landed hard, bruising the heels of my hands as I hit the walkway. Without looking around, I took off at a dead run down the street to our hangout. My friends would be there. They'd know what to do. Once I found them, I could start to calm down and think this thing through, and we could take care of this mess.

The door to the little house stood open, which wasn't a surprise. The house was abandoned and wasn't in a great section of town. Part of the roof had collapsed and a little paper sign on the door read that the building was condemned, but it was ours. It was a place we could go to get away from our parents, our kid sisters, school. It was a place we could drink as much as we wanted, smoke as much pot as we wanted, and no one could see. It was a second home to us, and I only hoped my friends were there waiting for me.

They were.

As five sets of milky eyes turned to face me, the thought came back. I knew why zombies scared people.

Droplets

Family Business

When I was just a kid, my daddy took over the family business from his daddy. We were distillers from long back, carefully guarding the secret of our family recipe from any prying eyes. Our particular brand of whiskey, called "Coffin Liquor," was strong enough to raise the dead, if our label's motto was to be believed. I was raised around the stuff, and no curious boy past the age of ten could ever resist taking a snort or two in such surroundings.

The deep brown liquid packed a kick, let me tell you. I don't know if it was quite enough to raise the dead, but it was surely strong enough to put a person under like a corpse if he drank too much. Still, it had quite a unique flavor that I came to love and admire.

Now, ever since I was old enough to follow my daddy through the warehouse, he always warned me off of taking even baby sips of what he called "the product." Dangerous stuff, he said, too powerful for a child the likes of me. Still, boys will be boys, and I couldn't help myself. One day when daddy was in the warehouse office, I snuck away, pried open a crate, and pulled out one of the fat glass bottles.

Coffin Liquor had been made the same way for as long as anyone could remember, and tradition followed even to the bottling process. Where other companies switched to plastic caps and paper wrappers, Coffin Liquor bottles were still stopped with a cork, the tops sealed with drippy red wax. Except for the labels, which were now printed by machine instead of hand-lettered on parchment, the process hadn't changed in nearly six generations.

As I pulled that smooth cool glass bottle from the crate, I goggled at the ochre liquid inside. It was, and remains to this day, my favorite color, warm and rich. My hands shook as I tucked the bottle inside my jacket and ran out the back door of the warehouse and around the corner. If my daddy'd found me, he'd have whupped me good, but I couldn't resist. That beautiful brown was too inviting, almost intoxicating even before it touched my lips.

I broke the seal and used my pocket knife to tear the cork to pieces until I'd finally managed to dislodge it, then I closed my eyes and inhaled the most delicious scent I'd ever smelled. Better than a woman's perfume or a batch of home-baked cookies. It burned my nostrils and made my eyes sting with the cold vapors, but I could also catch a hint of the taste in the scent, spicy and warm. It made me want to try it even more. When I couldn't stand it any longer, I put the bottle to my lips and lifted the bottle to the sky, letting just a swallow past my teeth. It bit into my throat as I swallowed it, burned all the way down until it came to rest, warm in my stomach. As that magic heat spread through my body, the feeling made me smile.

I managed to hide that bottle in the warehouse behind a few empty crates that seemed to always be lying about, and after a few months of visiting the warehouse every day, I managed to finish it off. Another bottle followed, as did another, and another as the years went by. If my daddy ever caught on, he never said. Only kept telling me that a good brewer doesn't drink away all his profit. At the time I thought I was putting one over on the old man, but now I figure he was letting me know that I wasn't getting away with anything.

When I turned twenty-five, my daddy asked me what I wanted to do with my life. I'd only barely managed to get out of high school, thanks in part to my family's whiskey keeping my studies from really taking root in my brain. College wasn't really an option, and besides, I told him, I only had one plan in mind. I wanted to follow in the family business. Coffin Liquor was my birthright, and although my father had never taken me to the actual brewery, I knew enough about the business end to keep carry on the family label. All I needed was the recipe and for my daddy to teach me the secrets of making that rich brown elixir I'd grown up to love. Yessir, I told him. A brewer was my father and his father before him, and a brewer I'd be just as well.

My daddy hung his head and nodded. He told me he'd hoped for better for me, but he understood. It was time I learned the process, and then for me to decide. I couldn't sleep that night. Visions of hops and barley ran though my mind along with giant copper vats and yeast, and my head fairly swam with the imagined scent of my family's life's blood.

Just after midnight, daddy knocked on the door to my room and told me to get dressed and follow him. It was time, he said. I didn't understand, but I was too excited about learning the recipe that I didn't really care that it was still pitch black outside. I was being trusted with the secret, just as he'd been trusted by his father before him. I hurried to pull on my pants and shoes and almost ran to the pickup truck where my daddy sat waiting.

We rode in silence for what seemed like an hour toward the outskirts of town and beyond. I didn't dare ask where we were going because I didn't want to spoil the magic of anticipation. When we passed the town borders, I began to wander just how secret the recipe must be, that it had to be kept so far away from prying eyes.

We pulled up at a stone wall that stretched off into the night. Parked along the wall were three other pickup trucks, all painted dull black without even a hint of shine. Daddy climbed out of the truck and motioned for me to follow. As we climbed up the wall, I saw three lanterns in the distance. Employees, daddy said. We were here to check on their progress. I never questioned why we were looking in on them at night, or what this place was. I assumed they were digging a special root from out of a secluded field that gave Coffin Liquor its distinct flavor. When one of the workers' shovel struck something solid, he waved the lantern, making my daddy's pace quicken. We made our way toward his light just in time to see the workers pulling a long metal box from out of the ground.

A coffin.

"Seven years," said the digger. "This one ought to be ready."

The other three hoisted the coffin from the ground and, as my father approached, shook it from side to side. From inside, I heard a sloshing sound.

It was part of the putrification process, my daddy explained. As the body began to rot, parts of it just turned to liquid. The longer a body stayed in the ground, the longer it fermented. It was a tricky process, though. Leave them in too long and all that was left was stained linen and dust. Not long enough and there would not be enough of the coffin liquor to fill a bottle, and it wouldn't pack the right amount of punch.

I watched in horror as my daddy took something from his pocket, a metal spigot with a spike on one end. One of the workers handed him a mallet, which he used to drive the spike into the foot of the casket. Never, he explained, take it from the head end. Driving the spigot from there ran the chance of piercing the skull, which would foul the whole batch.

The workers tilted the coffin toward the spigot, which poured the liquid into a bucket. When the last drippings were out, one of the workers handed my daddy a small dipper. He stirred the contents of the bucket then brought the ladle to his lips and took a sip. His body shuddered as the taste hit him, then he opened his eyes and motioned for me to do the same. The scent hit me first, that same burning and intoxicating scent I remembered from my youth, the one I'd never forget.

"It's a little raw yet," he said as he passed me the ladle. "Still has to be filtered, but have a snort."

Tasting Coffin Liquor from the bottle made me love it from my youth. Tasting the coffin liquor straight from the source, however, was a feeling I'll never forget, euphoric and sensual. It poured down my throat, warming my body like a lover, touching me in ways I'd never experienced, or even imagined, from mere alcohol. I opened my eyes to find my father's sad expression. He never wanted this life for me, but now that I'd tasted, I could never go back. He left the decision in my hands, and I wanted this life for my own.

I glanced back toward the flat smooth stone that bore the name and age of the cask. It was a woman's name, aged somewhere in her forties. The other lights waved, signaling the plucking of more casks from the ground. One was a man in his fifties, the other, a mere child of ten, each with their own distinctive flavor.

Droplets

——————————————

The Freakshow

As Sam walked down the dirt path, he sneezed. The stench of alfalfa and barn animals always made his sinuses act up. It was part of the reason he hated when the carnival came to town. The other was he didn't see much of a point to the whole thing. People paid good money at ramshackle booths to with cheep crap at fixed games, handed over by toothless sweaty men who looked like they'd seen a prison more recently than a shower. Carnival food also made him sick. Not that he was foolhardy enough to actually eat it, but just the thought of dirty hands touching inadequately-refrigerated sausage and stale pretzels made his stomach churn. In fact, there was only one thing that could make him go to the carnival, and she walked right in front of him.

Becky bounced as she walked, her blond pony-tail keeping perfect time with her gate. Though she was twenty-six, the carnival brought out the child in her. The dazzling lights and off-key calliope music brought a smile to her face as she went from booth to booth and begged Sam to win her another stuffed dog or a goldfish. Only for her would he endure the horrors, but even she couldn't make him enjoy it.

"Isn't it time we got going?"

"Oh, come on!" she pleaded. "Just a little while longer. I haven't ridden the Zipper yet! I'll make it up to you when we get home."

He sighed. It wasn't a battle he was going to win, and he knew it.

She smiled, kissed his nose, and bounded further down the midway. Carnival or no, she had him wrapped around her finger. If she weren't so damned cute, it might be a different story, but her big blue eyes had a hint of the devil in them, and her body knew just how to please his.

"Ooo! Funnel cake!" she squealed as they rounded a corner off the main midway, and ran to yet another booth where a greasy man dumped something beige and lumpy into a kettle of boiling grease.

"Step right up, don't be shy!"

The voice cut through the sounds of the crowd like a scream. The face attached to it was every bit the cliché. From his striped vest to the straw Skimmer on his head, the handlebar moustache and white spats, he looked more like a carton than a real person. He waggled his knotty bamboo cane toward a faded poster behind him.

"Behind this curtain," he boomed, "lies the most incredible, most cruel, most disturbing creatures that Mother Nature herself spat out! Direct from Vienna, after a long engagement performing for the crowned heads of Europe! You'll Ooooooo! You'll Ahhhhh! You'll scream! You'll cry! You've never seen anything like this in all your lives! For the price of one dollar, gaze into the true faces of horror!"

"You've gotta be kidding me..." muttered Sam.

"That looks like fun!" squealed Becky.

"Give me a break," he said. Two hours walking around in the heat with the stench of sweat and animal piss was enough. No matter how good looking she was, or how much sex she promised him, he was tired, and a freak show wasn't his idea of fun.

"Come on!" she whined.

"Everyone knows those things are fake," he said. "The dog-faced boy is just some guy with hair glued on his face, the human lizard is some woman with a bad skin condition. I bet the strongman even wears fake muscles under his leotard."

"Well I want to go," she said.

"But it's stupid!" He wished he could suck the words back into his mouth the moment they passed his lips, but they fell to the ground in front of Betty like a dead fish. Her eyes blazed, and he realized that any promise of "making it up" to him just became null and void.

"Oh, so I'm *stupid* for wanting to see the freakshow, am I? If you won't go with me, I'll just go by myself."

She stormed up to the barker's platform.

"One please."

"Yes indeedy, little lady," said the Carney with a salacious grin. "You're awfully pretty to be going into such a hall of horrors all by your lonesome. How 'bout you, young man? Care to take a peek at the natural horrors inside?"

"He doesn't want to go in," pouted Becky.

"I see," said the barker as he licked his chapped lips. "Too scared, eh? I don't blame you."

"Now wait just a minute..!"

"I'm just saying," shrugged the barker with a wave of his hand. "I mean *I* wouldn't let such a..." his eyes danced over Becky's frame and came to rest of her cleavage. "...luscious creature go in there by herself, but, hey, some people just can't handle what they see in that tent."

"You go ahead and wait outside," said Becky. "Go ride the teacups or something. I'll be out in little while."

There was a challenge in her voice that he didn't like, and the bastard behind her with his wolfish grin didn't help matters. Bad enough that she was already pissed at him, but he'd be damned if some weirdo in a straw hat was going to make him look like a wimp in front of his girl.

"I'm not scared," he blurted. He wrestled with the giant stuffed dog as he fished in his pocket and came up with a wadded up dollar.

"There's my dollar."

"Are you sure?" leered the Carney. "Some people come out of there laughing, and others are driven mad by the experience."

"Yes I'm sure!"

"Suit yourself, tough-guy," he replied. "You understand that the carnival cannot be held responsible for any emotional or psychological damage you may...and probably will...incur?"

"Whatever," spat Sam. "Just let us in already!"

"Very well, then." He lifted the tent flap with his cane and flourished his other hand. "Right this way, folks!"

When the flap fell again, they stood in darkness. Becky snaked her hand into his and held on tight.

"Why is it so dark in here?" she whispered.

"Now who's scared?" The jibe cost him an elbow to the ribs, but it was worth it.

Somewhere above them, a radio crackled, and the voice of the Barker came through tinny speakers.

"Welcome madame and monsieur," he said. "Please watch your step, no flash photography and remember...Don't touch the exhibits. No matter how innocent they may look, those bars are there for a reason. Step lively to our first exhibit."

Bright light and the fizzle-pop of a spotlight blinded them for a moment as the voice continued.

"Meet Bingo, the dog-boy," he said.

Inside the cage before them, a shape moved from shadow to shadow.

"Discovered in Borneo as a child, anthropologists thought, at first, he was some sort of missing link. Then they discovered that beneath all his fur, he was, in fact, as human as you or me. He was raised by wolves and keeps his feral temper. Please stand back...He has been known to bite."

Sam squinted against the light to get a better look. It was the size of a small man, or maybe a large monkey, and covered in thick course hair. When it rushed the front of the cage, Becky let out a giggling scream. It snarled and swiped through the bars at Sam. But in coming into the light, it lost its wonder. The zipper on the back of its fur coat glinted when he turned just right, and each of its teeth were filled with dental silver. From under the shaggy black, blue eyes stared out at him without a trace of ferocity. It was an act. A good act, but an act nonetheless.

"Nice coat," was all he said.

The light above them went out with an audible clack and another blazed a few feet down. They moved to the next cage, in which sat the largest woman Sam had ever seen. Four stools sat under her, two for each side of her massive posterior, and creaked as she smiled, eating a turkey leg. It's juice ran down her lips and into the thick black of her beard.

"That's just gross," said Sam under his breath.

"Meet Lola!" crackled the barker's voice. "The bearded fat lady! Weighing in at just under one ton, Lola is too much woman for any man. And it's just as well...She has to shave twice a day to keep her skin smooth! She's got a voracious appetite, both for food, and for love!"

The blobish creature in the cage turned her piggy eyes out toward them and smiled, grease glistening off her fingers and lips.

"A man!"

Her voice was low and sounded as fat as the rest of her. She shook as she waddled off her stools and clutched the bars. Sam wondered how she could hold so much weight on just two legs.

"Come to Lola," she bellowed. "Let me give you a kiss!"

Sam's stomach flipped as the glistening lips dripped grease to the floor.

"Sorry, sweetie!" said Becky with a grin. "This one's mine!"

"I can do things to you that twig can't even dream of!"

The back of Sam's throat burned with bile as he pushed Becky to the next exhibit. They stood in darkness for a moment until the light in front of the fat lady went out and the one above them came on, but darkness was preferable to looking into Lola's horribly hungry eyes.

"Now watch your step around these two, young lady," said the

Barker's voice. "Bob and Bill, the Siamese twins!"

In the cage before them, two men stood naked to the waist. They looked normal in every way to Sam, except for a single tube of flesh as big around as his leg that joined them at the midsection.

"Conjoined at the waist," continued the static-pocked voice, "Bob and Bill share *everything*. Food, drink...Even women."

What woman would ever want to screw a couple of freaks like Bob and Bill, Sam couldn't begin to guess, but the thought made his already-queasy stomach turn a little more.

"What one sees, the other knows. What one eats, the other tastes. And, believe it or not, they're married...To sisters! But watch out...When they argue, it's not pretty."

They moved on through the tent from cage to cage, seeing oddities, each more pitiful than the last. But it was just what Sam expected. The "lobsterman" was born with conjoined legs and deformed hands. The "pinhead" was either retarded or a brilliant actress. And the "human worm" was nothing more than a quadruple amputee who lay on the ground and wiggled. With every passing freak, Sam grew more disgusted. The fakes were bad enough, but the ones that were truly unfortunate mixed him with feelings of disgust and outrage. The sideshow exploited them, held them up for ridicule, and for what? So normal people like Sam could stare into their misshapen eyes and feel grateful for being born normal.

When they came to the cage where a man stood driving nails into his own sinus cavity, Sam could take no more.

"This is bullshit," he said. "I'm getting out of here."

"But we haven't even gotten to the shrunken heads or the two-headed calf yet," protested Becky. "I hear they have a Thalidomide baby in a jar!"

"You want to stay, be my guest," he spat. "This whole thing is disgusting and stupid. Everything here is either fake or just wrong."

"But..."

"Go ahead. Get your rocks off looking at freaks. I'll be outside."

"Not seeing anything to your liking?" The Carney wasn't talking through a speaker anymore, though how he'd slipped up behind them, Sam couldn't guess.

"This stuff is all bunk," he said. "All you've got in here is fakes and retards. Hell, half these people shouldn't be on display. They should be in homes or hospitals or something."

"I hear you," said the Carney with a shake of his head. "When you walked up, I said to myself 'There's a man with morals. There's a man who won't settle for the standard tricks of the trade. There's a man who deserves nothing less than...the real thing.'"

"What do you mean," asked Becky.

"Well," he said with a devilish grin. "There is one other exhibit. One we don't just let the average customer gawk at."

"What is it?" Her eyes lit up when she asked.

"It's something really special...Something so horrible, so foul, something that defies the laws of nature, and yet is one of her cruelest jokes. We occasionally find customers that are a little too...jaded...for the standard fare. We don't let the average customer see this exhibit because, well, frankly, they would find it too disturbing."

"Yeah, right," said Sam. He couldn't believe Becky was falling for his bullshit line again. What could they possibly have in another tent that was so horrible?

"I want to see it!" pouted Becky.

"No way. Enough with the hard sell, buddy. He's just trying to get more money from us."

"No sir," he said with a hurt expression. "For you and your lady friend, admission is free. And I'll tell you what I'm going to do. If you don't find what's inside that tent to be the most terrifying thing you've ever seen, I'll even refund the dollar you paid to get into the side show. Do we have a deal?"

"Deal!" said Becky before Sam could answer.

The barker lifted the tent flap between two cages and gestured with his cane.

"Right this way then," he said.

They followed him further away from the Midway until the lights didn't reach the path. Sam wondered why the ground felt wet, then decided he didn't really want to know. It hadn't rained in a few days, so whatever moisture saturated the ground couldn't be good. They came to a halt in front of a large box-car with a heavy door on the front. With a flourish, the Carney took an old key from his pocket and held it up for Becky to see.

"We have to keep this one locked for the safety of the exhibit," he explained. "And the public. Why, if this one got out..."

"Save it," said Sam. Enough was enough. "Just let us in and let's get this over with."

"As you wish, sir," said the Carney with a low bow. "After you."

Becky needed no prodding. Despite Sam's attempts to hold her hand, she rushed up the steps and through the heavy door. Sam fumbled with the giant stuffed dog and goldfish until, exasperated, he set them down outside the door.

"I'll be back for those," he warned.

"Of course, sir," said the Carney.

Sam stepped into the darkness of the boxcar and reached out until he felt Becky's hand. The door slammed behind them.

"What the hell?"

"I don't go inside," said the Carney from behind the door. "But no worries! I'll guide you through with the loudspeaker, just like in the freakshow tent. Don't worry, you'll hear me."

"This is creepy," said Becky. Her voice was tight. If he didn't know her better, he'd swear she was excited. But the truth was the dark scared her. The edge to her voice and the tightness of her grip spoke volumes.

Overhead in the darkness, a loudspeaker crackled and the Carney's whispered voice filtered down.

"Ladies and gentlemen, what you are about to see may disturb you. It may shock you. It may even terrify you. But I must ask you...no...beg you...do not listen to anything it says. Do not scream, and whatever you do, do not approach the cage. These creatures are to be considered remarkably dangerous. You have been warned."

"Oh give me a break," groaned Sam.

"I don't like this," whispered Becky.

Whispers and murmurs cut through the darkness, accompanied by the sounds of fidgeting and shifting feet. It almost made Sam feel better that they weren't alone, but that they couldn't see or find the rest of the audience.

"Ladies and gentlemen," came the crackled voice of the Carney. "I give to you...The Modern Man!"

A spotlight crackled as white light ignited, blinding Sam for a moment. As his vision cleared, he made out shapes around him. Bars. And beyond, bleachers filled to capacity. He cupped his hands over his eyes and felt his stomach turn to water.

Freaks. The bleachers were filled with freaks. In the front row, the exhibits from the side show sat clapping. Behind them, horrors Sam had not imagined joined the audience. Pinheads, midgetts, dog-boys and transvestites, hermaphrodites and vampires, fish girls and human skeletons. They clapped and whistled while Becky and Sam stared about, confused. Standing on a platform, microphone in hand, the Carney continued his narration.

"How cruel nature is to create such an abomination! Note his bloated sense of self worth! His exaggerated but frail ego! Her dependence on being in-dependent! One is not complete without the other, yet they both insist they are individuals. Just like everyone else!"

"Very funny," barked Sam. "Let us out, you freaks!"

"Freaks, are we?" sneered the Carney. "Take a good long look at yourself in the mirror! Day after day, doing the same boring thing. Nothing to make you different. Nothing to make you special! People look at us and remember us for our uniqueness. But you two? I bet no one could even pick you out of a crowd!"

"They're hideous!" screamed a woman's voice from the audience. "Horrifying!" cried another.

"Yes, my friends, this is what becomes of those who strive to fit in! This is what becomes of those who can't stand difference! This is what the world has made of them!"

"Please," said Becky through tears. "Let us out."

"Not so fun, being on the other side of the cage, is it?" spat the Carney. "See how the female of the species tries to act strong? But when faced with adversity, just like her modern man, she crumbles!"

"Okay!" shouted Sam. "We get it! You've had your fun, now let us out!"

"Oh," said the Carney with an evil grin. "I don't think so. I've never seen as perfect specimens of *bland* as you two. I've never seen anything so horrifyingly *trivial*, so disgustingly *normal*! As a matter of fact, I think we've finally found our greatest exhibit! Pull the cage boys!"

At his word, a group of a dozen roust-abouts came from the darkness and shoved poles through the sides of the cage. They smiled when Sam kicked at them and laughed when Becky screamed.

"You can't do this!" cried Sam. "We're not animals!"

"No," said the Carney, all traces of mirth gone from his voice and face. "You're worse. You're human."

Sam shook the bars and threw his shoulder against the door as the misshapen audience filed out of the box-car. The roust-abouts lifted the cage onto their shoulders and carried them to the far end of the chamber and covered the cage with a tarp. The last thing Sam saw was Becky's terrified face, heard was the off-key sound of a calliope.

The Girl Next Door

Late nights were just an accepted fact of life for Danny, a graduate student working for a Masters in English. Because he worked part time as well as got a small pittance from the college for student-teaching, he was able to afford his own place, but it was hard going and the neighborhood wasn't the best in town. The winding streets just off Hopkins could change from one block to the next, going from a family neighborhood to a street where drug addicts and gang wannabes practiced their particular crafts.

His house was, at one time, all the rage with builders in the area. A 1970's model duplex, it had fallen into less-than-perfect shape ten years ago. The landlord, an amicable fellow of wide eyes and big-talking dreams, worked as much as he could on his houses, but when maintenance issues arrived, he was clueless. Even with rent from five such run-down slums coming in, he could not afford to hire actual carpenters and electricians to do the much-needed work, so the houses continued to slowly fall apart and take on more tenants in the form of vermin and insects that burrowed into the crawlspace that every house built at that time seemed to have.

After his regular day of going to classes at 8 a.m. then riding his bike to the bohemian restaurant where he served kous-kous to art and theater students, he rode back to the college for his evening classes. At 9 p.m. he left for his little half-a-house, as he called it, threading through traffic on his mountain bike. Twice a week he stopped at the ugly yellow building off the square to buy a six-pack of imported beer, then carefully ride home to begin his homework at around 10 p.m.

Because the house was falling apart, Danny was able to talk the landlord, Barry, into giving him a break on rent in exchange for doing all his own maintenance. Saturdays were spent sleeping until noon, rebuilding whatever had managed to fall apart during the week until 4 p.m., and then riding his bike to the restaurant in search of that elusive customer who would leave the enormous tip. Sundays, however, he managed to have completely to himself, to catch up on whatever he may have missed or to simply watch one of the five channels his television received while he recharged for the next day.

The nights toward the end of summer were hot and sticky, a point not lost on Danny as the old duplex had no central air, only broken window units to keep him from sweating to death. He lay in bed in the early morning hours, and fought for sleep, listening to the loud shouts that came from wall he shared with his neighbors.

When he first moved in, he'd seen her watching him through the mini blinds in the front window. He knew it was a kid, a little girl of around eight, he guessed. She watched him pass by several times, unloading his few pieces of furniture from his friend's pickup truck, carrying his meager belongings into the house. It took him less than two hours to get everything he owned inside, and she watched the whole time. She'd pulled away from the window when he looked to see if she was still there, but she always pressed her eyes through as though afraid of his moving in next door.

It was that first night that he'd become acquainted with the neighbors through their yelling at one another and at her. He sat on the couch, drinking his beer in his boxers, half eavesdropping as the late-night television program showed highlights of the basketball game he'd missed while he was at work. It was more irritating than bothersome, he thought at the time. Their voices almost blended with the screams of the fans as a man in a Bulls uniform cut through the air like a hawk and slammed the ball hard through the hoop, but only almost. There were still some things he doubted even jaded basketball fans would say.

Why do you drink so fuckin' much?

You gonna tell me what I can do?

The little girl's father and mother fought almost constantly, each one calling the other the vilest of names. The father's gravelly bark rattled the walls as he boomed abuse on the mother, whose shrill tongue liked nothing more than to envenomate the husband with barbs designed to break him down.

He didn't mind their yelling at each other so much. After all, what married couple didn't fight? But when they ran out of cruelties for each other, they turned their attentions on the child. It wasn't his business, he told himself, as he heard them screaming at her and felt the walls shake as her body hit them. But the bruises he remembered from his own childhood struck a painful chord with every cry. When he could stand no more, he'd clicked off the television, part of him wanting to go next door and rescue the child. Instead, he went to his bedroom and closed the door, hoping he could escape the sounds of abuse beneath his pillow.

The next day was Saturday, work day, and Danny got up earlier than he'd intended. He was still groggy with sleep when he stumbled out into the back yard in his boxers with a cup of coffee in his hand. He grumbled at the garish morning as he pulled a cigarette from his pack and tucked them into the waistband of his underwear. As he clicked his lighter, he began to feel uncomfortable, as though he were being watched. Not that he was modest, but he didn't like not seeing whoever was observing him.

He glanced quickly around the yard until his eyes rested on a small hole in the wooden fence, and he noticed that not so much light shone between the boards as did between those around them.

"Hello?" he called, only to be answered by the sounds of quickly moving small feet in dead leaves and a slamming door.

Great, he thought. She'd probably gotten a good look at him in his underwear smoking, with his long hair sticking up every which way and his goatee and his earring and he'd frightened her. Just his luck. If he saw her again, he decided, he'd try to be nice, to let her know that the scary guy next door wasn't some kind of freak.

Later that day, he was standing on a ladder in the corner where the house joined the fence, sweeping leaves from the mostly flat roof when he got the feeling again. It was strange to him, that he could feel her gaze like fingers on his back, as he generally didn't care if people stared at him. But when he felt her eyes, there was something that compelled him to stand a little straighter, to watch his language. It was that she was a kid, he supposed, and somewhere inside he wanted to set a good example.

He turned and looked over the fence at her, sitting on a rope swing under a diseased tree staring at him. She had long dark hair, pulled back with a ribbon, and wore clothes that told of her family's financial trouble. He didn't see any bruises on her, for which he felt oddly relieved, but there was a sadness in her lamp-like eyes that tugged at his heart.

"Hi!" he called cheerfully. The little girl did not move, only continued to stare. "I'm Danny. I just moved in next door." It made him uncomfortable, the way she stared at him, as though she'd never seen another living creature before in her life. It made him need to fill the silence with something, even clumsy small-talk. "What's your name?"

"Amber," she said so quietly that Danny was almost unsure he'd heard it, then she leapt off the swing and darted into the house like a frightened rabbit, leaving Danny feeling stupidly alone.

"Damn," he muttered under his breath as he went back to work.

Over the next week, Danny followed his routine of rising before the sun and leaving on his bike in the dark, not to return until the sun had set again. Because of his schedule, he saw very little of the girl next door, except for the unshakable feeling of her peering through the blinds at him as he came home. Every night, however, the shouts and cries began again, and every night he returned to his room, his heart filled with memories and calling himself a coward for doing nothing. For nearly the entire week that he'd lived in his half-a-house he'd not slept well, and when he did, it was with the image of Amber in his mind as he heard the screams.

It was Friday night that, whether moved by a particularly violent fight or careless from lack of sleep, that he could take no more. One cry too many had pierced the wall between their homes, and Danny felt a rage that was wholly unlike him. He would make them stop, his tired mind told him. He would keep them from hurting Amber any more. She, who was like him, did not deserve such abuse, and here, in this neighborhood, no one cared.

He threw open his door and crossed the narrow walk between his side and theirs, pausing, his fist raised, before he pounded on Amber's door. What was he going to do, he wondered. He'd never seen her parents, though he'd heard them often enough. Her father sounded big, and Danny knew he was violent. Her mother he couldn't even guess, but she seemed perfectly capable as well.

He turned quickly, feeling all the more like a coward, and slunk back to his side of the house, locking the door behind him and retreating to his bed. *Don't get involved*, he told himself. *It's none of your business. Look out for yourself. You don't need this kind of trouble.*

Saturday, Danny didn't want to work. He felt ashamed of himself for turning tail and leaving Amber to her parent's cruelty, and, as a result, hardly left his bed for the entire day. He left an hour before he was scheduled to be at the restaurant for no other reason than he could not stand being in the house when the nightly row began. He stayed late that night, though his mood was quiet and he didn't get many tips for it, thankful that when he got home, Amber and her parents were already quietly sleeping.

Sunday was as Saturday should have been, in that Danny woke up and realized that there was work to be done, and to get to it he'd have to be in the back yard again. He stepped out toward the tool shed, praying that he would not feel those icy eyes on his back again. What could he say to her, he wondered, if he saw her? She already thought he was strange, but now she'd be able to tell he had been there. She'd see it on his face, he was sure of it. She'd know he was a coward that could have saved her but didn't.

He had opened up the crawlspace under the house and was searching with a flashlight for the pipes that he knew were leaking when he heard heavy footsteps come through the gate.

"What're you doing under there?" asked Barry, squatting down and peering in past Danny's feet.

"Pipe's leaking," he grunted as he wriggled out to meet his landlord. "What brings you over?"

"Well," said Barry, shuffling his feet. "I was thinking about our deal, about half off the rent for work on the house."

"Yeah?"

"You've been busting your ass on this house since you moved in. It shows."

"I've only been here a week," said Danny with a scoff. "How much could it show?"

"Enough." Barry had something on his mind, that much was obvious to Danny, but he wasn't good when it came to talking business, especially when he wanted something. He was a good enough guy, always willing to trade even or make it right, but for some reason he always seemed to be apologizing for deals, as if he felt he were taking advantage of Danny. "Look, how would you like me to knock more of the rent off?"

"How much more?"

"Down to two-fifty."

"What do I have to do?" He was leery of such deals, especially since they invariably made more work for him.

"Just what you're doing," said Barry. "Just to the rest of the house."

Danny felt his stomach clench at the thought of knocking on that door, like he should have done two nights ago.

"What about the people that live there? Don't they need a break on rent?"

Barry fixed him with a strange look, one that said he couldn't tell if Danny was serious or not.

"Nobody lives on that side," he said. "That side's been empty for more than a year."

He tried to understand the rest of Barry's hurried instructions, but nothing made sense to him. Of course people lived there. Amber lived there. He'd seen her, heard her and her parents. He barely even noticed as Barry pressed the key to the front door into his hand and made his way back through the gate. Danny followed him in a haze out to his car and waved as he pulled away.

He half ran to the other door and stood where he had before, only now the doubt that gripped his insides were different. As he put the key into the lock and turned the knob he felt his breath stop in his throat. *I'm going to open the door,* he told himself, *and I'll see her. I'll see them all, and I'll tell them what I think of them. I'll call Child Protective Services.* He pushed the door open and stood gaping in confusion.

Aside from the blinds on the windows, there was not any sign that anyone had lived here. There was not one stick of furniture, not one crumb on the floor. The dust on the windowsills had not been disturbed in quite some time and the air was stale from having no window units running in a long while.

He stepped into that half of the house and searched for any sign of Amber. Sunlight peeked in through the blinds and lit the house well enough, but it was cold for summer inside, and he passed in a dream state through the rooms. It was a mirror of his side of the house, and he passed from the smallest, first bedroom to the to the bathroom. There were rust stains on the porcelain sink where water had dripped and no longer fell. He went to the third bedroom, the largest, knowing somehow that the room he'd skipped was hers, was Amber's. When he stopped in front of her door, somewhere inside he hoped, prayed even, that he'd open it and she'd be there to greet him, but her room was equally empty. He searched the walls with his eyes for some shred of truth, proof that she still lived here, until his eyes rested on the closet.

The door stood open and the closet was empty, but on the outside, where none should have ever been, was a latch with a padlock hanging from it. He knew its purpose too well as his knees buckled and he dropped to the floor.

I should have knocked, he told himself bitterly. *Someone should have knocked. Someone should have not run away like a scalded dog in the night at the sounds of her screams.* Daniel sat in front of the closet for some time, sobbing for the little girl whom he was sure he'd seen, before he finally went back to his side of the half-a-house. He returned a short while later with a screwdriver and removed the latch and padlock and placed them reverently into his duffle with his packed things.

Heaven on Earth

June was always the month for weddings, according to southern tradition, though Chris could never figure why. In the dog days of summer, June was one of the hottest months of the year in Texas, particularly in the coastal swamplands. The heat weighed heavily down, bringing with it mosquitoes and slyly moistening the clothes with sticky perspiration. Though he'd grown up in Lake Jackson, a town built by a chemical plant on a swamp, he'd never gotten used to the humidity the way others seemed to have. Even clear and sunny days, a welcome break from the seemingly perpetual rain, were made tedious by the water steaming from the spongy ground, trapped beneath the canopy of willows and pecan trees.

Though it always seemed oddly fitting to him, that a chemical company would invade such an unfriendly environment to build a town, he still found it startling when real places of beauty were made known. Such was the case with "Heaven on Earth."

The large antebellum plantation house had been named in the early 1800's by its builder, a southern gentleman named Captain Maddox. It stood just outside Angleton, making its name less laughable as it was far enough away from the swampland that, Chris imagined, the land might have once been considered beautiful. Now, it looked out of place among the modern buildings and paved streets of a growing downtown, proud among the unremarkable.

Chris took his wife's hand as they crossed on cobblestones the freshly-cut lawn toward the great stained-glass door. Tina looked beautiful against the pink and white flowers of the crepe myrtles. The look of joy in her eyes made Chris smile. It was her sister who was finally getting married, and her husband-to-be wanted the ceremony to be perfect for his bride. He'd sought out the place through a network of friends who'd heard of it, and gave sterling reviews of their service.

Inside, they were greeted by a sharply dressed old Negro man, who bowed crisply as he opened the door and took their coats. They made their way through the main hall toward the chapel with awe. It was as if time had passed for every other place, but had been somehow tamed for this structure. A woman wearing a maid's uniform of the period stood attentively, adding to the mystique and illusion that they'd just stepped back in time. In every corner, great columns rose to meet the peaked ceilings, adding to the grandeur of the palatial estate. On every wall, portraits of fine southern gentlemen, women, and their servants hung, staring wordlessly from another age.

They made their way through the ornately carved hallway to the chapel, still in its original glory, where the wedding was to take place. Chris sat, paying no attention to the ceremony until cued with a well-placed elbow, admiring the splendor of an age gone by.

As he looked about the room, he noticed several people dressed in period garb, whom he assumed were employees of the mansion. Chris scanned the room, stopping at each of them to notice the finer details of their costumes. It wasn't until one noticed him that he realized that something in Heaven on Earth was decidedly more than anyone had bargained for.

As he looked about, he spied the man who'd opened the door for them, whose crisp bow and warm welcome had ushered them in with such formality. As his eyes lighted on the old steward's face, the man seemed to grow still, then slowly shifted his own gaze until their eyes were locked. For whatever reason, Chris felt his flesh begin to creep as the old man smiled broadly at him. There was something in his eyes, his smile that seemed unnaturally white and wide, even his movements, that seemed somehow unsettling. Not that the old man actually did anything threatening, but merely smiled broadly at Chris, then promptly faded into the woodwork like as much smoke.

Chris jerked his body uncontrollably back in his seat, his immediate reaction to flee, but a stern look from Tina, whose face flushed with embarrassment and anger, allowed him to reign in his fear. He did, however, spend the rest of the ceremony with an uneasy feeling in his stomach.

As the ceremony ended, Chris glanced nervously around the room. Bad enough that he thought he'd seen a disappearing steward, but crowds also set his nerves on edge. He'd screwed up his courage to attend, realizing that there would be nearly a hundred guests at the wedding, of which he would know scarcely a handful. Tina, bless her, had told him that he didn't have to come, but it was a blessed occasion. It meant so much to his wife and her family that he put his own aversions aside and joined them.

The guests made their way out of the chapel to the ballroom. Chris seized the opportunity, with Tina's blessing, to sneak to the garden outside to smoke. He lit a cigarette and sat on the great marble bench in the gazebo, trying to rationalize what he'd seen, or thought he'd seen, inside. Of course the porter had been real. He'd taken their coats, hadn't he? His quick disappearance had been a trick of the light. He'd probably just stepped into a shadow on his way back to some duty. Now, in the night air, away from the antebellum surroundings of Heaven on Earth and the crowd therein, he began to calm.

"Hello," he heard a tiny voice say from in front of him.

He lifted his head to see a little girl, no more than eleven years old he guessed, dressed in a frilly dress the color of the wedding party.

"Hi," he said gently.

"What're you doing out here?" she asked, smiling.

"I'm getting away from the noise for a moment. What're you doing out here?"

"Same as you, I guess. Wasn't the wedding beautiful?"

"Yes," he said. He had to admit, Heaven on Earth certainly lived up to its name tonight. He could remember no more beautiful a setting in any church. Rene was stunning in her wedding gown, and Tommy looked, for lack of a better term, quite dashing.

"I love weddings," she continued dreamily. "I can't wait until I'm old enough to get married. I want my wedding to be here, just like theirs."

Chris smiled. There was an innocence to the child that touched him, reminded him of when his own daughter was that age. Now, he knew, it wouldn't be long before he'd be walking down the aisle, giving her away to some man that he neither liked nor trusted. Though she was away at college, he still thought of her the way this little girl looked: In lacy dresses with sparkling eyes and a wondrous outlook on the world.

From the house, he heard music, heralding the entrance of the bride and groom. As the crowd began to cheer, the little girl took his hand and pulled.

"Come on!" she insisted. "Let's go back inside! The party's starting!"

He obediently followed, as he would've his own daughter, taken in by her unvarnished joy. As they reached the ballroom, she loosed her hand from his and happily skipped through the crowd, leaving Chris feeling warm and happy as he went to find his wife. He found her hugging the bride, her smile more beautiful than he remembered. He kissed her cheek and gave her a squeeze.

"You look like you're having a good time," she said, surprised by seemingly calm demeanor.

"I guess I am," he shrugged, taking his wife around the waist and leading her to the dance floor. "Remember the last time that Dina was a flower girl in a wedding? How old was she then, eleven?"

"Yeah, I think so."

"I wish she were here now," he smiled.

They danced together for several songs, until, at last, Tina needed a break. They danced to the edge of the dance floor, where she sat in a chair, laughing at how much fun they were having. Chris was enjoying himself as well, until he looked across the dance floor and saw the little girl. She was standing by herself, swaying despondently to the music, her face a wistful mask of want. He could tell by looking at her what she wanted, and as his dance partner needed a break and his daughter was several hundred miles away, he decided to grant her wish.

He pointed her out to his wife, who smiled and nodded approvingly at his gesture, then he made his way across the crowded floor to the little girl, who looked up at him with wonder in her eyes as he extended his hand.

"May I have this dance?" he asked sweetly, bringing a squeal of delight.

For nearly an hour he danced with her, teaching her the clumsy jitterbug steps he could still remember from high school, much to her delight. He would occasionally glance over to where Tina watched with gleeful approval. Then, without warning, the little girl stopped dancing.

For a brief moment, she looked very sad, then she gestured for Chris to lean down to her. She kissed his cheek and hastily said she had to go, then she ran from the dance floor toward the front of the mansion. Confused, and a bit concerned, he followed, but as he rounded the corner, he was surprised to find she was nowhere to be seen. He could only see one conceivable place that she'd have gone to leave the mansion, so he made his way to the front door, hoping at least to say goodbye to the little girl before she went home with her parents.

He reached the front door to find the porter who'd let them in earlier standing at his station. The sudden disappearance dismissed as illusion, he asked the old man if the little girl had run by.

"Little girl, you say?" he asked, chuckling. "'Bout eleven years old?

_____

Blond hair?"

"Yes. Did she leave this way?"

"We calls her Abby," he laughed. "She never leaves. She been dead for nigh on to a hundred and thirty years."

"What're you talking about?" demanded Chris. "I danced with her for over an hour."

"Mighty kind of you, dancin' with her. She loves weddings, but nobody hardly ever dances with her. Probably made her really happy."

"Look," he said, the irritation in his voice evident. "Don't feed me the tourist stories crap, okay? I just wanted to see if she was okay."

"You don't believe me?" said the old man with a smile. "See for yourself." He gestured toward a framed photograph on the wall.

Still not believing, Chris went defiantly to the photo. As he squinted to see the faded image, his expression changed from one of anger to one of shock.

The photo was dated 1868, and was taken in front of Heaven on Earth of old. Where now there were buildings of like plainness, there were only pecan trees stretching out of the picture. It was a photo of the house owners and staff of that time.

Chris looked until he found a single image. He stared in shock at the lacy dress and cheerful smile of the little girl with whom he'd just been dancing. As realization set in, he noticed a few other faces that bore familiar lines. In the photo were several of the wedding guests, as well as at least one woman whom he'd seen wearing the uniform of a maid in the parlor. Most disturbing to him, however, was the elderly black man in the steward's coat, smiling on the front row. Chris slowly turned to face the old man, who smiled at him and winked.

"We all love weddings," he said, then faded into a shadowy haze.

It surprised Chris, that he did not feel afraid after the encounter. Quite the contrary, there was a growing warmth inside him, a welcoming feeling that seemed to radiate from the mansion itself. He smiled to himself

_____

as he made his way back to the ballroom, where the party was winding down. He kissed Tina and hugged her when he found her, feeling a renewed sense of wonder at the old mansion and its beauty. Heaven on Earth, he mused. An appropriate name for a place where angels walk among men.

The tinkling of a glass rose over the crowd, signaling the bride and groom's departure. Before they left, Rene turned to the guests.

"Thank you all, so much. This is supposed to be, and was, the happiest day of my life. I wish we never had to leave."

Some never do, thought Chris with a smile.

Droplets

Jock Itch

Clattering metal and curses filled the air as the hulking wet mass that was Adam Bethel stormed between the lockers. It was late, he was tired, and he'd had enough of all the nonsense. His days were full with classes and he didn't care for most of the sports endorsed by the college, so he chose to lift weights and practice boxing at the student center gym when it was relatively empty, for that he could at least be thankful. There was no one in the locker room to see him sopping wet and stomping about in just a towel.

He looked down each isle of lockers and in both showers to find his tormentor, the one who'd stolen his clothes and announced his presence by popping Adam with a rolled up towel, but found no sign.

"Fucking imp," he said under his breath.

It had seemed like a good idea at the time, as did many things that Adam did that were ill fated. And, like so many other things, he'd done it to impress a girl, who now would not give him a second glance. Who'd have thought that magic was real, that demons and monsters actually existed? Who'd have believed that an imp could be such trouble?

She was pretty enough that his lusts were aroused by her. He'd tried to strike up a conversation and finally hit pay dirt with the subject of religion. She, it seemed, was a nuveau-witch. He didn't particularly care, only that she was to become another notch on his bedpost, so he'd played along, clumsily professing knowledge of things he'd never heard of. When at last she'd invited him to her room, he was cocky, sure that he'd just charmed his way into another girl's pants. But when they arrived, she lit candles and showed him books on the strangest of subjects. He soon realized that she'd not believed a word he'd said, and had brought him here to confront him with his ignorance. To save face, he defiantly snatched a book from her hands and read whatever strange words were written on the page. Much to his surprise, that was when Gnyutlek appeared.

He was small, even for an imp, and covered in oily black scales that seemed to change color at his whim. What hair he had on his lizard-like head stood in several tufts that seemed to sprout from wherever it wished. It had clicked its claws and swished its tail at them once the sulfurous smoke had cleared, and then fixed Adam with its nearly luminous green eyes and spoke.

"Master has summoned Gnyutlek, he has, and Gnyutlek must do his bidding."

Adam fell backward, shocked that this, or anything for that matter, had happened. Witchcraft, to him, was nothing more than a way for goth misfits to live in a fantasy world. But the proof stood on Bethany's bed in front of him, swishing his tail excitedly, his eyes dancing with fire.

Before he could say another word, Bethany had thrown him out of her room in a fit of fury, calling him an immature neanderthal as she slammed the door behind him. Gnyutlek had slithered through the door just as it closed and stood expectantly in the hall in front of Adam.

"Get away from me," he'd stammered as the thing stared at him.

"Gnyutlek cannot," it hissed. *"Master has summoned Gnyutlek, and Gnyutlek must do master's bidding."*

"What are you?" asked Adam, aware but uncaring that his tough-guy facade had dissolved the moment the little demon had appeared. "Please, don't hurt me."

"Gnyutlek is an imp, it is," it replied, almost managing to look offended. *"It cannot hurt the master. Gnyutlek loves the master, it does."*

Adam remembered the wave of terror that had crashed over him in the hallway. Even now, as he searched the locker room furtively for the creature, his every intention to wring its scaly neck, he felt some lingering fear that the creature, if provoked, could do him harm.

There were rules, it had informed him, by which it had to abide. Although its purpose was to inflict mayhem and chaos at his master's whim, it was unable to touch another living being. All its pranks, vicious as they could be, had to be limited to the victim's surroundings and environment. It also could not kill anyone, as it was only an imp and such matters were not allowed by his kind. It could, however drive someone insane, or to ruin, or even suicide if his master so desired it.

He remembered standing outside Bethany's dorm room as the imp became flat as paper and slid under her door, and the screams that pierced the air with the sounds of breaking glass and moving furniture. It had hit her room with the force of a hurricane, and had rocked gleefully back on its tail, laughing, when it had caught up to Adam again. Adam, of course, wanted no part of the thing. It was a mistake, a monster, and he'd told it as such. He'd begged with the little thing to go away, but the imp told him that so long as Adam was its master, it would stay by his side.

Adam stormed out of the locker room, much to the surprise of the others who used the gym at that time of day, wearing only a towel and shower shoes.

"Gnyutlek!" he bellowed as he looked wildly around.

The girl behind the check-in counter fought to keep her composure as he stalked to her station.

"Have you seen a..." A what, he asked himself. An imp? A demon? The receptionist blinked at him while fighting to stifle a laugh. "Did you see someone run out of here with my clothes?"

She didn't answer, only shook her head quickly. Exasperated, he rushed past her desk and headed toward the quad. His car was in the parking lot, but his keys had been in the pocket of his pants, which the imp had stolen. Also in his pants was his identification card, the magnetic strip on which was his key to get into his own dorm. The whole thing had gone too far, and, God help him, he could only think of one person who might be able to help.

As he passed people one the quad, he made laughing comments to their stares. Hadn't they ever seen a naked guy before, he said, and made light comments about doing laundry, but in truth he was plenty angry and embarrassed. He only hoped Bethany would speak to him. By the time he reached the tower that was West-Campus Dorm it was well after eleven and he wasn't sure she'd even be awake, but he pressed the buttons by the door until she finally answered. After a few tense moments, during which she repeated her estimation that he was a jock neanderthal and he revealed that he was standing in front of the door wearing only a towel, Adam finally convinced her to let him in. She met him in the lobby and together they went to the lounge.

"What do you want?" she said with tight lips and an irritated edge to her voice.

"Look, I'm sorry, okay?" Not the best of beginnings, he knew, but he was angry and desperate for help. "I didn't mean to call that thing into your room."

"Did you see what it did? Renter's insurance doesn't cover imps, y'know."

"I know..."

"Serves you right for messing with stuff you don't understand."

"I know..."

"See what happens when you let your dick think for you?"

"Are you going to help me or not?" he cut in, angry at the berating. "This goddamned thing stole my clothes, and I can't get into my dorm, my car, or my classes."

"Good!" she laughed. "My room is still trashed."

"I said I was sorry," he growled. "I didn't know. You're the only one I know who knows about this magic shit."

"You're his master," she said nonchalantly. "You deal with him."

"I'm not his master anymore," he said quietly.

"Excuse me?"

"He kept going on about me being his master and I didn't know what to do. I finally told him that I commanded that I wasn't his master anymore."

Bethany sat stunned for a few moments before she spoke.

"Of all the stupid...Do you realize what you just turned loose on this world?"

"I didn't," he snapped. "I didn't think it would come after me."

"Oh, so as long as you're fine, who cares about the rest of the world, right? You are such a dumbass."

"Yeah, well, now he won't quit bugging me," he said, his tone almost pleading. "He e-mailed porn from my computer to my mom and grandma from my account, he filled my pillow up with dogshit, and now he's stolen my clothes!"

"And? Why should I care?"

"Fine," he said, standing abruptly. "Just be a bitch then." He turned quickly, nearly losing his towel, and made for the door. Back out on the quad, Adam fumed, wondering what to do.

"Hey," he heard, snapping his head around to see Bethany behind him. "Look, I'm sorry," she said earnestly. "I'll do what I can, but I'm not sure what I can do."

Adam let out a long exasperated sigh.

"Thank you."

"First thing we do is get you back into your dorm," she said. "You need clothes."

The walk to Adam's dorm was a short distance, but, because he was wearing only shower shoes, it made his feet hurt nonetheless. When they got there, they walked past the dorm's receptionist without looking up.

"Why didn't you just ask her to let you in?" asked Bethany, referring to the pretty girl with red hair that sat behind the counter.

"She hates me," said Adam. "Thinks I'm an asshole."

"Another conquest huh?"

"Yeah," said Adam sheepishly. He'd gotten her when she was only a freshman, and a virgin to boot. She'd been too naive to be wary of campus predators such as him, so he'd deflowered her with relative ease. Then he never called her again.

"Pig," she said, not even trying to hide her disgust. "She's right. You are an asshole."

They went around the building to the far wing of the dorm, where the electronic lock guarded against unwanted visitors. Bethany placed one hand over the lock and took a quick glance around.

"*Resero,*" she said softly.

Adam gaped when the door clicked and opened slightly as she gave a satisfied smile and turned to leave.

"Where're you going?" he asked, still unsure of how she'd just gained access to his dorm.

"I got you in," she said over her shoulder. "I'm done. Good luck."

Adam stood perplexed in the open doorway watching her walk away. "Bitch," he said as she rounded the corner.

As he climbed the metal stairs to the second floor, he fumed to himself. She could have stayed, he thought, and let him thank her properly. She didn't have to be such a bitch to him. So what if he screwed a few girls? He was a guy. That's what guys did. And it wasn't as if the girls hadn't wanted it.

Adam rounded the corner of the stairwell and stopped dead in his tracks. The door to his room was ajar and wisps of black smoke were flitting from within. He ran to the door and pushed it fully open to find that Gnyutlek had already been there. Sitting on his bed were his clothes, clean and folded, but the rest of his room looked as though it had been hit by terrorists.

His television and VCR were sitting in pieces on the floor beside a large mound of tape that previously had been inside the casings of his movie collection. The stuffing of his mattress was strewn like snow about the room with festive tatters that had been his sheets hanging from the ceiling tiles. His computer looked as though some crazed beast with an axe had run amok over its casing, and there was a pile of papers smoldering in his garbage can that, on closer inspection, proved to have once been the term paper that was due the next morning.

"No!" he half sobbed. Adam walked, dazed, into his room and stood with a lost expression on his face as he surveyed the damage. Was this what he did to Bethany's room, he wondered. No wonder she was still pissed.

He was about to reach for his pants, the only pair he had left from the looks of things, when a rustling in the closet caught his attention. He felt his temper flair as he picked a broken boxing trophy from the floor and held it like a club. He jerked the closet open with a cry and found Gnyutlek defecating in his dress shoes.

"You motherfucker!" he shrieked as he brought the club down hard, missing the imp by a whisker.

"Mustn't touch it," the imp said tauntingly. *"Against the rules, it is!"*

The imp cackled with glee as it leaped from wall to wall, nimbly avoiding each crushing blow. Adam could feel his temples throb with rage as he continued to try to smash the little creature. Demon or no, it had gone too far and Adam was going to kill it.

After a few moments of dodging, the creature seemed to grow bored with the game and made to leap over Adam's head. It landed on the floor behind him, only to have his tail pinned in place by Adam's shower shoe.

"Let Gnyutlek go," it pleaded. *"It won't cause no more harm, it*

won't."

But the maniacal look on Adam's face told with no uncertainty that he was going to make good on his threat to kill the wretched little beast. He dropped the trophy and bent down, taking the creature firmly around the neck and lifting it so he could see into its eyes. Then he began to squeeze.

Gnyutlek squirmed for a moment and then began to cough. Adam felt very satisfied with himself until the coughing turned into a muted chuckle and the imp raised its eyes to meet his.

"*Warned you, Gnyutlek did,*" it said through a smile that was wholly too wide. "*Should never lay hands on one of its kind, you mustn't.*"

Adam had no comprehension of why the creature wasn't dying until he felt his skin begin to creep and tear. His eyes grew wide as the scales of Gnyutlek's body turned liquid and began to seep into his arms through his pores. Adam wanted to scream, to pull it off of him, but the imp was having none of it. Its face twisted into a malignant leer as it continued to seep into his body, burning him to the bones as it flowed through him until at last it was done. Adam stood, still only clad in a towel and shower shoes, in the center of his decimated room, staring blankly at the far wall.

"Good boy, Gnyutlek."

He turned to see Bethany, a wicked smile on her face as she leaned against the frame of the door.

"I knew I could count on you."

"*Gnyutlek loves its master, it does,*" hissed Adam. "*Gnyutlek has done well?*"

"Gnyutlek has done very well," she purred. "Do you like this new body?"

Adam nodded vigorously.

"Are you sure about this, Bethy?" asked the receptionist as she peered around the corner. "I mean, this seems a little harsh."

"He deserved it sis," she said coldly. "Stupid jock, thinking he could screw my sister, never call her and get away with it. He won't do that again."

"I meant Gnyutlek," she said with a smile. "I mean, he's been our imp for so long. What's going to happen to him?"

"Gnyutlek will serve its masters, it will," hissed Adam. *"Gnyutlek loves its masters."*

Droplets

_____

Mimes

Jack brooded over the days events as he walked toward home. He'd gotten up late because the alarm clock was set for 6:30 p.m., not a.m., been bawled out by his boss because of his consequential tardiness, and things just deteriorated afterward. His latest client wouldn't listen to him and insisted on dragging an unwinnable case out in court, which threatened another blemish on his somewhat impressive record. Lawyers weren't supposed to have bad days. They were supposed to cause them for other people. When five o'clock finally rolled around, he discovered his wallet missing, which made him unable to pay for a cab ride. His mood grew more sour with every trudging step.

He decided to cut across Central Park to get to his house, an old brownstone with spacious rooms. He'd bought the thing when he first moved to Manhattan Island because it was close to his office and, for the salary the firm paid him, he wasn't about to live like some middle class apartment renter.

He cleared the outer wall of the park and paused as he looked around. Central Park was no place to walk alone after dark, but there were still a few hours of daylight left, more than enough time to get home. He could easily avoid trouble if he just stayed on the official path.

He'd not gone halfway through the park when he saw the Mimes doing their shtick for the other passers by. He felt his disgust at seeing them resurface.

Droplets

Jack hated Mimes.

To him, they were the lowest part of society. They did nothing but walk against imaginary wind and pull non- existent ropes to panhandle for change that poor suckers tossed to them. He doubted any of them had homes and bet they used whatever meager change was given to buy some sort of drug that would help perpetuate their hallucinations of invisible boxes and other such nonsense. Also, he found them disturbing, the way they always smiled wide-eyed and never spoke. Were it up to him, he'd have them all arrested and put on trial for something, anything, so he could defend the whole lot of them in court. Though he liked to think of himself as one of the best lawyers in the state, he would gladly lose that case on purpose just to see them all sent to prison.

He hurried toward the outer edge of the park, and almost breathed a sigh of relief, when he noticed one of the Mimes following him. He turned to look at the leotard-clad stalker, who stopped, smiled grotesquely, and gave him a snappy cartoonish wave.

"Leave me alone," said Jack, just loud enough for the Mime to hear him, then he turned to walk away.

He hadn't taken five more steps when he realized that the hideous beast still followed him. It mimicked every movement, every gesture, with grotesque overexaggeration. His arm swing, his gate, even the way he stopped became something of ridicule.   Again he turned to face the Mime.

"Look," he said through a forced smile. "I've had a very bad day, I don't have any money to give to you. Now go away."

The Mime made an exaggerated sad face and balled his hands over his eyes as though crying, then wiped his gloved palms across his mouth to reveal that same sickening smile they all wore.

"Cute," said Jack. "Very cute. Now go away."

He turned his back on the bug-eyed grinning idiot and started off toward his home again. The Mime, not deterred, pranced along behind him in obscenely exaggerated ballet steps.

"I'm warning you," muttered Jack under his breath.

Jack took two more steps when he felt the gloved hand of the Mime fall on his jacket.

"That's your last mistake," he shouted as he whirled around and connected with a vicious fist to the Mime's nose. Something inside him snapped. All the day's frustrations, his client, his wallet, and now *this* asshole? Bad enough street performers clogged the city with stupidity and panhandling, but for one to lay a hand on him was too much. He reached down and took the man by his shirt and pulled him close to his face.

"You people are a bunch of Goddamned freaks!" he screamed, spittle flying into the Mime's face. Again Jack's fist landed against the Mime's cheek, sending him sprawling back to the asphalt. "You're worse than rats!" He kicked the fallen Mime in the ribs with crackling results. "You plague this city," Jack yelled, kicking him in the ribs again, "and you make me sick!" A final kick and the Mime lay before him, bloodied and gasping for breath.

Jack felt his violence subside, but not his loathing. He reached into his suitcoat pocket and flung a business card at the fallen man.

"If you ever need a lawyer," he said snidely, "look me up. I'm the best in the business."

He turned to walk away, then couldn't resist a final barb.

"Oh yeah," he said. "Get a job."

He felt better, as if the day's troubles eased with every blow. No one would care. Police didn't file assault charges against people for beating up Mimes. And even if they did, the stupid bastard touched him first. It was self- defense. At least, he could plead so, and most likely get off. He walked away with a spring in his step. He didn't see the other Mimes as they slunk out of the bushes and down the sidewalk to come to the aid of their fallen brother.

The first by his side gently cradled the fallen one's head against his breast, took notice of the blood he spat up as he tried to breathe. As their

---

numbers grew, more than a dozen painted faces looked with burning eyes down the path in the direction Jack had gone.

* * *

Jack arrived home in a far better mood than when he left work. What a wonderful way to end his day. That Mime had it coming as far as Jack was concerned, and maybe he and his sissy buddies would think twice about laying a hand on good and hard working people again. As far as he was concerned, he'd done the city a service.

He unlocked the door and was greeted by his purring orange tabby.

"Hiya Justice." He smiled as he picked the large feline up. "Guess what Daddy did today?"

Hours later, after dinner for both himself and the cat, he sat with a glass of wine in his leather easy chair, and listened to Mozart as he pet his cat in the dim light.

"Heh," he said to the cat. "Y'know, the funny thing was, even while I was beating him up, that damned Mime never made a sound! I guess they really can't talk."

Justice purred as he stroked his fur again. Jack picked up his cat and walked upstairs to bed. His terrible day turned out better than expected. He had a few things to tell his client and his boss in the morning, and he was feeling quite invincible. He put the cat on the bed and took off his trousers and shirt. "G'night Justice," he said as he crawled beneath the sheets and switched off the light.

* * *

Jack awoke early, rested and satisfied with a good night's sleep. He yawned and stretched and lazily rolled out of bed. He felt a little odd, fuzzy-headed, but that he attributed to residual sleepiness. It would wear off as soon as he got some coffee and got moving.

He took a long shower and shaved, neatly combed his hair and dressed in a dark wool suit. The memory of the previous day's events still brought a smile to his lips.

With thoughts of having Mimes banned from the park and city racing through his mind, Jack went down the stairs where he found Justice waiting by the door.

"Good-bye, Justice," he said as he reached to stroke his cat's head.

The cat laid its ears back and hissed, raised the fur on its back. Just as Jack's hand got within petting distance, the cat slashed at it with its claws and yowled.

Jack pulled his hand back in surprise. "What's gotten into you?" he said. As if in answer, the cat spat again, then ran to hide under the leather easy chair. "Weird cat," Jack muttered under his breath. He pulled his hat and overcoat from the hat tree and put them on as he turned and opened his front door.

Across the street from his house, a Mime leaned against nothing. Jack froze. It looked different from the other Mimes in the park. Where their smiles and faces were often somnambulistic, this one's eyes burned. His smile was just a little too wide, his teeth yellow in comparison to the starkness of his face. His firey eyes gave Jack goose flesh to feel their malignant weight on him.

The Mime gave Jack an exaggerated wave hello. "What the hell do you want?" The Mime raised two fingers, as a child might when

talking about scissors. He pointed at Jack, then snipped his fingers across his own throat. Jack clutched his throat as he felt pain in his larynx.

"What the hell...?" he wanted to say, but when he opened his mouth no sound would emerge.

His puzzled look sent the Mime into convulsions of silent laughter and he stood, soundlessly slapped his knees and doubled over. The Mime then skipped across the street toward him. Jack felt the fear rise up within him, chilling his blood in his veins. He began to walk briskly away, around the block and away from his devilish looking stalker. As he walked, he kept glancing over his shoulder to see if the grinning menace was still behind him. To his dismay, it was, and it kept perfect time with his step. He rounded the corner and felt the hat lifted from his head. He whirled around to see three more Mimes perched in the doorway beside him. They too waved at him, either by broad gesture or by wiggling fingers, and they too smiled that same malevolent smile. The one in the middle, the largest of the three, donned Jack's hat and gave it a rakish tilt, all the while smiling at him demonically.

Jack's heart raced. It couldn't be happening. Corralled and terrorized by a street gang of Mimes? Who'd ever heard of such a thing? They outnumbered him, but what could they really do? A bunch of skinny, tight-clad poofs? Nothing, he hoped.

Again Jack resumed his course, but much more quickly. He half jogged to the next corner with all four of the painted monsters in close pursuit. As he rounded the next corner, he almost fell over himself as he tried to stop at the sight before him. Another pack of Mimes stood at the end of the block, and upon seeing him, began their slow advance. Each of them walked differently, but they all had the same menacing gestures, the same air of evil. His only exit was the park. He would have to cut through Central Park to get away from them and try to blend in. Then, after he'd lost them, he reasoned, he'd go to the police and have them all thrown in jail.

He made for the gate at a dead run, as cold sweat poured down his forehead and neck. If they caught him, he was sure they would kill him. Street people lived by different rules. They had no laws, no real homes. They were not even real people to Jack.

From behind every bush and bench leapt still more Mimes to torment him. Had he his voice, he'd have screamed. As he ran past a lightpost, another Mime swung out and snatched hold of him by the collar of his coat. Jack wriggled out of it and fell to the ground, still trying to gain ground away from his pursuers. He looked up at the one who had his coat. It stared back at him, swinging his coat overhead, his mouth open in silent laughter.

With great effort, Jack righted himself and ran down the path. He looked behind him to see that the number of Mimes in pursuit had grown.

There were more than twenty white faces, and with each step their ranks swelled. His feeling of panic increased as he passed the edge of the clearing that was the center of Central Park. Jack's heart pounded, but it almost stopped as he saw thirty Mimes lined up before him, blocking the exit. They smiled in unison and began the slow but terrifying creep toward him. The Mimes behind him had stopped running and took slow deliberate steps. Jack whirled about, frightened and confused. He lashed out at the closest ones, hoped in vain he could fight his way clear and escape, but there were too many of them. Gloved hands came from everywhere and held him fast. His suit jacket was ripped from his back and his suspenders snapped painfully many times. Two Mimes wearing cowboy hats approached twirling imaginary lassos. Jack could scarcely believe it when they took aim and seemed to throw them at him, but his mind simply refused to admit that although he could see nothing, he could feel the weight and strength of the ropes which bound him about the shoulders and waist.

Jack was dragged toward a wooded spot in the park, one that seemed darker than the rest. No markers adorned the area, no statues nor water fountains. It was a place most people left alone.

The Mime in front, the one who met Jack at his front door, gave an evil smile and gestured for Jack to be led over to an old rusted park bench. The Mime leapt behind it and gave it a tug. Much to Jack's surprise, the bench tilted backward, slab and bolt, revealing a flight of stairs down a long dark passage. Bound as he was, Jack could not resist being dragged down into the bowels of the world beneath the park. As he walked, gloved hands pinched his cheeks and swatted the back of his head.

This can't be happening, thought Jack. When...If he got out of this mess, he would make certain that this place was gutted with fire.

The Mimes led him down for what seemed to Jack to be forever. They'd walked long enough to be under the city's subway tunnels. If his fears were correct and they were going to kill him, his body would never be found. Jack began to cry.

A Mime noticed Jack's erratic breathing and looked back at him. Then, as it opened its mouth in a look of feigned surprise, it held a mirror before Jack. Where ever a tear fell on Jack's face, a black tear formed as though drawn on his face by an invisible artist. A Mime's tear.

The tunnel opened up and became lighter as the ghoulishly quiet procession came to an immense cavern lit by torches. Jack immediately recognized the room for what it was supposed to be: A courtroom.

Motley colors and strips of cloth lined the walls in tatters, giving the place the look of a ruined circus. Stretching the length of the cave were stone benches, twelve deep, that encircled him. Not one seat was empty as faces painted in white with hideous black lips smiled and stared down upon him with demonic bulging eyes.

A Mime wearing a badge and a police hat came and took Jack to the center of the great hall where stood a platform and rail. He was meant to stand trial for what he had done.

The bailiff gestured and every Mime stood reverently as the last entered the room. He sat atop a great pedestal behind a bench: A Judge. He wore a white powdered wig that curled over his shoulders and the black robes that Jack had come to know through his years. The only real discernible difference between this and the other Mimes was his face. While most of the Mimes' faces were white with black lines about the mouth and eyes, this one's face was a lesson in contrast, half his face in white, the other in black. The eyes and mouth were drawn with the appropriate colors with lines drawn to give the Judge a scowling countenance.

He sat and gestured, giving the other Mimes permission to sit. The Judge raised his empty hand, as if holding a gavel, and brought it down sharply. Jack flinched as though the sound of the invisible gavel echoed in his ears.

Two Mimes, one in red tights and the other in an ill-fitting suit, approached the bench and bowed deeply. The Judge nodded and the two went to either side of Jack. The one in red stepped forward and began to gesture wildly about. It was then that Jack realized what was going on. The two Mimes were lawyers. The one in the bad suit was his defense, the other satanic looking fellow, the prosecutor. Jack struggled against the non-existent bonds.

As the prosecutor wriggled about, Jack began to understand what he was trying to say. He watched in horror as the Mime thrust an accusing finger toward him, then motioned for his first witness. The broken Mime from the previous day was brought forth in a wheelchair. With broad, sweeping movements, the prosecutor questioned the witness. After a lengthy show of "walking along," performed using only his hands he put his fingers to his mouth in a silent whistle. Two more Mimes ran to his side, one roughly the size of the witness, the other obviously made up to look like a grotesque caricature of Jack.

The two proceeded to perform the altercation in broad detail. Every strike, kick, and insult replicated, but amplified as though looked at through a warped mirror. In horror, Jack watched himself pound on the poor man with devilish glee. Then, when the charade was finished, the two Mimes got up, bowed deeply before the Judge, and went back to their seats. The prosecutor spread his hands and arms wide, indicating that he would now rest his case.

The room around Jack was a cacophony of movement. Jack instinctively put his hands to his ears to block out what would have been a deluge of angry sentiments from those in audience.

The Judge gestured toward the defense. Slowly, the lawyer turned his head and fixed his gaze into Jack's pleading eyes. As though inspecting him, the Mime looked Jack all the way up and down. He turned back toward the Judge and shrugged.

Jack stood in disbelief as the lawyer turned and sauntered broadly over to the prosecutor and shook his hand. He wanted to object, to call for a mistrial, to scream bloody murder, but although his mouth formed the words, no sound would come out.

The harlequin Judge again raised his imaginary gavel and gave what would have been a viscous strike to the bench. He began a long gesticulated frenzy that Jack could not even guess at the meaning of until he began to hear a voice, a whisper, buzzing inside his head.

. . . *Found guilty of the persecution of our kind, and are therefore sentenced to life as one of our kind. . .*

Jack shook his head and stared, for though the Judge's lips did not move, the words were becoming plainer to him. He was being sentenced. . . . *Furthermore,* the voice continued, *you shall be kept in containment for the duration of your life, set symbol for all who would follow your example.* The voice faded, and, as if to punctuate the last remark, the judge drew a square with his fingers in the air then once again snapped the vaporous gavel to the bench. This time, Jack could have sworn he heard its report.

At once, all the Mimes in attendance leaped to their feet, congratulating each other in silence for their victory over such persecution. The two Mimes in cowboy hats reappeared at Jacks sides and, taking hold of the invisible ropes which bound him, dragged him back toward the tunnel, followed by a female Mime with a small satchel and two whose movements suggested they were carrying something heavy.

When light finally broke into the tunnel, Jack was hauled up to the great open area of Central Park where people most liked to spend their lunch hours and feed pigeons. There the Mimes tied the imaginary rope to a tree. Though Jack struggled to free himself, the phantom bonds held fast.

The female Mime then reached in her bag and produced a tin of whiteface and a cake of black greasepaint and began applying them to Jack's face. She carefully lined his eyes and eyebrows, then smeared more of the black paint on her own lips. Taking the sides of his head in her hands, she kissed him forcefully, leaving her imprint on his lips and completing his Mime's mask. She covered her mouth with the tips of her fingers on one hand, as if to stifle a schoolgirl giggle, and skipped away into the park.

The other two Mimes lifted whatever it was they were supposed to be carrying high above their heads and stepped to either side of him before lowering their arms to the ground. Both then waved in broad comedic fashion, and walked away against an invisible wind. The cowboys both tipped their hats, coiled their invisible lariats, and walked away, swaggering side to side.

Unsure of what the Mimes had actually done to him, Jack took two steps and ran into an invisible wall. Slowly he began to realize that they had put him in a box. He'd seen Mimes try to get out of imaginary boxes hundreds of times, but now he knew. The boxes were real.

Jack fell to his knees sobbing. He was sorry he'd beaten up the Mime. He was sorry, in fact, that he'd ever even heard of Mimes.

"Mommy! Look at the funny clown!" A young, golden-haired child's blue eyes looked up at him.

"That's not a clown, dear," replied a tired-looking woman. "That's a Mime." "What's the difference?" asked the child. Exasperated, the mother replied "Oh, I don't know.

Mimes don't talk, I guess." Jack wanted to scream and beg them for help in getting out of this box, but no sound would come from his severed vocal chords. All he could do was bang helplessly against the sides of his small invisible prison.

"Aw. . .," said the boy. "I've seen this gettin'-out-of- the-box thing before." His interest lost, the boy took his mother's hand and walked away, pointing out whatever new wonder caught his eye as they walked.

Jack's eyes followed them down the path as he continued to try to smash his way through the walls. He watched them walk away and stopped pounding. He stared in disbelief as she saw dozens of Mimes, each dressed in the suits or uniforms of the casual passer-by, lined up along the pathways, each of them furtively trying to find a way out of prisons made of air.

Droplets

Monotony

Jason got up, just like he did every Saturday morning. He slapped the alarm clock three times, stubbed his toe on the edge of his bed, and stumbled to the bathroom, just as he'd done every Saturday morning in his memory. He didn't bother taking his watch into the bathroom anymore. He didn't need to look at it to know he would spend less than a minute emptying his bladder, a minute and a half brushing his teeth, fifteen minutes in the shower, and another ten dressing and brushing his hair. He knew his routine.

He left the bathroom and took sixteen stairs down to the kitchen, cooked two eggs and four sausage links in the small frying pan, drank a small glass of juice, and was done and ready for work in twenty-seven minutes.

There was never any change. Every Saturday was the same, predictable as a matinee. He locked the door on the way out to the garage and backed his car out. He sat for a moment, counting. Three...two...one... Mrs. Willis walked out the back door of her house to get the paper. In his rear-view mirror, he saw Mr. Johnson walking Petey, his bulldog. He counted to five and the dog lifted his leg and marked Jason's mailbox, just as he'd done every Saturday. Nothing ever changed.

He backed out of the driveway, put the car in drive, and made his way to the end of the street. Five seconds. He turned left, drove for another seventeen seconds, then turned right. Same path, same street, same traffic, same time. Everything was the same.

On the way into town, he counted. It was a game he played often, but one that seemed so monotonous to him now. By sixty, he went on the overpass, and the morning train was right on its boring schedule. By ninety-five, he saw the hands working the McCullough ranch. They never seemed to work another section of field. But that was impossible. They had to work other sections, otherwise it would be a poor excuse for a farm. Still, when the blond boy with the pasty body stripped his t-shirt off, Jason knew it was going to happen. Knew it, because he'd seen the same thing at the same time every Saturday he could remember.

He used to remind himself of his schedule as he drove, but now it was more reflexive action. Past the tracks, past the pasty kid, exit by the count of two-hundred-five, pull into the doughnut shop by the count of two-sixty. In and out in five minutes, then on to the mega-store.

When did life lose its spontaneity? When did the rut first wear into his schedule? Most people longed for weekends when they could do something other than work. Jason, however, wished his employers wouldn't limit him to forty hours a week. At least at work, there was the occasional panicked phone call, customers who didn't know a computer mouse from a foot-pedal. Most folks called computer phone support boring, but it was the most exciting and least predictable thing he did. Weekends were stuck in a neverending loop that started on Friday at five p.m.

At the megastore, he parked all the way at the back of the parking lot. Sure, trying to find a closer place might have been a change, but he wasn't stupid. The subtle line between challenging and irritating was not one he cared to cross too often. From his car, it was three-hundred-six steps to the front door, then another thirty-eight to the hardware department. Just like last Saturday, he needed garbage bags and tape.

The trash bags he found without even looking. They always sat on the same section, bottom shelf, middle of the row. The box never changed either. Generic red with a photo of the bag overflowed with leaves. Five steps, turn left, eleven steps, turn right, seven steps to the tape.

At step eleven and turn right, he glanced up and stumbled. Something was different. The section was the same, but the colors were different. He took the last seven steps with caution. Change was good, so long as it was expected. But this...This changed the whole day. The row of tape, dull grey and neat, was now one shelf down. In its usual spot, more tape sat, but instead of matt-silver, there were colors. He counted at least five of them. Yellow, blue, red, white and electric, screaming pink. He felt his spirits rise. A choice! Something different! Something unexpected! It might throw off his whole schedule, but he didn't care. What a wonderful surprise!

He took longer than his usual two-and-a-half seconds to choose a color. In fact, he spent six, maybe seven, before he pulled a roll of hot-pink down and made his way to the front of the store. At the register, he smiled, broad and giddy at the young woman with a ring in her nose. Of course, she was the same girl who rang him out last week and the week before, but she wasn't important anymore. Pink instead of silver! What a bold step!

He bounded back to his car, all thoughts of counting steps and seconds forgotten. When he backed out, everything around him seemed off by a few seconds, and he reveled in it. Everything felt new, different.

Jason pulled back onto the highway and continued down the road. Only a few seconds' difference, and already he saw things he hadn't before. The way the light, a few seconds later, cut through the giant elm that sat at four-hundred seconds on the highway, struck him as completely different. The way the traffic congealed near the tunnel took him by surprise. Only a few seconds earlier and he might've missed the jam-up. In fact, he knew he would've because he'd done it every weekend for years. But he grinned as he sat in traffic. It was so novel, so new, it brought out a renewed hope in him. He was only a few seconds behind, but in those few seconds he saw the world differently.

He exited just past the tunnel and zoomed off toward the back road with a song in his heart. The traffic jam cost him time, at least fifteen minutes, and the hills looked so different for it. The colors were darker in some areas, lighter in others. Shadows ran just a fraction longer, but enough that he noticed. When he pulled into the gravel drive of the tiny cabin in the woods, he marveled at how different it looked in the late morning light. The front door stood in shadow, the walk darker than he remembered it being. He parked in his usual spot, gathered his purchases, and went inside.

"I'm back," he announced. "And I've got something new! Look!"

He opened the bag.

"It's pink! The tape is pink today! Isn't that wonderful? It'll look so much better than that dull silver."

He knew what she'd say before he pulled the tape off her mouth, but did it anyway. But the day was so full of new experiences, maybe she'd surprise him.

She didn't.

"Please," she wept, just like every other girl. "I don't want to die. Let me go."

He sighed, crestfallen at her repetitive response, then pulled a section of pink from the roll and slapped it over her mouth. On every other Saturday, he stuck to his schedule like clockwork. One minute, twenty-three seconds to take off his clothes, fold them, and put them in the cabinet where they wouldn't be covered in blood. Two minutes of suckling each soft breast, ten lapping between her legs, another two rubbing his hardened penis across her taped face. Then four minutes raping her holes.

The hacksaw wasn't even a challenge anymore. Seven strokes to cut through her throat, thirty seconds for her to drown in her own blood. It usually took hours to cut through all the pieces of her body, but he counted off strokes and seconds until he was finished. Two garbage bags, fifteen minutes to load them into the trunk of his car, then nineteen seconds to run to the stream behind the shack. Two minutes to wash all her blood off, then fifty-two steps back to the shack to redress.

But today was different. Maybe today, inspired by his unintentional change of schedule, he'd do things differently, change things up a bit. A few minutes difference and a change in color showed him a new perspective, maybe a few other changes would do wonders for him as well.

"Normally," he said as he reached for the hacksaw, "I'd rape you first, then kill you. But today..."

He pressed the blade down to her neck and thrust it forward in a spray of arterial crimson. The girl's naked body convulsed as she tried to breathe, but her lungs drew in blood and every gurgled sound came out as pink froth from her smiling neck. It looked almost the same as every other time he'd killed a girl, but her eyes were different this time, defiant and afraid to the last moment when they lost focus. On a normal day, their eyes were already dead when he killed the girls, broken and hopeless. Her hatred, her fear, the look when hope passed from her eyes, thrilled him. It made him wonder what else in his rigid schedule he should change.

Cleaning up before sectioning the body was stupid, as was putting the parts in the garbage bags before he'd had his way with them. But maybe he should cut them up, *then* have his way with them. Would it make a difference? Would it make things easier or more difficult? So many changes yielded positive results, he decided to go ahead and try.

With every stroke of the hacksaw, his pulse quickened. He sawed slowly at first to try to savor the sensation, taking her hands at the wrists, then working to her elbows and shoulders. When he reached stopped to survey his handywork, sweat dripped from his body. The effort always left him exhausted, but now, with the job half done, he stank of lust and blood. He was hard as a teenager, so much so that it hurt, but at the same time his pain brought ecstasy from anticipation. Just a few more cuts and he'd give himself the release he craved.

He started again at her ankles, sawing through first one, then the other. His breathing came short and shallow, as he pumped his hips with each stroke of the hacksaw. At her knees, he sawed faster, his cuts jagged and rude, and grunted with each thrust of the blade. When he came to her hips, he almost stopped, but the thought of unhindered access to her holes drove him over the edge. He cut frantically, as if his existence depended on separating her limbs from her body. With a final grunt, her last remaining leg fell to the floor and he could no longer contain himself. There she was, no longer the usual collection of shoulder-length brown hair and brown eyes, no longer a wriggling mass of fright and desperation. She lay, reduced to only the parts he needed.

He climbed onto the blood-slick table and entered her. Her blood made him slide in easer, and he grabbed a peach-sized breast in each hand and used them to pull him in deep. But something was wrong. She didn't fight. He didn't have the difficulty of her trying to close her legs, but there was no fire, no passion there. He looked up to where, on any other day, hate-filled eyes pleaded with him to stop, but saw only the bloody stump of her neck.

Maybe the other side, he thought. He turned the slab of meat over and felt his heart sink. Again, no bucking, no struggling. There weren't legs to pry apart anymore. In fact, half her butt was gone, still attached to the tops of her legs. Still, he'd come this far. He pressed himself into her pucker, and was disappointed. It was supposed to be tighter. Without her to fight, it wasn't the same. She couldn't milk him dry with her sobs of pain.

He pumped away, but his heart wasn't in it anymore. He didn't even reach climax. Without the fight, he went limp and withdrew, his mood blacker than the day before. Too much change, he decided, wasn't good. And change for its own sake robbed him of his one monotonous but joyful feeling of the weekend. He sighed as he climbed off the table.

Her body, he had such a hard time thinking of it as hers now, lay in pieces around the room, useless to him. Damn him for being so overzealous. A few longer shadows got the better of him. A different hue of tape and suddenly he threw his whole plan into chaos. He sunk down into a corner of the room, feeling sorry for himself. No more toy for the weekend. He had to be at his sister's tomorrow for a family lunch, so there would be no time to make up the mistake. Another week he would have to wait before satisfying himself. He looked down at his limp penis and cried.

Next weekend, he decided, it would be better. Maybe a different colored tape, maybe a different leaving time, maybe a blonde or a red-head, but the differences stopped there. No more diddling around with order. Things had to be done in sequence. He stood and gathered the pieces into his garbage bags, then placed them outside the door. Then he pulled the hose from off the wall, took two steps, three turns to attach it to the sink, twenty-three minutes to hose the blood into the drain. Nineteen seconds to run to the stream behind the cabin. Two minutes to wash all her blood off, then fifty-two steps back to the shack to redress. Ten minutes to redress, then fifteen to load the bags into the trunk of the car. Eighty miles to dump them, then back to his townhouse in the city. Eight hours of sleep. And the whole process would start again.

Droplets

————————

Of Moss and Bullfrogs

The trees of the darkened swamp forest loomed like grasping hands as Sarah fled across the leaf and slime covered floor. They were close behind her, she knew, but did not know or even stop to imagine how close. Her only thought as she clutched the tattered parcel tight against her chest was to escape, to get away before they caught up with her. As the marshy ground splattered beneath her feet, she almost dared to hope. Surely the main road could not be far ahead.

She chanced a glimpse behind her into the pitch that was the swampland night, but saw no sign of her pursuers among the moss that swayed to a windless rhythm. They were still back there, she could feel them like spiders under her hair, even if she could not see them. Not far now, she told herself, as she continued her painful lope toward what she hoped was safety.

Since she was a little girl in that south Texas town, she'd heard stories of strange doings in the untamed swamps. It had always seemed impossible to her, that any part of the land remained untouched in the wake of the sprawling chemical plant that built her home town. Up till then, children like her always considered them legends, folklore, stories told by the old folks to keep the young'uns in line. Stories of the cursed brothers for whom the town was named and of the giant race of Indians who used to roam these parts were told by every father and grandmother.

As she raced further into the humid night, she neither recalled those stories nor the smiling faces that told them. All she knew was that Michael was dead, skinned and half eaten. Worse awaited her too if she couldn't find his truck that was parked on the road. She sobbed as she ran, each painful breath forcing another torrent of anger and bitter sadness from her soul. It was her fault that he was dead. She felt it as deeply as she had known that she'd loved him.

In the darkness she stumbled and landed face down in the muck. Damn her ankle, she thought, as she squirmed to her back and wiped the dripping mud from her eyes. Through the velvety night, she imagined she could see a hundred eyes pinning her to the ground, waiting for her to die so they could feast on her carrion remains, but she heard nothing. Her terror had made her hearing sharp as a cat's, and even the smallest of noises would have made her spin and scramble farther into the night, but there were no sounds. The cicadas that usually filled the air and the bullfrogs that barked and sang throughout the night were strangely silent. Even the air was still and pressed heavy and wet against her skin as it crawled more than she thought possible.

She turned and dug through the mud until her hands found the tattered cloth of the parcel that she dropped in her fall. Quickly as she dared, her quivering hands unwrapped the cloth to make sure that the box inside, and its strange contents, was still intact. As she recovered her cargo, a sound snapped her head up and sent her diving into the deeper pitch of the tree line. Though she couldn't be sure what she'd heard, she was too terrified to take any chances. The swamp was home to many creatures, gators and snakes to name a few, but she had bigger things to fear than a cotton-mouth.

She lay in the mud for what seemed like hours, until she was certain that the sound would not repeat, then she crawled skittishly from the relative safety of her hiding place. The swamp stretched out in all directions around her, every tree identical, every vine the same, and she felt panic begin to grow as she realized that she had no idea in which direction the main road lay. Now, as she slowly got to her feet, she strained but could not tell which direction she'd been going. The fall, the dive for cover, her quick speed had all disoriented her, and now a hopeless feeling began to settle in her stomach as she knew she was lost.

When you're lost, she'd heard her father once say, *stay where you are and someone will find you,* but that was the dread that made her bladder weak and her heart feel as if it would burst. They'd find her, she told herself, and do to her as they'd done to Michael, or worse. It was best, she decided, to keep moving and pray that she found the road and her lover's truck.

The night was hot and brought out more mosquitoes than she'd believed existed. With every limping step, dozens of the tiny vampires pricked at her skin and drank their fill, but she dared not swat at them, as the sound of slapping might bring them again, diving out of the curtain of blackness for her. She cursed herself as she walked, cursed the box, cursed them, whoever – whatever – they were. Time was distorted to her from exhaustion and hunger and fear, and she continued walking through the night until she came to a place where the darkness congealed, as if a physical thing, and pressed its weight down on her like tar. As she struggled to free herself and push past, she felt her stomach knot and her knees buckle at the clearing in front of her. She'd found her way back to the cabin wherein Michael still remained hanging on a hook while bits of his flesh were savored by the monsters that had killed him. Sarah screamed as a leathery arm encircled her neck and waist and threw her hard against the ground. As she looked up into the absence of eyes, she could feel more hands grabbing at her legs and arms, snatching the dirty parcel from her trembling hands, and they bore her up high and carried her back to the cabin. Too tired to struggle, or to weak with fear, Sarah felt her body go limp as her unblinking eyes looked through the moss-covered branches at the pinpoints of stars in night's curtain.

At the threshold of the cabin, she found some small reserve of strength and fought them to keep her body out of that house. The stench was nearly overwhelming, as her stomach convulsed and heaved empty. The cabin stank of death and decay. She grabbed for either side of the doorjamb, only to have her fingers broken with two swift blows by her captors, sending pain arcing through her body and making her sob anew.

They dumped her roughly to the floor, knocking the breath from her lungs as she struggled to right herself, to fight back, to run. In the cabin's dim light she could see them more clearly now. The immense creatures were men, dressed in tattered and filthy rags, their faces covered by strips of cloth that seemed to hold them more together than they should have. They shuffled as they walked, dragging their feet as though hobbled, and none of them uttered a sound. They didn't seem real to her, like some creature made of foam or plaster, but their cold skin touched hers, left trails of slime it its path. She'd smelled the rotted flesh in their breath, and looked into their eyeless heads. These creatures could not be alive, she told herself of the blasphemous abominations.

"Naughty child." The crackled rustic accent came from over her shoulder and brought with it a stale wind that choked her and brought the hairs on her neck to attention. "Thought you could run from me?"

"No, Grandmother."

"Now give me back the box," the old woman commanded. She took it from one of the shambling hulks and unwrapped the cloth gingerly. "Nasty things, souls," she said. "You're better off letting me keep this one." She placed it high on a shelf with several others while Sarah looked on, helpless with tears streaming down her cheeks.

"Now you hush that up," said the old woman sternly as she stooped to examine Sarah's ankle. "Serves you right, shirking your chores and running off like that. Made me call up a dozen rotters to get you too."

The old woman's touch on her granddaughter's ankle was gentle, despite her swollen knuckles and skin like tree bark. She knew the old

---

ways, and the ankle would be healed by morning.

"He wasn't right for you. Too clean. Makes a fine stew though." She went to the fireplace and spooned out a generous helping into a bowl. "Eat up. We'll find someone for you some day, then you can have that nasty thing back. When you're ready."

"Yes, Grandmother," said Sarah.

Droplets

One Night,
in New Orleans...

The crowded streets pulsed as Billy fought his way through the throng of partiers celebrating Mardi Gras. Amid the women who flashed their breasts for beads and men who stood wolfishly by, hoping to catch a glimpse, or better, a cheep feel, it seemed nothing could be wrong. Not to a college boy like Billy. The scene of drunken debauchery and hedonistic pleasure was what he'd heard stories about all his life, and now that he was here, in the middle of Bourbon Street, he could think of nothing but to run, to hide from the zydeco and blues filled air and beer that ran through the streets.

Only half an hour ago, he was one of them, a drunken, nineteen-year-old, a perpetual erection with more money than brains. Twenty minutes ago, he walked through an old French-Quarter cemetery hoping that the creepy vibe would further loosen the morals and pants of the girl he'd met. Only ten minutes ago, he stopped to take a leak, neither paying attention, nor caring, who saw or where he was. And only five minutes ago, he watched the girl, whom he'd hoped to bed, or at least molest in the cemetery, break out in painful sores all over her body before the creature that seemed to form from congealing shadows tore at her neck with its teeth and drained her dry.

It wasn't a vampire that emerged from the shadow of Marie Laveau's crypt, at least, not one like he'd ever heard of. It was hideous, well over six feet tall and hunched over, drooling as the sores that covered its body ran with puss and slime. It seemed to just appear behind her, while she giggled at the sight of him standing there with his member in his hands, relieving himself against a graffiti-marked wall. He didn't even have time to zip himself up when the creature pounced on her and left her twitching against the concrete crypt.

He ran, unsure of the direction he was going. It seemed the farther he ran, the faster his feet kicked, the more crypts sprang up around him, obscuring the night sky. He glanced behind him, stumbling over smaller stones for doing so, only to see the disgusting form leaping from marker to marker, leaving a trail of infectious slime on whatever it touched. How he managed to get back to Bourbon Street, he could not say. Only that he ran until he came to the bent and ruined iron gate and pushed through a breath before the creature slammed into it, slashing at him with its wicked claws.

He did not turn again, certain that to do so would mean to see the thing bearing down on him. As he ran down Conti, he could hear the thing coming after him leaping from the bottoms of the overhanging balconies, gaining every step of the way. When he reached Bourbon Street, he pushed his way through the blissfully unaware faces and drunken smiles, screaming until he tasted blood. Of course they paid him no mind. They pointed, laughed at the kid who'd drank too much. But he was stone sober, terrified of the touch of the creature that followed him.

The party swept him along for several blocks until, in a thin spot in the crowd, he turned down a side-street called Dumaine. The street, though still packed, was empty in comparison to Bourbon. He hoped he could make better time on a less-trafficked street, if the thing was still after him. He slowed, his chest heaving with the strain of running, sure that he'd vomit up all his precious beer any moment. The street behind him was empty. The creature had not followed, he thought. He'd not seen it since leaving the old cemetery, only heard it pursuing him. Maybe he'd lost it after all.

He fell back, wheezing on the pavement until he realized that he was still running about with his tackle hanging out. He quickly zipped up and sat on the sidewalk.

"Find somewhere else to cool your heels, boy," he heard a voice say from behind him. It was the owner of the shop whose stoop he was using for a stool, a tall thin woman with long strait hair and a necklace with skulls for beads.

"Please!" he panted. "I'm being chased...Horrible...Ate a girl...It's coming!"

"Wait a minute," she said, cocking an eyebrow. "Ain't you that boy what pissed on the grave of Madame Laveau? Cou me chere, you fucked it big didn't you?"

The fact that she knew what he did would not register in his mind, as it was competing with the images of the creature that still loomed heavy and the name that stuck in his mind like a metal sliver.

"W...Who?"

"Don't tell me you never heard of the great Marie Laveau. It don't seem right! The greatest Vodu priestess in history, and you never heard of her none? Where you from, under a rock?"

"Utah," he replied, sill in shock.

"Oh. That explain alot," she smiled. "So what she call up on you, eh? Zombie? Vampire? What?"

"I don't know what it was," he said, his voice quaking. "It was covered in sores! It ate...It ate..."

"You din even know her name?"

His eyes fell to the ground as he shook his head.

"Dumb dumb dumb," she said. "You come on inside, chere. Sadie gonna help you."

"Why?"

"Heh! N'Orleans got enough problems without some dumb-dick kid goin' spreading the stories. And the last thing we need is someone with a Sousson-Pannan chasing him all over hell and back. It's bad gris-gris."

Billy followed Sadie into the shop, constantly glancing over his shoulder to see if the...whatever it was... was following him.

"No worries in here, boy," she said without turning. "You in Dark Sadie's Juke Joint now. Ain't no bad gris-gris getting past my charms. I done saw to that."

The shop looked like a flea-market record shop, with posters and fliers as old as fifty years adorning the walls and vinyl records lining the bins. Had he not been terrified beyond rational thought, he might have been impressed. Past the dozens of bins that obscured the back of the shop there was a red curtain, which Sadie parted and gestured for him to follow. It was here that her real business was done, he decided.

The small room was a testament to the Voodoo religion. Adorning the walls were severed chickens feet and strange markings, canisters of every size containing herbs he'd never seen before, and was not sure were entirely legal. In the center of the back wall was a large altar, lit with dozens of burning votives and in the center sat the Papa-Loa, the father spirit of Voodoo.

"Don't touch nothing," she said as they passed through the curtain. "What you done, boy you fucked yourself bad, you know that?"

"You said that already. What is that thing?"

"Heh, sounds like a Sousson-Pannan to me." She rummaged around beneath the counter until she came up with a large book. "Dis will tell us what we need to know." She flipped through the pages, scanning for the right entry. Finally, her face lit up as she found that which she sought.

"Aha!" she shouted. "Yep, I was right! It is a Sousson-Pannan. Oh, bad loa this thing. Says here they drink blood and are evil to the core. Once they get your scent, they don't never stop coming for you."

As if on cue, the front door of the shop rattled as powerful fists began banging on the outside. Through the glass, Billy could see the sticky smears where the fists hit, and he knew that the Sousson-Pannan had found him.

"Oh God! Oh Jesus!" he cried, desperately looking for a way to escape.

"Shut your mouth!" barked Sadie, clearly unruffled by the creature's presence. "I told you, ain't no bad gris-gris getting past my charms. Now shut up and listen. You safe in here."

"Can I just stay until it goes away?"

"Shit no!" she shouted. "Thing like that is bad for business. I won't sell no records that way! Besides, what you gonna do when it comes time to go back to your home and find that thing under your bed. What then, eh? No, you better just face it now."

"What can I do?"

"Better," she said. "Now, it say here, that thing loves two things, and only two things. Blood..."

"Oh God..." moaned Billy.

"And Rum. You give that thing a good bottle of rum, he leave you alone...for a little while."

"I don't want a little while. I need to get rid of it for good! How can I kill it?"

"Stupid boy!" she growled. "You can't kill nothing what's already dead! Don't you know that? You want it gone, you gotta make peace."

"With that?"

"With the Madame Marie Laveau."

Billy gaped at her. Peace? With a Voodoo priestess that had been dead for God-knew how long? She had to be joking.

"I don't believe in voodoo," he said. "I don't believe in ghosts, or demons, or Sousson-Pannan, or any of this shit! I'm a Christian, and this stuff just isn't real!"

"Oh?" she smiled. "Maybe you'd like to go outside and tell that thing that you don't believe he's real. Go ahead. I'll wait. And when he's done draining you dry, you be just another body to wash up in the gutter what partied too hard. See if I care."

Billy looked out the window at the creature, who even now left slimy prints on the glass as it was trying to get in. For just a moment, it caught his gaze and it stopped pounding. The thing cut through him with its yellow eyes and smiled coldly at him, telling him how much it would enjoy every life-draining moment that it spent sucking the blood from his body.

"What do I have to do," said Billy, near tears.

"Good thought kid," said Ellie. "First, you need rum. Lots of it. You want that thing to drink until you done making peace with Marie."

"Okay, rum. Then what."

"Then what? First, I'd start by washing your piss-stains off her crypt. I think I'd be mad too, if I found you pissing on my bed."

"Okay, then what?"

"Then you gotta make peace with Marie with an offering. Give her something she wants, something that she crave."

"Like what? She's dead."

"Dead don't mean nothing in New Orleans, boy" spat Sadie. "You don't never disrespect someone just a'cause they dead."

"Sorry. So what should I give her?"

"Marie, she's what we likes to call a Loa, a spirit. She's like what you folks call a saint, in a way. Our Loa, they miss their earthly pleasures. Drink and food, that sort of thing. What Marie loved in life, as well as death, are cigars. She loves to smoke."

"Rum and cigars. Okay, fine. Then what?"

"Heh...Then you pray she accepts before that bad boy outside tears your head off."

Sadie showed Billy a back way out and told him the quickest way to a liquor store that might turn the other way at his lack of good judgment, then slammed the door behind him. He didn't look back as he ran as fast as he could.

The fellow at the liquor store, a fat surly man, would sell him nothing until he mentioned Sadie by name. Then he smiled.

"Sadie helping out another stupid kid, huh? Okay. What you need boy."

"Rum and cigars."

"For what?"

"I'm being chased by a Sousson-Pannan."

The shop-keepers face went ashen.

"Shit, boy? Why didn't you tell me that when you came in? I don't want that damned thing coming in here! Look, you want good stuff, not no cheep rotgut that it might not like. If it's bad rum, he'll kill you slow. How much money you got?"

"About two hundred in cash," said Billy.

"Give it. I'll give you two bottles of the best I got in the house and a box of the best cigars you'll find in Louisiana, then you get the hell out of my store."

Under any other circumstance, Billy might have argued. Two hundred dollars, apart from being all he had left to get home on, was a great sum of money to him. However, seeing the logic in the shop keeper's argument, and seeing as he wanted to actually see his home again, whether he had to hitch-hike or walk, he wasn't about to haggle. He handed over the money, and with a sponge and a bottle of water that the shop-keeper threw in out of pity, ran from the shop as quickly as he could.

When he arrived at the cemetery, it was well past two o'clock in the morning. Back home, he mused, the bars would be long closed, but here, the sounds of Mardi-Gras still echoed through the air. He jogged as quickly as he could manage while carrying his parcels until the great stone structure rose up in his vision.

He slowed his pace to a brisk walk, his stomach churning with apprehension as the tomb loomed closer. When he was less then ten feet from the place where he'd angered the Loa, he heard a sound that was unmistakable to his ears. He whirled in horror as the Sousson-Pannan lumbered into view, dripping filth and disease from every open wound on its body.

Billy froze, wanting to run but unable to make his legs move. As the creature drew nearer, he remembered the words of Dark Sadie, and quickly snapped open one of the bottles of rum, splashing just a thimble-full into the air. The creature came to a dead halt, mere inches away from his face, his rotten breath feted in Billy's nostrils. Its glassy yellow eyes went wide, then narrowed dreamily as it inhaled the scent of the sweet rum that wafted from the bottle. Billy cautiously raised the bottle to eye level, letting the creature see it in his hand.

"Ooooh..." said the creature with a voice that sounded like hamburger being dragged through gravel. "That's gooooood...."

It took the bottle and shambled off to lean against a tall stone tomb and it sat with a heavy thud and took a long pull off the bottle. Billy stood watching for a moment until his brain finally began working again and kept him to task. It took him only fifteen minutes and the full bottle of water before he felt sure he'd washed away all of his own filth. What he'd mistaken for graffiti, he discovered, were tiny red crosses, prayers from those who'd come to visit the grave. He glanced over to see that the Sousson-Pannan was nearly done with the bottle, and when it was done, Billy was certain, it would come for him.

He rushed to the door of the great mausoleum, setting the box of cigars and the remaining bottle of rum at the threshold. Then, as Sadie showed him, he took one cigar and lit it, blowing the rich smoke toward the vault. He opened the bottle and took a mouthful, then spat the rum on the door in a fine mist. Then, laying the lit cigar across the top of the bottle, he dropped to his knees.

"Madame Marie Laveau," he said with great reverence. "For any offense I have caused, I am truly sorry. Please accept these gifts of drink and smoke, and forgive my ignorance."

He looked toward the creature, expecting it to leap up and tear him to pieces. Instead, it finished the bottle and raised it in a toast to Billy.

"Thanks," it said. "S'good drink."

The creature melted back into the shadows, leaving only the bottle on the ground and the sweet scent of rum in the air. Billy turned back to the crypt to find the bottle now half-empty, and the lit cigar gone.

Droplets

_____

Ouija

"Now you place your fingertips on the planchette like so," said Allyson with a mischievous grin.

Noelle barely breathed as she reached her trembling fingers out toward the heart-shaped stone as if she were afraid it would bite her. Her eyes never left Allyson's. In the candle light, she seemed almost completely alien, the girl she knew from school replaced with this gleefully wicked creature. At school, she was the quiet Goth-kid who wanted nothing to do with the popular crowd. Or the unpopular crowd for that matter. Everyone knew who she was, and everyone whispered.

Allyson was a witch, they said, and she worshiped Satan. She ate kittens and had sex on their bloody carcasses with any boy or teacher that would pay her. But Noelle never paid attention to rumor. As the new girl at a new high school, Allyson had no friends, and Noelle, having once been the new girl herself, felt sorry for her and took it upon herself to befriend her.

There were other teens at the high-school that dressed like Allyson, with pale foundation and black lipstick. They only wore black, only listened to death-metal or synthesized dirges. So full of angst and self-loathing. They littered the halls like cockroaches. And they were fake. Most of them were trying to get attention or for some vague form of revenge on their parents for some imagined crime. Others streaked their hair because it was cool. Noelle could not stomach the sight of them. Their rich parents' only crime was giving them freedom, as far as she was concerned, or not showing them what it meant to have real pain. Let them have a real feeling, she often wished. Let them know what I've felt. Let them lose their mother.

At first, she mistook Allyson for one of their clique, with dark clothing and a hunched, furtive shuffle when she walked. But she shunned the other goths, regarded them as ridiculous parodies of emotion. While they were essentially children playing dress-up, Allyson was real. Far from being chronically depressed, she showed a real lust for life and experiences. There was a suspicious glint to her eye as she passed the other students in the halls though, and she never lingered long enough to make connections, only to get from one class to the other where she would sit in the back and take copious notes on whatever the subject.

After a time, wherein Noelle managed to gain a precarious trust, they became friends of a curious sort. They neither dressed nor acted alike, with one preferring pop boy bands to the other's classic rock and metal, but they began to keep each other's company more and more.

It was after only Noelle stood up for her and stifled a few sniggering classmates that Allyson decided that she was different from the others. Afterword, in the girls' locker room, Allyson took her into confidence. Not all the rumors, she revealed, were lies. No, she wasn't a whore and she didn't worship the devil or torture animals. She did, however, dabble with the occult. Actually, she thought of herself as Wiccan, an honest-to-goodness modern-day witch, and being such wasn't a bad thing. Magic, she explained, was nothing more than the manipulation of energies. Spells were similar to Christian prayers. Everything in nature had such forces inside them, and all life, she considered sacred. It wasn't long before Noelle's curiosity burned, and she began to learn from her friend.

"Now," said Allyson in an authoritative tone. "All we have to do is ask a question."

"Like what?"

"Anything. If there's someone listening in, they'll answer it."

Hundreds of questions vied for prominence in Noelle's consciousness, each tumbling over one another until they flowed like a river. But there was only one question that she wanted to ask, only one person she wanted to contact.

"You go first," said Noelle, her voice shaking. She wasn't sure of herself, or of what was happening. What if it wasn't real, like she'd heard a thousand times, or if Allyson pushed the planchette, or if she accidentally offended whoever might be listening? She might ruin the spell and never get the answers she craved.

Allyson sighed deeply and closed her eyes.

"Are we alone in this room?" she asked aloud.

Noelle's heart pounded in anticipation. She jerked her head around to scan the room. She didn't know what to expect. If movies told the truth, there'd be a wind and purple lights and howling monsters would burst through the door.

The planchette pulled beneath her fingertips. It seemed for a moment that they, neither one, breathed, each afraid of breaking the spell that now slowly drug the heart-shaped stone across the board and over a single word.

NO

"You're pushing it," accused Noelle.

"No way," replied Allyson, her eyes wide and dancing. "This is too cool to fake."

Their gazes met and for the first time, Noelle saw a chaotic fire in her friend's eyes. "Ask it something else," she whispered.

"Are you the only one?" she said, a little too bravely.

The planchette waited for a moment, as if considering, before it slid across the board. It had not gone far, only an inch or so, when it made a slow arc and returned. Noelle felt her hair bristle as the hole in its center rested over the word *NO*.

"Tell me you pushed it," said Noelle, an ember of dread growing in her stomach.

"No! I swear!" said Allyson with an excited laugh. "This is so cool! Can you see us?"

The planchette crawled across the marble surface until it reached the other side and came to rest over the word *YES*.

"All the time?" asked Allyson with a wicked grin.

Yes.

"Awesome!" she said with more exuberance than Noelle would have liked. She cringed at the thought of the dead voyeurs staring at her in her sleep, watching her bathe, watching her grieve.

"Mommy?" said Noelle quietly. Her voice shook as tears gathered in her eyes. "Mommy, are you there?"

It was the one question she'd wanted to ask for the past ten years, the one that even now she grieved over. Her mother died when she was only five, and though her father dated and even tried to remarry once, no one could take her place. Her mother was her world when she was five, and Noelle felt incomplete, empty even, without her. When she died, and every day of the years that followed, she felt alone

She held her eyes firm on the planchette, willing it to move, to shift, but there came no answer.

"Mommy," she repeated. "If you're there, please let me know."

When the planchette refused to move again, she lifted her reddened and tear-swelled eyes toward Allyson, who sat gaping like a fish at her friend's questions.

"You didn't tell me..."

"Why doesn't she answer?" demanded Noelle. Her friend's expression told her that Allyson didn't know, but more importantly, that Noelle's sudden transformation from normal teen to sobbing wreck had taken her completely by surprise. "I'm sorry," she said, embarrassed. "I didn't mean to."

"It's okay," said Allyson cautiously. "I mean, you freaked me out, but it's okay. You never told me your mom was..." Her voice trailed off before she finished the sentence.

"Dead," completed Noelle coldly. "She's dead. Died ten years ago. I don't like to talk about it."

Allyson looked at her through different eyes, Noelle felt it. She'd never spoken of her mother, and the subject was never broached. Though they'd been friends for over a month, Noelle had never met Allyson's father, who worked late shifts as a security guard. Nor, now that she thought of it, had she ever met her mother, who now lived in Montana. It was always her stepmother, Doreen, who cheerily greeted the pair and brought them snacks. It just seemed normal to have one parent perpetually absent. The thought of death had probably never occurred to Allyson.

An uncomfortable silence filled the room while they both stared at the unmoving planchette. Just a wiggle would have satisfied either of them, a shift. It was Allyson that first bridged the void.

"Hey," she said awkwardly. "Why don't we go do something?"

"Like what?"

"We could go to a movie, or to the mall. Anything's better than hanging around the house on a Friday night."

"Okay," Noelle shrugged. "Let me get cleaned up first." She rose and headed for the bathroom while Allyson extinguished the many candles in the room. At the bathroom door, she paused for a moment to look back at her friend. Allyson moved the planchette and mouthed something to the dormant ouija. She longed for something from the great slab, an answer or some sort of validation, but it had not worked for her. She closed the door behind her despondently.

The mirror of the oddly-decorated bathroom was mostly covered in photos cut from magazines, drying roses, and other bric-a-brac that Noelle had come to expect from her friend. For someone so outwardly tough, Allyson could be more girly than any cheerleader. It was a wonderful luxury, that this bathroom was solely Allyson's, one that Noelle envied. Her parents had donated the entire basement to their daughter's need for privacy and space. This cavernous room was sacred to the girls, safe from little brothers or adults or anyone else who would not understand the things that went through the teen-aged mind.

The mirror was particularly cruel this evening, as it showed the great raccoon-like rings formed by Noelle's mascara and tears. She swore under her breath as she dabbed at her eyes with tissue and attempted to regain her composure somewhat. When at last she felt decently disguised, thanks in no small part to Allyson's make-up bag and some borrowed eyeliner, she emerged to find her friend had gone upstairs, probably to secure money and a ride from Doreen. She crossed the room slowly, almost fearfully, toward the carved marble slab.

She had, of course, seen an ouija before, but never one like Allyson's. Most that she'd seen were meant to be children's games, made of cardboard or wood with a plastic planchette. The one that sat before her, however, was no child's toy. Into it's pink and grey marble surface was carved numbers and letters, the words yes, no and goodbye. In that respect, it was much the same as any other. But the carvings on the board were truly breathtaking, with Celtic dragons writhing around one another to form knots which framed the board. The letters themselves were of startling intricacy, and were filled with a red substance that could very well have been candle wax dripped into each cavity. The entire top had been glossed over many times, making it very smooth to the touch.

The planchette was of similar material, with ornate carvings and little bits of white among its main pink hue. Its legs were capped in white felt, to allow for easier sliding and to keep from scratching the board on which it sat. How appropriate, she thought, that it was shaped like a heart.

She absently traced the path of one of the dragons with her finger. Why didn't her mother answer? Maybe Noelle really was alone.

"You ready?" came Allyson's exuberant voice from the top of the stairs, breaking Noelle's reverie. She snapped her hand away from the board as though unaware that she was touching it.

"Yeah," she said, her eyes still on the smooth pink and white surface.

"Are you okay?" There was a sincerity to Allyson's voice that was reassuring, genuine.

"I'm fine," she sighed. "I just don't understand why she wouldn't answer."

"It doesn't work that way," replied Allyson as gently as she could manage. "Ouija is like an open transmitter. You never know who's going to come through. It's really hard to target one particular soul."

"Maybe she just wasn't listening."

"I doubt that," replied Allyson with a frustrated scoff. "It just wasn't our night. Come on. We'll miss the movie."

During the course of the evening, Allyson made every attempt to take her friend's mind off the events of hours past. Since the movie theater was located inside the mall, they stopped at the food court before going inside. There, they sat talking of generalities that had no real weight or bearing on one's emotional state. Allyson tried, but Noelle's mood wouldn't be lifted. It was her intention to lull her back into a good humor, after which she might open up. But no matter the subject, nor the feigned interest and revitalized mood, Noelle still had the great slab in the back of her mind, pressing all its impressive weight down on her psyche. She imagined that basement room filled to the brim with wispy figures in tattered shrouds, all of them trying to speak, to be heard, but among those tired drawn faces she could not find the one face she so desperately needed to see, her mother.

By the time they returned to Allyson's house, they were both emotionally exhausted with the evening's events. Allyson's mother offered to take her home, but the thought of her empty house depressed her. Noelle didn't want to be alone with her thoughts, and left a message for her father that she was spending the night.

Later, as Allyson snored softly in a deep sleep, Noelle lay on the tattered sofa in the dark with a strong urge to try again, to give one more effort at finding her mother's spirit somewhere. She quietly pulled the quilt aside and crept toward the great marble slab, trying not to wake Allyson. What would Allyson say if she woke up to find her dabbling with her things? Weren't these things supposed to be sacred to witches, or Wiccans, or whatever she was? She felt strange, like a child stealing a cigarette from a parent's drawer, but she couldn't bring herself to stop. She knew if she turned away she'd just lay there for the rest of the night, wondering.

A single candle would be enough, she decided, to see the board without waking her friend. As she struck the match, shadows leaped around the room like living things escaping the candle's dim glow. She knelt beside the low table and gingerly placed trembling hands upon the planchette, fingertips only, the way Allyson had shown her. Her stomach fluttered a bit as she took a deep breath to try to steady herself to ask her questions.

"Mommy?" she whispered. "Are you there?"

The hairs on the nape of her neck prickled as the planchette tugged under her fingers toward the word "Yes." It felt the same as it had earlier with Allyson, but this time there could be no doubt as to who was pulling it. There was such force behind its motion that it nearly pulled itself from under her fingers. As it centered over the word, her heart fluttered in nervous joy.

The air around her fairly hummed with electric anticipation of the next answer, the question to which burned to escape her lips. She glanced again toward the sleeping witch. A trick of the candle light made the darkness seem thicker, obscuring her view. Allyson's breath was deep and steady, still under the spell of sleep. Her heart raced as she returned her attention to the board and pointer.

"I miss you," she whispered, her voice quaking with tears.

"I miss you too, honey," came a breathy voice from across the room.

Noelle's head snapped up, immediately fearful that she'd been caught. The darkness parted like a curtain, letting the flickering candlelight spill throughout the room. There, sitting upright on her bed, was Allyson.

"Oh my God," she said, jerking away from the planchette and board. "Ally, I'm so sorry. I didn't mean to..."

"It's alright," said the witch. "Allyson is still sleeping." Her eyes were still closed, but her lips moved with a voice that was not her own.

"I'm sorry I couldn't speak before," the sleeping form said. "I so wanted to. I've missed you."

"Allyson?" stammered Noelle.

"You called me," she said. "I came."

Though the body was that of her friend, the voice sounded strange falling from those lips. It wasn't Allyson's light and energetic voice that came through, but an older, tired sound. Although she could not remember from ten years ago, she knew instinctively that the voice that came from the sleeping face was her mother's.

"How?" she asked. The question contained a thousand questions in itself.

"You opened the door," said the sleeping form as she raised a finger toward the ouija. "Your friend was sleeping. Easy to slip inside."

There was so much she wanted to say, so many things she'd wanted to ask over the past ten years. She wanted to know if her mother had ever really left her, and why she was taken away, and if she was proud of what her daughter had become. In that moment, however, none of her questions would come as she was overwhelmed with emotion. She fell to her knees, sobbing in her friend's lap as though she were praying to her.

"Shhh..." chided her mother's voice. "You'll wake your friend. I just wanted to tell you that I am still with you. I have to go. We'll talk again soon, alright pumpkin?"

The pet name "pumpkin." It was her mother's favorite name for her, and although her father often called her by that name, his way was a poor substitute. Only her mother could make that word seem less an item of produce and more of a beloved thing. Hearing the voice say it to her made her heart ache even more. She sobbed aloud while clutching Allyson's hand.

Droplets

"Get back to bed quickly," said the voice. "I can feel her inside, waking up. Put out the candle. Hurry!" With that, Allyson's form gently slumped back to the bed, once more her own. Noelle leaned forward and kissed her friend's cheek softly, then hurried back to the couch and beneath the quilt. As she snuggled deep into the blanket, she heard Allyson shift and mumble in her sleep, the voice her own. Noelle smiled to herself as she drifted into warm and secure slumber for the first time in years.

It was nearly noon before they awoke. Noelle's eyes fluttered open to the warmth that came from inside. She'd spoken to her mother. Although she'd not gotten the answers she wanted, she was euphoric. She expected to have questions answered by the sliding planchette, but to hear her mother's voice again, to touch her through her friend's flesh, was more than she ever hoped for. She wished she could keep the feeling always, or at least have it again.

She rolled to her side and looked across the basement. It looked different with small dust motes dancing in the sunlight filtering through the tiny wall-top windows. The spell of last night was broken by daylight, she decided. It no longer seemed to her to be a secret place of magic, where witches cast spells and the dead spoke. It was, during the day with the garish sunlight streaming in, simply a goth girl's room.

She climbed down from the couch and went to the bed where Allyson still slept. She no longer saw just Allyson in the sleeping face, though. She now held a genuine affection for her closed eyes and pale cheek. Allyson's sleeping face was now, to her, the face of her mother, and she hesitated to spoil it by waking her friend. Just another moment with her, she thought, then they could begin the day.

She gently climbed onto the bed and lay next to her mother's face, tracing the lines of her eyes and hair. She brushed Allyson's cheek softly, but pulled away, embarrassed, as her eyes fluttered open.

"Hi," she yawned.

"Good morning," said Noelle cheerily.

"What're you doing?"

"Just waking you up. It's almost noon."

"Wow," said Allyson with a great stretch. "I haven't slept that hard in a long time."

They got up and dressed, climbed the stairs to the kitchen for a late breakfast, then said their cursory goodbyes to Allyson's step-mother. A Saturday was a day of play for them, and Noelle was in a particularly good frame of mind. As the day wore on, she caught herself staring at her friend's face, searching for signs of the sleeper inside, and regarding her differently, almost fawningly.

Noelle invited Allyson to stay at her apartment that night. After all, one night at one's house deserved a night at the others. And Noelle still didn't feel like being alone. They returned to Allyson's house to gather a few necessary items, and as she stuffed her toiletries and a change of clothes into a duffle, Noelle awkwardly suggested she bring the ouija along. Although it was cumbersome, she readily agreed. She pulled a large zippered case from her closet and slid the board into it, pausing for a moment as she picked up the pointer. Although she said nothing, it seemed to Noelle that she'd seen something that she found disquieting on the surface of the board. She slipped the planchette into a side pocket on the case and zipped it.

"You want to bring it," she said, "You get to carry it." There was a teasing tone in her voice that Noelle found endearing, but as she slung the carrying strap on her shoulder, she grunted under the weight.

"This thing weighs a ton!" she said.

"Actually," replied Allyson. "It weighs just under fifty pounds. It's solid marble."

The conversation on the ride to Noelle's apartment was largely one-sided, with Allyson explaining the history of the ouija and, in particular, the origin of her board. It belonged to her grandmother, although where she got it was open to anyone's guess. They found it in a cupboard when she died. According to at least one family source, she'd found it in a garage sale, but the generally accepted origin was that it was in the family for many years before Allyson's grandmother came to have it, with no thought as to where it was before that. The intricate designs and painstaking details denoted craftsmanship that was seldom seen anymore, and Allyson treasured it. Though most of the family wanted the thing destroyed, she'd managed to keep it safe and convinced her parents to let her keep it as an object d'art. It wasn't until the first time she used it that she realized how powerful it truly was.

She revealed that she'd been dabbling with ouija boards for some time, even though such things were frowned upon by other Pagans. They were dangerous, open channels. One could never tell who or what was coming through. But Allyson was fascinated by the prospect of talking to the deceased and continued to experiment. By the time they reached Noelle's apartment, she was anxious to try the board in her room, though in her heart she knew she'd have the best success when her friend was asleep. They breezed into the apartment, saying only brief hellos and explanations to Noelle's father, and went to her bedroom.

It was later that night, after they'd watched a rented video and Noelle's father was at work, that they uncased the giant slab and set it on a plastic crate to begin.

She sat breathless as Allyson lit several candles she'd brought and said a quiet prayer, asking for protection. Noelle and Allyson put their fingers gently on the stone pointer and stared into each other's eyes. There was a giddiness to them that was brought on by the step into the taboo, one part recklessness, one part calculated risk. They asked a few questions, mainly focusing on whether or not there were any spirits present, but Noelle took care not to mention her mother. It wasn't long before the answers began to flow freely from planchette to board.

"Why are you here?" asked Allyson to one particularly insistent presence. They watched at the pointer drug across the board toward the alphabet and singled out letters spelling a word.

"Danger," said Noelle, looking nervously into Allyson's eyes as recognition dawned on her.

"Who's in danger?" asked Allyson intently.

They felt the pointer pull at their fingers until it rested under a letter. "U?" asked Noelle.

"You," said Allyson grimly. "It's saying that one, or both, of us is in danger." She turned her attention back to the board. "Who are you?"

Again the planchette began to pull, this time faster, stronger than it had ever been. As it slid back and forth between letters, Noelle frantically tried to keep pace, forming words from letters in her mind. When the pointer's movement ceased, it took her a moment to arrange the letters into a cohesive thought, but when she finished they both felt their blood freeze with the cryptic phrase.

"Not who you think," said Noelle aloud jerking her hands away from the pointer. Her heart pounded in her ears, a sudden palpable dread seizing her spine.

"Put your hands back!" hissed Allyson, her eyes wide. "Don't break the circle until I close the path!"

Though her hands trembled with fear, Noelle did as she was told. She was so anxious to get away from the board that she didn't hear the quiet prayer the witch said, nor did she notice where the planchette rested when she was done. As Allyson raised her head, Noelle retreated across her room and sat quivering on her bed, staring at the ouija with unblinking eyes.

"Are you alright?" asked Allyson. This was twice in as many days that she'd caught glimpses of closely guarded sides of Noelle.

"I'm fine," she lied. "What did that mean? 'Not who you think.' What did that mean?"

Allyson smiled reassuringly as she sat next to her friend.

"It's like..." she began, formulating her words into a reasonable analogy. "It's like a chat room on the Internet. You have a bunch of people with usernames, but how do you know they're who they say they are?

Sometimes they lie."

"So what was that? What're they trying to warn us about?"

"I don't know," she said, frowning. "Maybe nothing. I've gotten stranger messages."

Noelle understood, but could not shake the feeling of dread. Her system still pumped with the urge to flee. Who had warned them? Who was not who they thought? Did this have something to do with the conversation last night with her mother?

"Can we do something else? Something less spooky?" she pleaded, her tone pulling a laugh from Allyson.

Allyson nodded, smiled, and together they crept to the kitchen where ice cream lay waiting. They retrieved their treats and returned to Noelle's room to watch another movie.

Just after three in the morning, Noelle woke from a fitful slumber. She'd dreamed of menacing shadows in paper masks, pretending to be someone she loved. She could not figure what had awakened her but was now aware of just how dark her room could get in the night. It seemed the moonlight refused to come any farther than the window. Were it not for Allyson's faint snoring, she'd have thought she was alone. As she strained her eyes to try to make out any familiar detail, she became aware of a faint whispering that buzzed in her ears like a gnat.

Not words so much as a feeling, the buzzing grew louder. It pulled her attention through the darkness toward a particular corner of the room. She silently rose from her bed and went to large zipped case. She glanced toward where Allyson slept, and felt her stomach knot as she quietly pulled the zipper. Inside, the great granite slab seemed to glow in a rich shade of purple she'd never seen before. It took her considerable effort to remove it from its case silently, but she couldn't risk waking Allyson. She slowly, carefully, placed it on the plastic crate and set the planchette on top. Then she took a candle from her friend's duffle and lit it. The sudden stark brilliance of flame made her squint until it finally settled into a dim glow.

Then she placed her hands on the planchette and took a deep breath.

"I'm here, mommy," she said nervously.

The board glowed brighter as the whispered buzzing in her ears doubled. The hairs on her arms stood straight out against her creeping flesh.

"Hello pumpkin," she heard as the whisperers became silent.

Noelle went to the bedside, elated that her plan had worked a second time. Over the course of the day she had made a mental list of questions to ask her mother should she speak to her again, when she was not in the throws of such an emotional first meeting. So many questions, but where to begin?

"Why did you leave me?" she asked as tears began to well in her eyes.

"I didn't," said her friend with her mother's voice. "I was taken from you, but I never left. I've been with you your whole life."

"What's it like, you know, being dead?"

Allyson's body shuddered at the question. Noelle took her hand and found it cold to the touch, as though blood no longer flowed through it. It made Noelle's skin crawl.

"I feel nothing," her mother said, "except for the pain that I can't be with you. I miss touching your hair."

Noelle considered a moment. She'd always been taught that death was a release, that when a person died all her questions were answered. It had never occurred to her the logical step that if personalities survived, they might be unhappy in the afterlife. It pained her to think of her mother as an unhappy soul, angry at being taken too soon from her side. For so long she'd only been aware of her own anger. She'd never considered the other side of the coin.

She took up Allyson's clammy hand and placed it in a thick shock of hair at her shoulder and pressed her cheek into its palm.

"Can you feel this?" she asked.

Allyson's face gave a rapturous smile. "Yes," she said. "I can feel things through your friend's body. So soft." Tears fell from her closed eyes.

"I love you, mommy."

"I love you too, pumpkin." Allyson's hand pulled suddenly away, making Noelle jump. "She's waking up," said her mother. The voice was strained, as though it took great effort to maintain control of the body.

"No," pleaded Noelle.

"Quickly," said her mother. "Put out the candle and put away the board. If she finds out, she'll never let me speak to you again."

"But..."

"Now!" she hissed, sending Noelle scurrying to follow her edict, all the while great tears rolled down her face. It took her only seconds to put things right. It was easier to replace the board's cover than to remove it, and as she returned the thing to its corner, she turned to see Allyson's body swaying as though dizzy. She rushed to her mother and took her hands.

"Don't leave me yet," she pleaded.

"I'm sorry, pumpkin. I have to go. Your friend is too strong."

"But there's so much more I want to know."

"Kiss me goodbye for now, and we'll talk again later."

Without hesitation Noelle pressed her lips to Allyson's and hugged her tight. "I love you," she whispered in her ear.

She raced around to the other side of the bed and slid between the blankets. Once there, she took one last look as Allyson's body slumped back onto her pillow and went limp. She pinched out the candle and sobbed quietly in the darkness until emotional exhaustion bore her into sleep.

Allyson went home the next day, saying she felt strangely tired and not entirely herself. As it was Sunday, she could not have stayed another night anyway, nor could Noelle at her house. Both their parents were like-minded in that school was a priority, and there would be no overnights when the next morning was school.

Noelle remained sullen for the rest of Sunday, snapping at her father several times. Unlike many fathers, he felt he understood her emotional state and gave her room to breathe. With every biting remark, he simply sighed and left her to her own devices, an act that made her feel instantly guilty and plunged her mood deeper into blackness. She was restless, yes, but not because of teen-aged angst or hormones. She wanted her mother. The simple taste she had gotten was not enough for her, and she was greedy for more. The fact that her life and school got in her way infuriated her.

The next week went by slowly for Noelle, with days spent in a deep funk and wishing the weekend would arrive. She feigned interest in her classes poorly, and her teachers noticed. While they spoke of Hawthorne and Algebra, Noelle silently brooded and planned the coming Friday night. When she did see Allyson, it was as if a weight had lifted off her back, and she seemed happier, though there was something different in the way she regarded her friend. She tried not to, but couldn't help but to see her mother's face every time Allyson walked into the room. There was genuine love there, and an unhealthy attachment that added fuel to the already rampant rumors throughout the high school.

By the time the weekend came, Noelle was filled with nervous energy. She and Allyson had already made plans for sleepovers, first at Allyson's house, a practice they'd made common for several months. Noelle had only to wait until the evening hours, when Allyson was asleep, to talk to her mother again, but patience was not her virtue, and waiting made her seem cross to everyone but Allyson.

Late Friday night, after they'd finished their ritual of watching rented movies and snacking until their stomachs felt unnaturally full, Allyson finally fell asleep. Noelle crept to the ouija, lit a candle, and placed her fingers on the planchette, this time with no hesitation. She knew precisely what she wanted, who she was looking for. She knew she could get the answers and validation she so craved.

"I'm here, mommy," she said again, and was shocked as the pointer began to quake violently beneath her fingertips. She tried to pull her hands away, but found them firmly adhered to the planchette by some unseen force. As it sped around the board, she watched and noted the letters to which it pointed. When it had pointed to the last of the letters, it did not stop, but continued to drift on the board in an infinite loop.

"'Not who you think?'" she asked, a gnawing at the base of her spine growing. "Who the hell are you?"

The whispers began almost immediately, starting at what sounded like a great distance, then closing in, growing louder and more painful by the second. Her skin crawled at the sound of the spectral voices. In their breathy buzzing were words, a confused din of pleading whispers, each one begging for her attention. Though she could not understand most of what she heard, certain words rang out, their meanings confusing but potent. Among the hissing voices she heard cries for help, the words *trickster*, and *danger.* Most disturbing to her, however, was the realization that one whisperer in particular kept repeating a single word: *Noelle.*

As the din grew louder in her mind, she tried to cover her ears only to find her fingers still firmly held on the planchette. She felt as if she would scream, but a single voice cut through the pandemonium. Though the voice was in the room with her, the voices in her head stopped almost immediately.

"Enough," said Allyson's sleeping body with a scowl.

Noelle's eyes snapped open as she felt the hold on her fingers suddenly released. Allyson sat as she had the week before, sleeping but animated. She rushed to the bed and threw her arms around the cold body that spoke to her.

"What was that?" she asked, her heart still pounding with terror.

"I won't be able to come back like this much more," said her mother's voice. "They keep trying to get out, and they're getting stronger."

"They?"

"Souls. Unhappy souls."

"They said my name."

"They'll say anything to get out." There was a bitter, angry tone to her voice that Noelle didn't like. Something in it revealed a darker side to the afterlife, something she had not considered.

The thought of her mother being unable to contact her gave her a glimpse of sorrowful panic. She would beg, plead, to whatever power existed, if only she knew to whom.

"You can't leave me again," she sobbed. "I just got you back. You can't leave me again!"

"There might be a way," said her mother's voice.

"How?" she asked breathlessly.

"I need a body," she said plainly, as if it were something a person would say every day. "You can see how easily I can slip into this one while your friend is asleep. In a body without a soul, I wouldn't have to leave."

"Where do I find a body?" It was a ridiculous supposition, that a fifteen year-old girl could find a corpse suitable for her mother's soul. She began to feel hopeless.

"I've grown quite used to this one," came the voice from the sleeping witch's lips.

Noelle raised her head slowly to look into the sleeping face of her friend. What it asked was plain, but hideous. The life of her friend for the life of her mother, stolen away for ten long years. If it were possible to have her mother back, did she dare to put the act into motion?

Her attention was drawn by the ouija across the room, which now pulsated with violet light. The planchette began to spin, turning up on its point, the light from its centered crystal growing brighter as it gained speed. As it spun, the light drew inward like smoke, until a hazy outline began to form. Wisps of light reached like tendrils through the icy air toward the two girls, as a thousand voices' howls began to build in Noelle's mind. She felt as if her head would split from the pressure, as if the screaming voices had substance inside her head.

"They've found me!" wailed her mother's voice. "They've come to drag me back! I don't want to go! I want to stay! You have to help me!"

Droplets

The ribbons of violet light streaked out and pierced the sleeping face through her nostrils and ears. The body convulsed violently, and then sprawled backward as the violet light streaked out, dragging behind it a sickly green mass of vapor. As the green tried to gain a hold on something in this world, the violet pulled it toward the ever-shrinking tempest until at last the planchette stopped spinning and the room was silent. Allyson slumped forward coughing in labored breaths.

"What's happening?" she demanded.

"Nothing," replied Noelle through fought-back tears. "You were having a nightmare. I woke you up."

Noelle had her own nightmares later, after she'd managed to get the witch back to sleep and exhaustion claimed her body from consciousness. In her mind's eye, her mother was as she remembered from photographs, without Allyson's body, her face contorted in terror as the unnamed presence entangled her. Her screams cut the air as violet tendrils pulled and stretched her body toward the abyss. Allyson stood behind her, her face twisted into a cruel smile as she pushed her mother toward the clutching hands that erupted from the pulsating ouija. And in the midst of it all stood Noelle, dressed as she had been at five years old. She cried and screamed for her mother, begged her not to go, pleaded with the unnamed thing to leave her alone. But the image of the witch laughed at her cries and pushed harder, sending her mother hurtling down the rift in the board into blackness.

She awoke drenched in sweat and tears just as early daylight began to stream through the tiny window at the top of the basement. Allyson breathed deep in sleep. It made her angry. Her mother said the witch was strong and wouldn't let her stay. Was it so much to ask, to sacrifice one so her wrongly-taken mother could live again? It seemed to her that the dream held more truth than distorted fiction, that Allyson, in her selfishness, was what kept Noelle from her mother. She fumed as she made her decision, that her mother would be free.

For the remainder of the day, they followed their teen-age rituals and agreed that Noelle would spend another night in Allyson's basement room. Noelle feigned interest and good humor while Allyson shopped for clothes or combed the thrift stores for something unusual, but in her mind she looked on her friend with bitterness, as though it were her fault her mother wasn't with her now. She laughed in the appropriate places and pretended to listen, but she was anxious to get to the deed tonight.

Later that evening, movies watched, popcorn eaten, the two settled down to sleep. On the couch, Noelle's nerve tightened as though she would split her skin if she didn't move quickly. For the better part of the day, she'd been contemplating how it was to be done. Her mother was beautiful in her memory, therefore she had to be careful not to spoil the features of her new body. Slashing the wrists, hanging, strangling, and other methods were, therefore, out of the question. The best course, she decided, was to smother her with a pillow. There would be no blood loss, and the downy stuffing would muffle any screams. It would, she knew, be difficult. After all, she'd never killed a living creature before, let alone her best friend. But it had to be done. If her she was to have her mother back, it had to be done. Her mother would be back by her side, and what else did she need to know?

When she heard the familiar light snoring from Allyson's bed, she crept out from under the blanket, pillow in hand. Though it was very dark in the room, she could still see well enough, her senses sharpened by the act she was about to commit. She took a final look into the witch's horribly peaceful face. Her stomach twisted at the thought of Allyson pushing her mother back into the abyss, and she used the pain to strengthen her resolve. She quietly positioned the pillow over the sleeping girl's face, the pressed down upon it with her full weight.

For the longest three minutes of her young life, Noelle felt Allyson struggle against her. She fought and thrashed until Noelle had no choice but to straddle her body to pin her arms down with her knees. As she pressed the pillow hard against Allyson's head, she had no thoughts save for that of her mother returning to her. She sat squarely on her chest to force the air from her victim's lungs, until the body went limp. Only then did Noelle begin to understand the severity of what she'd done. The realization that she'd murdered her best friend gripped her like an icy shower, her nerves clattering, but she knew the time for turning back was past. Nothing more to do, she decided, than to go forward and reclaim her mother.

The body twitched slightly with the last electric impulses of life as Noelle climbed off and hurried to the ouija. She placed her fingers on the planchette and took a deep, nervous breath.

"Mommy," she said aloud, her voice quivering. "I'm here. I've done it."

At once, the body that was Allyson sat up, opened its eyes and smiled at Noelle. It breathed deeply and ran its fingers over its skin, a look of exquisite joy crossing its curiously twisted face.

"Thank you, pumpkin," it said, its smile growing wider. "Thank you so much."

Noelle felt a nervous joy in her heart, knowing she'd committed the most heinous of crimes, but that her sin had been rewarded. As she shifted to rise and hug her mother, the ouija erupted in violet light so brilliant it hurt her eyes and threw her backward. The whisperers shrieked louder than ever, their cries threatening to burst Noelle's head from the inside. As they increased in pitch and volume, a single voice cut through them like a razor, sending Noelle crumpling to the floor.

"No!" it shouted as the violet tempest swirled from the ouija's center.

"This body is mine," snarled the thing on the bed as it crouched like an angry cat.

The purple storm split, a silver light emerging from within it. Noelle watched as Allyson, now a being of pure luminance, drifted forth to face the caterwauling thing within her body. She knew what was going to happen. Allyson was going to fight for her body, aided by some force from the deadlands. Rage grew inside her, hatred for the witch who wanted to take her mother from her again.

Before she could act, the light from the violet tempest shot forward and pinned her to the ground. It burned against her skin and she struggled to free herself, but it was as though it pierced her body and held her fast, a butterfly on a board, and try as she might, she could not get free.

Allyson raised her hands toward the creature on the bed. Arcs of light erupted from her outstretched arms and burned through the thing on the bed. It howled in pain as they ripped across its body.

"Mommy!" cried Noelle. She needed to help her, before the witch reclaimed her body.

As she fought, the violet tendrils snaked up her body until they waved in front of her like seaweed. She pressed her head back hard against the floor, as though it would give way and let her keep them from touching her, but a single tendril shot forward, piercing her forehead with light and casting her into her own mind, where time had no meaning and the light took on a familiar form.

"Mommy?" she asked.

Her mother looked as Noelle had remembered, but with a stern expression on her face.

"I tried to warn you," she said without speaking. "You didn't listen."

The being of light raised its hands to Noelle and took her face in its hands. On contact, she saw everything that had transpired, not as they happened to her, but from the point of view of one whose judgment was not tainted by emotions. She saw herself, the stupid girl, inviting this entity into her world, the murder of her friend. She saw the truth behind the lies it told and realized with soul-wrenching horror that it was not her mother that now inhabited her friend's skin. She saw her mother trying to warn her from the other side, struggling to free herself from peaceful nirvana to correct the mistake that her daughter had made. Within that tiny span of time, she had a moment of sorrowful clarity. How stupid she had been, she thought. Of course it wasn't her mother. Her mother would never have suggested murder. Her mother would not have been in a realm of torture, a hell from which escape was planned. Had she not been blinded by her own pain, she might have seen.

Noelle sobbed openly in both worlds, begging her mother to tell her what to do. How could she, she pleaded, set things right?

Her mother's image became clear to her again as it drew its hands away and smiled sadly at her.

"You opened the gateway," her mother's voice said in her mind. "You must close it."

At that, she was again on the floor, no longer pinned, watching as the being of silver wrestled with her own body.

"Allyson!" she cried. At once, she knew what she had to do. The conduit must be closed. She only hoped things could be set right and her friend could forgive her when, if, it was all over. She scrambled to the ouija, ignoring the pain in her arms as violet electricity coursed through her body. The tempest raged and sent fiery tendrils from it's gaping chasm haphazardly throughout the room. It centered over the planchette, its winds tearing at Noelle's hands as she reached for it. As her fingers made contact, power coursed through her body, and burned it from the inside. Every hair on her arms, every twitch of her flesh Wracked her body with pain.

"Momma!" she pleaded. "Help Allyson!" She watched in horror as the being of light climbed through Allyson's mouth and into her body. As the body shook and convulsed, Noelle could only imagine the battle inside, both souls locked in fierce combat for their existence. The seconds took an eternity to pass, until viscous green oozed forth from Allyson's nose and mouth and congealed on the floor.

"Now!" she cried. Violet tendrils struck out toward the lumpy mass that formed in the slimy pool. The green struggled against the entangling ribbons of light as it was dragged back into the maelstrom above the great slab. Noelle was thrown backward, leaving her wide eyed and gaping as it howled in protest. It clutched at the edges of the board, trying to keep some hold in the world of the living, until at last it was wrenched downward leaving the room in relative darkness.

Noelle scrambled to her feet as the last of the green mass disappeared into nothingness, and breathed a silent prayer as she moved the planchette to the word "goodbye." Then she lifted the cumbersome board from its stand and slammed it to the ground, breaking it into rubble. She sat for only a few moments, sobbing until her legs found strength again. She'd gained the knowledge she'd sought for so long, but at what price? As quickly as she could manage, she went to the bed where Allyson's body lay inert.

There was no blood, no bruises, no other sign that there had been a struggle. Had she not seen it, Noelle would have thought Allyson was simply resting peacefully. However, her lack of movement conjured her innermost fears as she slowly began to realize what she'd done. It wasn't so much what would happen to her now, when Allyson's family found her dead in the basement with no believable explanation forthcoming, nor was it that she'd never talk to her mother again. It even occurred to her that she might have damned herself. It didn't matter to her, however, what consequences lay in wait for her. Now all she wanted was to take it all back, to revive her friend. Now, with the clearness of hindsight, she should have known, and it gnawed at her that she would so easily murder another being, let alone her dearest friend.

When she did not see Allyson's chest rise with breath, she lowered her head, clutching her friend's cold hand against her cheek. She pleaded silently to God, to her mother, to whomever might be listening to right what she'd done, all the while sobbing in remorse, until, at long last, she felt Allyson's hand grow warm again, and opened her eyes to find her friend sitting up next to her.

"Allyson!" she stammered. "You're..."

"Alive, no thanks to you," came the cold reply.

"I'm so sorry..."

"*Sorry*?" she said incredulously. "Sorry for what? Pretending to be my friend? For using my magic and good will for your own selfish games?

Sorry for breaking my ouija? Or maybe you're sorry for killing me!"

Allyson jerked her hand away and stood on shaky legs.

"If you wanted to talk to her so bad, you could have asked me, you know," she spat. "Maybe I could have come up with some other way than to try to kill me!"

She turned with snap and went to a large cabinet on the other side of the room. From its top she retrieved a large bottle full of salt water and began sprinkling bits around the room, all the while fuming.

"I can't believe you'd do this. If I'd have known..."

Noelle sat dumbly staring at her feet. She deserved to be yelled at, hated, and more. She deserved to go to jail, but worse. She'd betrayed a trust and had no excuse other than that she was blinded by emotion. Her stomach churned with remorse and fear with the knowledge that she'd destroyed any trace of a friendship with Allyson. She dreaded what Allyson would, or could do.

By the time Allyson stopped muttering to herself, she'd finished cleansing the room and turned her attentions toward Noelle, first splashing her with the saltwater, then dousing herself while saying a prayer that Noelle did not recognize. When at last she opened her eyes, there was sadness instead of anger behind them.

"You have to leave," she said bluntly.

"I'm sorry," said Noelle quietly. It seemed like a clumsy, inadequate thing to say, but she couldn't think of anything else. But Allyson's face remained hard. No amount of pleading or justification would change her mind.

"Sorry's not good enough. I trusted you."

"I know." She knew she was crying, but didn't care. She understood her friend's position, and would have felt the same. She slowly got up and gathered the few belongings she had brought with her. As she walked to the staircase that led to the rest of the house, she turned to face Allyson. "I didn't mean for any of this," she said. "I wasn't thinking right."

For a brief moment, hope flickered inside her as she saw Allyson's expression soften. Allyson went to the crumbled mass that was the great ouija and took a piece.

"Take this with you," she said. "Think about this the next time before you do something stupid."

Noelle took the piece without looking at it and hugged her friend tightly before rushing up the stairs. As she closed the door behind her, she found Allyson's stepmother in the kitchen looking tired and peevish.

"Where're you going at this time of night?" she asked as Noelle came through the door.

"I'm...not feeling well. I need to go home."

"Do you want me to drive you?"

"No, thanks," she said, hoping the dimness of the room would hide her tears. "The walk'll do me good."

"What was all that screaming down there?" she asked, obviously irritated at being awakened by the noise.

"I'm sorry," said Noelle. "It was a movie. Things just got out of hand."

Doreen nodded, still angry, but at least satisfied by the answer. She gave a cursory wave as Noelle went out the door into the night air.

She walked quickly until she made it back to her apartment, then stopped, unwilling to go up the stairs, back to her lonely life. She sat on the stairwell and pulled the piece of the ouija Allyson had given her from her pocket to examine it. Though any piece would have done, Allyson had chosen a piece that would, as if she would ever need to be, remind her bluntly of her trespasses. As she turned the polished stone over in her hands, she traced the word with her fingers and sobbed openly, feeling very alone. The piece had only one word on it. It was marked "goodbye."

Droplets

—————————

Rakshasa

I never really believed my Great-Grandfather's stories of India and his adventures on safari. He was, as I recall from my youth, a dottering old Brit with many tall-tales, designed to capture the imagination of children and elevate him to some mythical status in our eyes. True, his collection of Indian antiquities and trophies was quite impressive, but many of his objects could very well have been purchased from street vendors rather than won through, as he called it, honorable combat in the untamed wilds.

As I walked through his study on the eve of his death, I could still hear his tired voice retelling stories that I'd heard a hundred times, with little variation. I passed by the glass bells and remembered tales of each piece, how this dagger came from a "spritely little blighter who took to collecting human ears" and that sari was from "the Maharaja's personal concubine," and all I could think was how I would miss the inflated stories and how perhaps someone should write them down, sell them for what they were, stories to thrill children.

I was astounded by the sheer number of attendants at his funeral, which was done with all the regality of his military post in Her Majesty's Royal Army, and at the vast differences in origin of the guests. Though the majority hailed from England, and were, no doubt, fellow servicemen, I noticed several whose accents placed them as coming from America and

Australia. One rather large group, I found curious in their attire until I realized that I'd seen it before, in the photographs hung in the Colonel's study. They were unmistakably from India. There were five of them, four women and one man, clothed in the most elegant of fashions. Two of the women carried a large chest, obviously meant as a gift, but to whom I had no idea. I was astounded when the group approached me, proffering the box as a way of honoring my Great Grandfather.

"He was, to my village, a great hero," said the man with surprisingly good English. His accent, though heavy, did little to obscure his words. "We are saddened by his passing, and bring this, in tribute to his family line."

The two women placed the box before me and lifted the lid, revealing what I at first thought to be a robe of blue.

"Rakshasa," said the man. "It belonged to the Colonel, a prize won in honorable combat. It seemed only right that it pass to the hands of his family."

It was the phrase, so exactingly my Great-Grandfather's, that caught my attention. In that instant, it occurred to me that I may have been mistaken in judging the validity of those tall-tales. I had heard him mention before the word rakshasa, but it was with such quiet reverence that it seemed that even the mention of whatever this thing might be chilled him to the marrow.

I reached gingerly into the box, laying fingers on the blue material and realized instantly with wonder that what I was looking at was no robe of silk or cotton, but a raw animal hide, the color of the sky during spring, with small tufts of hair dotting the edges. There was no mottling of the color, no trace that the pelt had been dyed, and so it was left for me to wonder what sort of curious beast of nature could grow with such a vivid hue.

When I inquired as to the nature of the beast, the Indian replied very simply that it was a great and ancient evil, and that the Colonel had vanquished it from his village. I spent the rest of the day in the Colonel's study, the strange pelt in my lap, gazing at his many treasures, wondering just how much truth there was in each of his stories. By day's end, I was so enraptured with the idea that perhaps my Great-Grandfather was indeed some sort of hero, that I decided the best course of action was to journey to his most favorite of foreign lands and see for myself what terrors this "rakshasa" could possibly hold.

That very night, after the burial, I spoke with the Indian and his servants and made arrangements to accompany them back to their homeland, as a way of honoring their hero's memory. I packed quickly but thoroughly any item I might need, including an electric torch and my own pistol. Then, with visions of India and my Great-Grandfather drifting through my consciousness, I settled down to try to sleep before my long journey.

The first and longest leg of the trip, which was made by ship from the British isle, around Africa, then back up to the Arabian Sea, was, in the beginning, spent with little discussion other than memories of the Colonel and how much he meant to his village. It was not until the second day out that I learned the Indian's actual name, Ajatashatru, which means "without enemies" in his native tongue. It was determined that, as we were to be traveling companions for some time, that formalities were without merit. He introduced me to his four companions, the servants Apala, Malati, and Vajra, and his wife, Sarasa. We were, he revealed, to travel by ship to the port at Marmagao, after which there was several days trek to their village, just south of Bhopal.

It was a fine time for me, learning all I could glean about their culture and language, cursing that I'd not paid more attention to the Colonel's stories. I even managed to learn, with some proficiency, the art of swordplay with one of their long, wickedly curved blades. It was only when I pressed for more information about this rakshasa creature that my host became quiet, refusing to discuss such a thing with an outsider. Though I tried plying him with money and drink, he simply would not discuss the species with the blue pelt, saying that there were things that English eyes dared not see. Frustrated, yet still keen to learn more, I waited, patiently testing the boundaries of their divulgence.

It was after more than a week had passed that I was aroused from my slumber by a faint knock at my cabin door. I pulled on my robe and slippers, calling for the knocker to wait, then opened the door. There, beautiful against the moonlit ocean, stood Apala, her eyes darting about conspiratorially. Without waiting to be bade enter, she slipped quietly into the cabin and closed the door behind her.

"It is dangerous," she said. "The information for which you ask. Rakshasa is not spoken about, and for good reason."

She told a tale that could only be described as miraculous and hard to believe, of the old gods and how, in the Hindu belief, the world was formed. Of terrible monsters and vengeful demons, of creatures that drank the blood and ate the flesh of humans. Though it was obvious to me that her mind was clearly entrenched in superstitious folklore, there was a real element of fear with which I could not help but sympathize.

The Rakshasa, she said, were as old as the world itself, their race feeding on ours like cattle. They were immense creatures, possessing an unbridled ferocity that most men feared and those who did not, fell prey to. In addition, she told of their other mystic powers, that of shape changing, a gift attributed to many of the mystical creatures of Indian folklore, and of their ability to glide silently into darkness. Such was her fear that I sat, astounded until she'd finished her tale, and sat quivering in the lounge chair.

She bade me never speak of the Rakshasa again and returned to her cabin, leaving me to ponder her tale. I went to my suitcase and pulled from inside the pelt. It was soft in my hands, like fine silk, although it felt as tough as any boot I'd encountered. It was cut so I could only discern its size, nothing more. There was no head attached, nor were there paws. Only the broadness and length of the creature, more than two meters from shoulder to buttock, were evident. I shuddered to think of my Great-Grandfather facing such a fearsome beast, whether real or mythical. Moreover, I wondered what I would, or even could, do should I come face to face with one. It was, after all, the reason I was going to India, for the validation of the Colonel's fantastic yarns.

It took longer than even I expected, with time stretching to the point that I no longer recalled with any certainty what it felt like to be on dry land. When we finally did arrive at the port of Marmagao, it was with great relief that we disembarked. From the moment we set foot on Indian soil, however, I could sense that something was amiss. Perhaps it was that I was too used to the swaying of the ocean current, which, after a fashion, I managed to convince myself. Now, in hindsight, I know that I should have trusted my instinct and gotten back on board that ship.

My host and his servants procured transportation by train to Bhopal, after which we would travel by motor to his village. From the moment we stepped on the train, I somehow got the notion in my head, whether from the exotic setting or the strange people, that our party, or more specifically I, was being watched. It was for this reason that I kept my pistol firmly tucked beneath my jacket.

As the train began its laborious journey into the heart of India, we retired to our respective cabins. An air of excitement surrounded us, they, for bringing the ancestor of their hero to the village, me for finally finding the truth in my Grandfather's ramblings.

It was during that first night that I was roused from sleep by a noise both peculiar and fearsome. It was akin to that of a large cat, a mountain lion or jaguar, screeching across the distance. Strange it seemed, that such a noise could penetrate the chugging rumble of the train's engine, so that I thought the originator of the sound might be right outside my cabin door. I rose from my bunk, pistol drawn, prepared for the worst, but when I threw the door open, I saw only the empty hallway. The noise continued unabated, however, until it roused every cabin in our car. Only my hosts seemed to know the source, as the serving girls looked fearfully to each other and Ajatashatru cast a glance of concern to his wife. Although none of them gave voice to their concerns, I knew what they believed the sound to be.

Droplets

Rakshasa.

"They follow us," said Apala to her master, who silenced her with a withering stare.

"Nonsense," he hissed. "Back to sleep."

I spent the rest of that night sitting in my cabin, eyes open, listening to the cries of creatures I imagined to be hued of blues and greens.

Daylight brought with it a sense of relief, as the cries stopped with the dawn. We breakfasted together, with no mention of the sounds of the previous night. They spoke of the many wonders of their homeland, and with pride of their village, but no one even dared broach the subject of the rakshasa or of the strange cries in the night.

The evening came, and with it a palpable fear that hung heavy over the sleeping car. The cries in the night came again, louder this time than last, but no doors opened to investigate. Doors were, in fact, locked and braced against intruders. I spent the evening with the pelt in my hands and my ears acutely attuned, trying to imagine what sort of creature could produce both sound and skin such as these.

At some point during the night, I must have drifted from exhaustion, as I was awakened with a start by pounding at my cabin door. It was Ajatashatru, looking fearful, as he revealed to me that the train's last car had been ransacked during the night, and the lantern-man who held his post there was most brutally butchered. As he spoke, he glanced downward to see the pelt that I, having fallen asleep, was using as a blanket. His brown skin turned ashen at the sight of the thing, and he demanded to know why I'd brought it on the journey. I explained to him that I meant no harm, that I wanted to bring it as a connection to my Grandfather and his apparent greatness.

His words grew loud and fast, slipping between English and Hindi, his anger and fear evident. Thought I could not understand most of what he said, due to my ignorance of the Hindi tongue, I did manage to figure that I'd been wrong to bring the rakshasa pelt, and that the death at the back

---

of the train was somehow my fault for doing so. He bade me throw the damned thing from the train immediately, an act which I was not inclined to follow. They were tracking us, he said. They could smell the skin of their slain kind, and they would take revenge on any who possessed it.

While I do not consider myself to be foolhardy nor particularly brave, it disturbs me to no end to be thought the cause of so great a tragedy as a death. And so, pistol in hand, I went to the rear-most car to discern for myself just what had happened. As I crossed between cars, I marveled at the Engineer's reasoning of not stopping the train. While it was true that a crime had been committed and procedures needed to be followed, he maintained that, if indeed we were being tracked, the last thing we should do is stop and make ourselves easy prey. On the other hand, if, as I asserted, there was a madman onboard, he also did not wish to stop and give the criminal the chance to escape.

The rear car was, as reports stated, in a state of remarkable disarray, with smashed furniture strewn about and stains that were now brown and sticky covering the walls. The lantern-man's body was, I was thankful to find, covered by a sheet to the side, a trail of crimson leading to where it lay. I was, I will admit, greatly disturbed by the condition of the room, as I've never been privy to such carnage before in my life. There were, I found on inspection, great slash marks carved deep in the walls of the car, many as far as apart as two finger's width. The back door of the car had been smashed from its hinges inward, and now stood upright only by the careful placement of a bench.

I stooped beside the body, both fearful and repulsed by the act which I had to commit, but needing to know, nontheless. As I gingerly drew back the sheet, I felt my gorge rise in my throat at the sight.

The man had been, in life, quite large, though any real features were torn away with vicious precision. His right arm, still clutching a rifle, was detached and placed across his chest. Across his body were several slashes, in sets of four, similar to those that covered the walls. It became apparent that this man perished while doing his job, protecting the rear of the train from any who might wish to gain access. I examined the chamber of the rifle to see that the bullet and housing were still intact, indicating to me that he'd not even been able to get off one shot.

I placed the sheet back over the corpse and continued around the room, hoping for some shred of evidence that this was not what my traveling companions, and, in truth, I, feared. When I came to the back door, I pushed aside the bench and set the door aside, feeling the warm air rush past into the car. The iron stoop and rails were grizzly testaments to what had happened, as there were large pools of blood where the unfortunate man had undoubtedly been found. I could scarcely imagine what it must have looked like to the person who discovered the tragedy, his large body draped over the rail, his arm laying in the pool of blood to my right.

I turned and went back into the car, feeling sick with the thought that perhaps I was to blame. This was not the work of a madman. To be certain, it seemed more and more like the deed of some large animal, a big cat or some such thing. Perhaps rakshasa.

Before I could shake the ridiculous thought from my mind, my eyes alighted on something I had not seen before, and would not have save for the light from the broken doorway. Amidst the gore and splattered flashes, there was a stark patch of blue pinned to the wall by a dagger.

As big as the palm of my hand, the patch proved to be what resembled the ear of a large cat, blue and hairless on the outer skin, tufted with white on its inner folds. My stomach cramped with recognition as I pried the blade and pinned slice of flesh from the wall, as I knew at the touch where I'd seen such a thing before. It was the same as the pelt which even now lay folded in my cabin.

It became clear to me what had happened, and a great sadness washed over me for the man who had fallen in his duty. The creature attacked, tearing his arm from his body and the man fought to the end, taking the beast's ear in the process and hurling it, wounded, from the train. It was thanks to him that the creature had not gotten to the rest of us, or to me.

I closed the sliding door behind me, making my way quickly to the car where our cabins were. I neither knocked nor waited to be bidden enter before throwing open the door to the Indian's room, startling him considerably. I threw the bloody ear in his lap and, in no uncertain terms, advised him to tell me what he knew of this raksasha creature, before it killed us all.

He was, understandably, angry, but more frightened I think. In that moment, for him to realize that the train was, indeed, being tracked, as he'd asserted, was more terrifying to him than I could have dreamed possible. At long last, during which time he staunchly refused to speak, despite the pleading of his wife and servants, I finally wore his resolve and he began to tell what he knew of the creatures.

"They are brutes," he said, his voice quaking. "Immense creatures driven by hunger and hatred. The one your grandfather killed terrorized my village when I was a child. Each night it would return, each morning, another child would be missing."

He took a deep breath and motioned to one of the serving girls, who brought him a glass of water.

"Their forms can change," he continued after a long drink. "They can take any shape they wish, but their color stays the same. They drink the blood of men, and eat the flesh to satisfy their hunger."

This much I knew already from Apala's covert explanations. More, I wanted to know how to kill the infernal beasts, and how my Grandfather managed to get away with the pelt.

"They die as does any creature," he said. "Through honorable combat, but care must be taken. For although they are but brutes, there are few who have seen one and come away alive."

A shrill howl filled the air, deafening in its ferocity. The creature was again following us, as the sun had slipped below the mountains. I snatched up the ear from the Indian's lap and bade them lock the door, then

Droplets

I ran to my own cabin. As I reached the door, I felt a sudden lurching of the train, and then the Indian night seemed to turn inward on itself. The train careened off the tracks and drug itself sideways to a stop amid the sounds of screams from passengers and howls from that which would eat them.

I have stated before, I am not foolhardy nor am I brave, but I do know when something is my fault. I did know what had to be done, and, loath as I was to do so, I knew is was I who had to do it.

I crawled upward, into my cabin, and found the bundled pelt. Whether it was a sense of irony, stupidity, or even justice, I do not, nor shall I ever, know, but I tied the thing around my neck like a cape and dropped through to the hallway. With my pistol in one hand and the long curved blade of India in the other, I crawled through an open window and into the night air.

What I saw will, I dare say, haunt my subconscious forever, for the main engine of the train lay twisted, nearly in half, on its side by the tracks. It was obvious to me that some large creature had rammed it, knocking it from the track.

I recall that it was deathly still, with not even a wind to disturb the silence, save for the beating of my own heart as I set out to fulfill what it seemed was my duty as the heir of the great Colonel. I wondered how he felt, what he had done that night, so many years ago, and if he prayed to God or his own ancestors for strength as I did now.

From behind me I heard a noise, a fearsome growl that I knew was the beast that I sought. I turned to see it, recognizing the blue pallor of its skin as the same as that which I wore on my back. It looked, however, not like a beast at all. It had taken a form that doubtless caused fear in the peoples of India, that of their Hindi god Vishnu.

"I am not of your country!" I bellowed at the beast. "I am English! And no such trickery will prevent me from claiming your hide!"

At that, Vishnu crouched and revealed its true form. It was an awesome, terrible sight to behold. Like an enormous hairless cat, with long jutting fangs over its flat face and fiery slits for eyes, its head seemed to split in half as it roared, revealing rows upon rows of razor-like teeth, slashing with wicked, curved black claws.

I fired my pistol, emptying the chamber at the creature. Though I know at least one of the six shots struck its mark, the beast did not fall, nor did it seem to even notice, as it leaped toward me, screaming in a way that I shall never forget.

What happened in the next few moments is a blur to me now, as the whole exchange could not have taken but a few seconds. As I slashed with the Indian blade, it tore at me, knocking the blade from my hand and opening a wound that began at my shoulder and traveled downward toward my elbow. I fell to the ground, blinded by pain and fear as the monster lumbered toward me. I could feel its hot breath as it sniffed the pelt around my neck, smell the rot in its maw. It reared back, preparing to strike the fatal blow, when I felt a splash of warmth across my face, and the creature recoiled and turned away. Through my pain-induced haze, I saw the cause, and its new target. There, behind the creature, her eyes wide with terror as she held my fallen sword, stood Apala.

The beast's muscles coiled beneath its taught skin as it sounded its fearsome cry. I watched as she held the blade in front of her, flailing at the monster with reckless abandon, but to no avail. It raised a mammoth paw and struck her, knocking Apala to the ground. I felt my English temper rise and my blood boil at the sight of the monster bearing down upon her. How I found the strength, I'm certain I shall never know, but I somehow managed to get to my feet and found myself striking at the creature's back with my bare hands, screaming all the while.

It seemed not to notice my blows, as it opened its mouth wide, spraying Apala with sticky saliva. As it was about to bite down and end her life, I reached with my ruined arm and dug my hand into the bloody wound where the creature's ear had been. It howled in pain, shaking me from its back with enough force to send me sprawling.

Droplets

For but a moment, the creature seemed in a quandary about which of us to claim first. When at last it set its great body toward me, I was certain I would be joining my Great Grandfather in the afterlife.

Out of the corner of my vision, I saw Apala holding the fallen sword. She cried out and threw the blade to me, and, as the creature pounced, I pressed the blade upward, piercing it through the soft pallet of the monster's skull. It slumped on top of me, twitching, but otherwise quite dead.

That was many years ago, and now I look and see the same disbelief on the faces of my own grandchildren. But, unlike the Colonel, I proudly wear the scars on my withered arm as testament to the creature I defeated in honorable combat. When my grandchildren look on me with disbelieving eyes, I simply smile and kiss the hand of my wife, her dark skin soft beneath my lips. She smiles and tells the children of how we fell in love, and of how I took her for my wife and we returned to England, I with my blanket, and she with a coat of curious blue hide.

Rats

"Strange old house, isn't it?"

Brian Oglethorpe struggled with the rusted doorknob and heaved with his shoulder.

"I mean, it's cool and all, but it's just...I don't know...Weird."

Becky smiled as she watched him struggle. Thin an nerdy he might be, but he was still cute for a lawyer.

"Yeah," she smiled. "Look, are you sure? I mean, there hasn't been some mistake?"

"No ma'am," he said between grunts. "My firm researched the documents as well as we could. Everything is in order."

"Then this house really is..."

"Yours," he huffed as the door came open. "It really is a prime piece of real estate, even if you decided to tear the place down. I mean, the house itself is worth a small fortune, but the land itself? Developers would kill to get their hands on this piece of property. Do you have any idea how many apartments they could fit on this lot?"

"I can guess," she said, distaste evident in her voice. The high ceilings, peaked doorways, the ornately paneled walls. The very idea of cookie-cutter stucco cubes replacing the beautiful artistry that defined the antebellum mansion made her cringe. Mistake or no, it was her house now, her mansion, and no developer was going to tear it down.

"Well, if you do decide to sell," said Brian as he disappeared into the dark foyer, "We'll be more than happy to get you a fair price for it."

A loud click later, the entry way lit up, revealing the splendor of a bygone age. In the stifling darkness, the house was foreboding, as if every shadow were a living thing that pressed down upon them. Now, with the power restored, Becky felt as if she were in a dream, a castle the likes of which she'd only read. No longer was she in modern Galveston, but was transported by the magic of antiquities to a distant time. It seemed rude that she should be called Becky instead of her given name, Rebecca, in these walls. Even Miss Schiflett. The old woman who'd owned this house, who died here, was a true lady, Southern Royalty in every sense of the title.

"I don't think I'll be selling."

"Suit yourself," said Brian. "If you change your mind, give us a call. That goes for all the furniture as well. Could fetch a handsome price at auction."

"I'll keep that in mind," she said as she peered up the stairwell. "Breathless" was a term she'd heard overused over the years, but as her gaze passed from one marvelously-carved edifice to another, she understood its true meaning.

Brian shook her hand and left her in the cavernous hallway with the dying echo of the heavy closing door. There was so much to be done, but all she wanted to do was stare wide-eyed at her new surroundings. She'd only been in the house once before, but she didn't really remember it. It was too long ago, when she was only two years old. Now, twenty years later, she couldn't help but wonder about the identity and motives of the woman to whom the house once belonged, her great aunt.

The first order of business, she decided, was to explore, then to take inventory of every room and its contents. There were eleven in all, not counting common areas and bathrooms, each furnished with headboards and chests of oak and cherry. On every wall hung yellowing photographs of formally dressed people in the Galveston that was. And God only knew what treasures lay hidden in the closets and dressers. The weight of such a daunting task pressed on her, but she decided to give it her full attention. Tomorrow. Today, she wanted to get her bearings, get a feel for the house before she and her legal pad reduced the beauty of the old mansion to endless lists.

Becky threw the curtains of the sitting room open. In the sunlight, the air seemed almost solid with motes of dust that flitted about. Their dull, flat scent combined with the salty air smelled of age and antiquity, somehow appropriate for the old house. She dragged a finger across the oak tabletop. Years of humid brine left its mark in the form of small pits eaten into the surface. Gingerly, she traced the stiff fabric of the sofa with her fingers.

She left the sitting room and made her way to another set of heavy doors across the hall. When she pushed against their dark-stained bulk, they groaned in protest before opening. The scent from the room beyond was one she knew well, and loved. Old paper, combined with the subtle scent of mold and dust. The room was lined with shelves that went from floor to ceiling, all neatly stacked with books. The house library. She lingered for a moment before moving on.

Further down the hall stood the stairway, wider than the space in which she'd parked her car. She giggled as she looked up to where it split in the middle and followed the carved railway around the landing. Like many girls, she dreamed of being a princess in a castle, and when she dreamed as a child, it was of a house like this one. As she made her way up the stairs, she imagined she could hear a string orchestra, their lilting sounds guiding her gently upward. At the landing, she turned and looked won across the entryway and laughed aloud. The sound of her echoed voice startled her a bit.

Before long, she found herself in the east wing. There were five bedrooms on this side, six on the other. Every door she opened revealed similarly decorated rooms, each with heavy bedposts and vanities, but each distinct enough in design and color that they could easily have been called the "red room" or the "Chinese room." Each held its own wash basin and fireplace, and several adjoined by way of a connecting bathroom. They also had access to the kitchen by way of dumbwaiters.

Perhaps a bed and breakfast.

She moved across the next suite to the French doors that led out to the balcony. As she pushed the curtain aside, it crumbled in her hand, a victim of decades of the saltwater air.

The sun fell long before she realized the time. She was so caught up in the splendor of the house, and in her treasure hunt, that by the time she reached the master suite, she was physically exhausted. But her mind jumped from item to item and found more things to keep her eyes from closing. As she pushed the door open, her breath caught in her chest. Where the other rooms had like designs and similar furnishings, this one was unique. From the canopy over the bed to the personal items that lay on the vanity, she knew this to be her great aunt's room.

There was still dust everywhere, but it lay in a thin layer instead of the thick blanket in the other rooms. The curtains were still soft and pliable in her hands. It even still had the slight odor of rosewater instead of dust and stagnant air. How long, she wondered, had her aunt lived alone? Alone in such splendor was still alone. She wished at that moment that she'd known her great aunt.

Without thinking, she stretched out cross the bed and smiled at the softness of goose-feathers beneath her head. She felt like a princess in a castle, maybe Southern Royalty herself. Miss Rebecca. She giggled and drifted into a deep sleep.

She awoke with a start in strange darkness. It took her a moment to remember where she was, but when her memory forced its way through the thick haze of sleep, she sat for a moment and listened for some sound that might have startled her awake. She glanced around the room, half-expecting to see some specter or ghost to walk out of the closet, when she heard a strange sound. Scraping, somewhere in the room, quick and light. Tiny paws skittered across plaster. She closed her eyes and focused on her hearing as she tried to find the sound's origin, until she realized it was coming from behind her. Her eyes snapped open and she slowly turned her head, her eyes focused on the wall behind the headboard. The hair on her neck prickled against her creeping flesh as she recognized the sound.

A rat. There was a God-damned rat in the wall. Apart from being disgusting, the disease-carrying beasts were hard to get rid of.

She got to her feet and put as much distance between herself and the creature as possible. Rats. Well, she reminded herself, the house seemed too perfect anyway. One call to an exterminator, then she could open her bed and breakfast. She glanced at her watch. It was past eleven in the evening. Becky made a mental note to look up the number of a reputable exterminator in the morning as she hurried out of the room.

* * *

It seemed strange to her as she turned the iron key in the door and shouldered it open. Only yesterday morning, she didn't even know the house existed, and now she had such plans for it. But all those plans revolved around getting rid of the rat. She glanced down at the amber eyes that stared up at her through the top of the carrier.

"Wait'll you get a load of this place, Chester," she cooed. "Lots of corners to sleep in...rats to chase..."

Inside, the house appeared unchanged. She expected there to be at least an odd smell, but the air still held the sweet perfume of rose-water and dust, mold and brine.

"Now see if you can catch a few of those rats," she said as she snapped the front of the carrier open. The cat poked his head out and sniffed the air, ears twitching. For a long moment he waited, listened to sounds that Becky couldn't hear. Then he crept from his cage, orange fur bristled.

"Go on," she coaxed. "Go get 'em."

As if he understood, Chester darted across the room, a blur of orange against the moldy carpets, and disappeared down a long hallway, the jingling of his collar fading into the darkness.

She set her satchel by the door alongside the carrier and pulled out a pen and her legal pad, then made her way up the grand stairway. Start at the top, she figured, in the wing she already knew, then work her way down. Besides, she wanted to spend more time in her great aunt's room. Su much fascinating history, so much about the woman who owned the house that she didn't know, it seemed the logical place to start.

Inside the master suite, she felt giddy, almost voyeuristic, as though by going through this old woman's things, she were peeking in at the most intimate details of her life. She sat at the vanity, entranced by the carvings around the mirror and drawers. The silver-handled brush was cold in her hand, its horsehair bristles soft under her fingertips. How strange, she thought, that she should be here holding things that belonged to a dead woman she didn't even know.

A sound drew her attention from her aunt's toiletries and made her focus on the ceiling. It was the same sound that woke her the night before, the same light-stepping claws that dug behind the plaster. It was still here, in the room with her. As she lowered her eyes, she saw a dark shape near the floor shoot past the door. Her legs mimicked her heart as she leaped off the stool and spun to face the creature, her legal pad held out like some sort of flimsy shield. Her throat tightened in a scream as she stared at the doorframe, ready to run from whatever came around the corner, whether it was a tiny rat or the Hound of the Baskervilles. For a few terse seconds, she heard nothing, saw nothing, then she heard a soft tinkling noise as amber eyes looked at her from around the corner.

"Chester!" Relief washed over her as she released the breath she wasn't even aware she held. "Oh, you scared me, you bad kitty!"

Chester slunk into the room, his ears ridged and alert to any sound. He ignored Becky, but instead focused past her. The fur on his back and tail bristled, and a low feral mewl croaked from his bared teeth. It was not something Becky was accustomed to.

"Chester? What is it boy?"

His attention shifted to her for only a moment, then went back to whatever invisible thing he stalked. He crouched, tail twitching, only a few feet inside the doorway. Then she heard the noise again, and knew his prey. The damned rat. Its tiny paws clawed behind the plaster, then the sound darted down the wall. Chester flew into a rage. He spun and dashed through the door in pursuit of the vermin.

"Go get 'em!" she called as the tinkling bell on his collar faded down the hallway. She took a deep breath and turned back to the task at hand.

Nine pages of yellow paper later, she felt as if she'd only just scratched the surface of the items in the room. The roll-top desk held more hidden treasures than she could've believed possible, as did the vanity, the dresser, and the armoire. Each item had to be carefully documented for tax purposes, but she'd be lying if she said she didn't find each new discovery fascinating. She sat in the middle of her great aunt's giant bed, thumbing through a box of photographs. The familiar tinkling of Chester's collar brought a smile to her face.

"Did'ja get him, boy?" she cooed without looking up. The jingling grew louder until she espected the cat to leap onto the bed with her. When it did not, she raised her eyes to find that, though she could hear him, she couldn't see him.

"Chester?"

The metallic jingle grew louder still, as though the giant orange tabby sat mere inches from her face, but as she turned to look around the room, her hands began to shake and sweat in cold recognition. The sound moved past her. She followed it with her eyes until there could be no doubt. Behind the headboard, where only last night she'd heard the faint scrapings of rodent claws, Chester's collar jingled from within the wall.

"Chester?" Her throat tightened around the word. "Kitty? Is that you?" She crept to the wall and pressed her ear to the plaster, hoping to hear her cat's familiar raspy mew. Her stomach fluttered and then tied into knots at the sound of claws running across the boards within the walls. Worse was the sound of wet sliding along behind the plaster as well, as if the little monster were dragging something behind it. From the sounds she heard, she knew what the dragged something was.

"Chester!" she screamed, banging her fist against the wall. The blow ignited a fury of movement, as the sounds of skittering claws grew louder and less distinct. She backed toward the center of the room, as far away from the walls as she could, her eyes reeling, trying to pinpoint a single source for the horrifying din. There had to be hundreds, thousands even, each of their paws scratching within the walls, overhead, beneath the floorboards. She could feel them watching from cracks, smell their foul odor as the sound grew louder still. She spun and ran toward the door as she tried to get away from the noise, but every direction she found blocked by the horrendous sound of scratching feet. It was so loud she couldn't focus. The room seemed to spin around her as her eardrums throbbed. The walls seemed to wriggle with all the fury of the rats they hid. She turned and lunged for what she thought was the exit, only to discover it was the closet door. With a stifled cry, she threw the door open.

They fell from above, crawled from below, a living wriggling tide of vermin who seemed to have built in a wave within the closet. She had only time to scream as the great hairy bodies dropped on her, smelling of droppings and urine, their hungry mouths snapping at whatever they came into contact with. She flailed against their claws, knocked bodies left and right, unable to scream as several found their way beneath her hair and began chewing at her sweater collar. Becky closed her eyes and pitched her body wildly, trying to sling them off of her. She felt them nibbling at the tender area of her thigh, as some had climbed up her pants legs. She shook and kicked, peeling off her jeans and sweater, striking her legs and back and neck with open hands, anything to get them off her.

She had to get out. There had to be a way. A door to close between them and her. But there were so many. Had she not been in such a state of panic, she might have been awed by their sheer numbers, blackening the floor and flooding into the hallway. As it stood, all she could think to do was to get out, to get them off her. She felt a stabbing heat at the nape of her neck as one took a bite. Becky screamed and raked the creature from her body, then ran through the French doors, out onto the balcony, slamming them shut behind her. She slumped against the rail and screamed, her body spasmed in uncontrollable sobs.

Inside, hundreds of tiny feet scurried about, only slightly softer than the sound of her own heartbeat in her ears. She crept toward the door as the sound faded, unsure if she could bring herself to open it and go back inside. Even with the sounds gone, would they be? Were rats crafty enough to be silent and ambush? She pressed her ear against the glass pane and strained to hear squeals or chatter or any noise that might betray their presence. A moment of silence from the other side prompted her to raise her trembling hand to the handle. As her fingers closed around it, she heard the sound of splintering wood. A quick look toward the glass showed her hundreds of hungry mouths with jagged teeth, each biting another for a chance to get out and at her tender flesh.

Becky scrambled backward, her legs kicking madly away from black soulless eyes in the glass, until she found herself at the guardrail with nowhere else to go. As a single whiskered nose poked through a fresh notch in the door, she screamed. It was a long way down, but she'd rather risk broken legs than be nibbled to death by rats. She clamored over the rail and made a desperate leap without any thought of what she would do once she was airborne. She landed hard on her back on the ground below, knocking the wind out of her. For seconds that seemed unending, she lay on the ground, gaping like a fish, unable to draw breath. Then, with a stabbing pain in her gut, her diaphragm gave and she gasped.

Becky struggled to her feet, still certain that at any moment she would be covered with a rain of fur and tails. She ran as fast as her body would allow until she got to her car. She slammed the door shut behind her, thinking only of escape, of getting as far away from the house and the rats as possible. If developers wanted the land, they could have it. Hell, burn the place down for all she cared. It was only when she realized she'd left her pants, with her keys in the pocket, upstairs that she allowed herself to collapse into the seat, screaming and crying. She could still feel them on her, wriggling and biting her flesh.

She sat, for how long she didn't know, until she was capable of rational thought. She needed to contact someone to come and take her to a hospital to treat the rat bites. Then she needed to find an exterminator, if any felt they could handle such a job. But first, she decided, she would need clothes.

She stared at the front door of the house and debated whether or not to go inside for her satchel. Going upstairs was out of the question, but could she brave enough to even open the front door? At the thought of breathing in the smell of so many vermin, her stomach turned and her arms pimpled with gooseflesh. No, she couldn't. Not alone.

Becky searched the car, looking for something useful in any way. She found her cellular telephone, still plugged into the cigarette lighter, where she'd left it to charge. For the first time in a long while, she was thankful she had the thing instead of thinking it a nuisance. Becky didn't relish the thought of dialing the only local number she knew, but she found the idea more appealing than walking several miles in her underwear, in the dark, to the hospital, though not by much. Thirty minutes later, when Brian the lawyer pulled up in his black sedan, she felt more humiliated than she thought possible.

"Miss Schiflett?" he called as he got out of the car.

"I'm over here," she replied from behind her car, waving. He stopped a few feet from her vehicle, his face flushing crimson as he noticed her state of undress.

"Uh...I'm sorry...I didn't...Uh...Here." He lobbed a plastic shopping bag with clothes in it over toward her.

"Thanks," she called out as she caught it. It seemed ridiculous to her to try to maintain any sense of modesty, given the situation. She even found it charming that he seemed more embarrassed than she at her state of undress. She quickly donned the contents of the bag, a pair of sweat pants and a t-shirt, before coming from behind the car.

"Thank you, Mr. Ogletree," she said as she handed him back the bag.

"Um...You can call me Brian," he said, still refusing to make eye contact.

"Brian, can you drive me to the emergency room?"

"Sure," he said with an enthusiastic nod. He seemed grateful to be doing something other than standing about trying not to stare.

The hospital cleaned her wounds and gave her a series of injections of rabies immune globulin around each bite and one, just for good measure, in her thigh. When she emerged from the treatment room, she was sore and more angry than frightened anymore.

"How're you feeling?" Brian stood as she came into the waiting room.

"Like a pincushion." She managed a weak smile. "They said I have to come back over the course of a month and get five more shots of the rabies vaccine."

"Ouch."

"Yeah. Thanks for staying."

* * *

"So how many did you say there were?" asked the older man with "Roy" stitched on the oval patch on his overalls.

"All of them," said Becky with a shiver. "It seemed like all the rats in the world were in there."

Roy looked at her over the tops of his glasses.

"That's a lot of rats," he deadpanned. He made a few scribbled marks on the form on his clipboard. "Tell you what," he said, looking up at the old house. "We'll go inside and have us a look, see what's best to do."

"How much will it cost?" Ever the lawyer, Brian couldn't keep his mind off money.

"Depends," said Roy rubbing his chin. "If it's as bad as you say, we may have to tent the house. That'll cost you a pretty penny. Plus, you'll want to move all your stuff out. Don't want to get Cyanide gas all over it. Stuff's dangerous."

Becky groaned at the thought of having to clean out the house before she even knew what was in it. Moreover, the cost of storing such a large number of items would be tremendous.

"Isn't there some other way to get rid of them?"

"I'll know after I look," smiled Roy. "Take me to where you saw them."

Her skin prickled and crept as she pushed the front door open. That the exterminator and Brian were by her side did nothing to calm her nerves. Every creek or rustle sounded to her like skittering feet. Every dust mote that hung in the air reminded her of hungry eyes. Even the scent of salty air and mold now smelled more foul to her, as if the air itself was saturated in the creatures' urine. Her companions seemed not to notice, but then, they weren't there when the creatures attacked. Theirs weren't the pants-legs the little monsters ran up. They weren't the ones that took a flying leap from a second-story balcony. She could feel them still, as if their claws still tickled her arms.

They climbed the stairs and made their way to the master chamber. Becky stopped outside, unable to force herself to open the door.

"In there, huh?" said Roy. She nodded. "Best stay back then. I been doing this for a while."

Becky felt her stomach knot as he turned the knob and pushed the door open. For a tense moment he said nothing, then he straightened and turned toward her.

"How many rats you say you saw?" Without waiting for an answer, Roy disappeared into the room.

She came around the door and her breath caught in her chest as the room came into view. The floor was carpeted thick in droppings, as was the bed and the other pieces of furniture that lay toppled. Becky stood in the doorway, unwilling to step into the foul stench of the room. Her eyes shot from the floor to the walls where deep scratches marked the plaster and spots where the vermin nibbled were evident. The closet door stood ajar, giving her the feeling that the little beasts were watching her from within.

"We best check the other rooms," said Roy loudly.

"Why? They were in here..."

"Yes ma'am," smiled Roy. "But I didn't notice any other rat-sign on the way in here, did you?"

"No, I told you, they were only in here."

"Ma'am, I been in this business for a long time, and I can tell you, this many rats don't stay in one room. Your whole house ought to be covered like this here."

That the rest of the house showed no sign of infestation had not occurred to her, but now set her mind wondering why. It was true, she realized, that in her wanderings she'd not seen one other sign of vermin. It was not until she was in this room, alone, that they ran between the walls and gnawed at the plaster.

It took them nearly two hours of methodical searching to cover the rest of the house, yielding no trace of the creatures that should have, by all rights, been teaming at every turn. When at last they returned to the master suite, they were tired and confused.

"You said there were hundreds of them, right?" said Roy, his brow creased in thought.

"Yes," sighed Becky. "They came out of there." She pointed toward the closet.

_____

"And you say they were all piled up and came falling out on top of you?"

"That's what she said," said Brian as he put his arm around her shivering frame. "So? You're the expert. Where'd they go?"

"Good question," said Roy, pulling a flashlight off his belt. His boots made squishing noises as he crossed the waste-strewn floor toward the closet. At the door, he paused for a moment and locked eyes with Becky, then pulled the door open and shone his beam inside. He crouched deeper within the closet and began tossing old shoes and filth-covered boxes out into the room.

"Hey! Take a look at this!"

Becky could feel her innards knot and the hair on her arms prickle, but crossed the threshold into the sewer that was her bedroom and stared into the darkness. She tried not to think about the filth encrusting her shoes stepped to the closet door with Brian close behind.

"Ugh," he said. "These are ruined."

She glanced behind to see him scowling at his loafers.

Inside, the stench was greater than in the main room, as if all the fetid rot of thousands of rodent droppings were compressed into this small space. She felt her stomach lurch at the smell and dragged the tail of her shirt over her nose and mouth. Though her eyes teared with the acrid air, she could see plainly enough the hole in the floor of the closet.

"That's where they went, I'll bet," said Roy. He backed out of the closet and stood, his filth-smeared hands on his hips, staring inside for a few moments. "Don't go nowhere," he said as he turned and went out of the room. "Be right back."

She heard his boots thudding down the stairs and said nothing, only stood and stared at the jagged planks that formed the toothy mouth of the rats' hole. She could smell them, the disease-carrying lot of them, down there, and she was sure they could smell her too. The stinging air that seemed to breathe from the hole turned her stomach and burned her nostrils,

_____

but she couldn't force herself to back away.

"Becky?" she heard somewhere at the back of her consciousness. It wasn't close enough for her to comprehend, more like a whisper behind her ears. She stared intently at the hole, certain that if she were to look away, they would come flooding out and swallow her whole.

"Hey," said Brian, laying a hand on her shoulder.

The sudden contact made her jump, as surely as if one of the rats dropped from the ceiling onto her back.

"Christ! Brian!"

"Sorry," he grinned.

"Okay!" boomed Roy, clomping back into the room. On his belt he had several small canisters that resembled grenades and a pry-bar. "Let's see if we can figure out where those little bastards got off to!"

He handed Becky and the lawyer filter masks, which they immediately pulled over their mouths and noses. The smell didn't seem to bother Roy at all as he pushed his way past into the closet and, instructing Brian to hold the flashlight steady, jammed the prybar at the wooden floor of the closet.

Becky's heart pounded in her ears with the sound of squeaking wood and rending timbers. As she watched, her breaths became shorter and more shallow. At last he stopped pulling and leaned back to survey his work.

"Well I'll be..."

"What?"

"You should see this, ma'am."

She crept forward into the closet to find Roy sitting at the mouth of a gaping hole that fell into blackness.

"I don't understand," she said. "We should have broken into the kitchen..."

"No, this here's called a floodwall. Lots of old houses like this one have 'em. Only for rich folks though. See, here, in Galveston, we get lots of hurricanes. The bay floods, and well, lots of houses get washed away. This here gives water a place to go when it comes up."

"Comes up from where?" asked Brian.

"Gulf of Mexico, I expect," he said. "Usually from one of the caves below. See, this wall's made of rock. Real sturdy. I guess Galveston's seen at least fifteen hurricanes during this house's lifetime. And she's still here to tell about it. Miracle really."

"What's down there?" asked Becky, her fear of the rats surpassed by her curiosity.

"Only one way to find out," said Roy with a shrug. He shone his light straight down into the pit. "Yep. Good," he said. He slid his lower half into the hole and let himself drop.

Becky felt the air sucked from her lungs as his head disappeared below the floor.

"There's stairs!" she heard from below. "Workers must've built them into the wall. Like an access tunnel. Come see!"

The thought of putting her body through the gaping mouth brought back all her fears of thousands of wriggling bodies and twitching noses. She could almost feel them on her again, brushing her skin with their oily pelts.

"No, thanks," she said.

"I want to take a look," said Brian, as he hung his jacket on a hanger. "No telling what's down there."

Before she could even form the words to stop him in her head, he'd already clambered through the jagged hole and into darkness. Becky stood for a moment in the awful quiet. She glanced around the closet walls, remembering the wave of rats that poured from all around her, and did not want to be alone. The darkness, with only a flashlight, an exterminator and a lawyer, was preferable to being up here alone, with imagined sounds of tiny claws to plague her.

"Brian!" she called as she slid into the chasm. "Wait for me!"

The slick rock beside her glistened in the darkness as the thin beam of the flashlight cast strange shadows on the walls. The staircase was steep, and several times she lost her footing, only to be caught by Brian's sure hand. They continued downward without speaking, as if fearful of their own voices, until Roy stopped and held up his hand.

"Mother of God..." he whispered.

He shone the beam around the walls of the vast cavern that opened up below them. It seemed to Becky that she was no longer herself, no longer Rebecca Shiflett in Galveston. It was as though they stared into the belly of some great primeval beast that had swallowed them whole. It roared as the salty bay water rushed inward and then receded against the rocks.

Roy held up his hand, a signal for them not to move, then clicked the flashlight off. Becky felt her breath sucked from her lungs again as the cavern lit with strangely glowing lichen and kelp. It was, in it's own way, both frightening to her and beautiful. The luminous molds traced the hanging rocks into insane teeth while the splashing water dripped like saliva from its hungry maw.

She was so caught up in the spectacle of it that she almost didn't notice when smaller lights began to flicker on, two by two, in the darkness below.

"Roy," she whispered. "The light."

The flashlight clicked on, revealing the wave of water dissolving into a tide of vermin. For a moment neither human nor rat moved, neither seeming to believe what they saw. Then a thousand shrieks like the sound of rending metal joined the ripple that began at the back of the sea of glistening eyes as the creatures advanced.

"Run!" cried Roy.

Without conscious thought past the tide of rats on her heels, Becky stumbled backward, scrambling up into the darkness. She could hear Brian and Roy screaming, hear their quick steps slipping against the algae-slick stones. The flashlight played spastically against the darkness, giving her only strobes of what was in front of her. Against the beating of her own heart she could hear her companions behind her, clamoring for footholds, and the awful sound of skittering claws on stone. When she reached the hole in the closet floor, she fairly jumped through and scrambled out of the way as Brian and Roy emerged behind her.

"Grab some clothes!" shrieked Roy as he pulled two canisters off his belt. He pulled the pins on them and threw them down into the darkness, then began stuffing garments into the opening. When the hole was choked with lace and taffeta, he shoved Brian through the closet door and dragged Becky behind him by the arm.

The only sounds were their own beleaguered breaths and grunts as they fled the room and down the great staircase. As they cleared the front door, at last, Roy broke stride and collapsed, wheezing, on the lawn.

"Cyanide canisters," he gasped. "Nasty shit. Had to get out of there."

"Did you get them all?" huffed Brian as he looked back toward the house.

"Bet so," said Roy. "Won't know for sure till I go back in and look. Can't do that for a couple of days, though, till the poison's disipated."

Becky sat on the lawn, her hands shaking and bloodied from the climb. She wanted nothing more to do with the house, nothing to do with its inhabitants. She only wanted to be away from them. She hugged her knees close under her chin and rocked gently.

* * *

It was nearly two weeks since the last time she'd set foot in the old house. Now, as she stood in the shadow of the overhang, she felt her stomach wriggle as if full of rats   "We've had the whole house gone over," said Brian as he clumsily rifled through his briefcase for the correct folder. "No signs of rats anywhere. We had the hole in the master suite sealed and repaired, and made sure there were no toxins left. We even had the floor professionally cleaned."

"What about the rest of the house?"

"Roy checked. Nothing. He says the house is clean."

"Thanks," she said, her eyes never leaving the front door.

"Hey," said Brian. "Are you sure you want to do this? We can still sell..."

"I promised myself a bed and breakfast," she smiled. "I'm never going to get this chance again."

"Let us know if we can do anything." He shook her hand warmly and gave her the envelope containing the final paperwork for the house. She smiled as he went down the walk toward his car.

Becky looked up again at the door and took a deep breath, steeling herself. She looked down at the large brown carrier at her feet.

"You ready for this, Malachi?" she asked of the green eyes that twinkled back at her. She took the carrier by the handle and adjusted the load in her arms so she could open the door, then stepped across the threshold. The cat was different from Chester, not nearly so small or sleek. Malachi was a large, black, fearsome-looking beast with a head bigger than Becky's fist. Though Roy said there were no rats left in the house, Becky wanted a cat anyway, just in case. She let him out of the carrier and started up the stairs.

Outside the master suite, she glanced down to see if the cat still followed her. On finding him still at her heels, she opened the door.

The room inside was very different from the last time she saw it. Gone were the garments that hung in the closet. Gone were the rugs and most of the furniture. The draperies no longer hung over the windows, having been replaced by mini-blinds temporarily. The room showed no sign of ever having been invaded. Even the trim on the French doors looked neat and clean and smelled of fresh paint. She dropped her parcels to the floor and plugged in a portable radio. As it crackled to life, the music washed over her, helping to ease the fear associated with the room. As the band in the box played, Becky began the task of claiming the master suite for her own.

* * *

Droplets

It was late, Becky thought as she drifted back into consciousness. The day went well, quickly and with no sign of anything unusual. Malachi stayed with her all day, and when evening fell and Becky got tired, she took a comforter from another room and made a pallet for herself in the master suite. It was, after all, her room, her house. She shifted in the darkness, unwilling to open her eyes and admit to herself that she was actually awake. Open eyes meant more work to be done. The fog of sleep cleared from her head slightly, just enough to make her wonder what had awakened her. It was then that she heard a faint sound. It seemed to be coming from behind her head, a dull scratching noise somewhere just out of the reach of...

She froze beneath the blanket. Scratching. She heard scratching. No, she thought. It was just her imagination. It had to be. The house was exterminated, their entrance sealed. It was a trick of her mind in the darkness.

The sound grew louder until she was certain it could be no hallucination. They were still here, running within the walls, skittering between the boards. But how?

She clamped her hands around her ears, trying to shut out the noise as it grated at her spine. Her breath grew taut in her chest as she squeezed her eyelids harder, tears leaking onto her pillow. Where was Malachi? They'd stand no chance against...

The scratching behind her head stopped abruptly. She lay for a moment sobbing, her breath coming in ragged gasps beneath the blanket. When she realized the sound had stopped, she felt the hair on the back of her neck prickle. At the base of her pallet, she felt heavy feet touch the blanket.

"Malachi," she sighed, as she slipped her hand out from under the blankets. Her fingers touched the giant cat's black fir, but found it wet and sticky.

"What..?" she said as she pulled the blanket away and opened her eyes to find the dead cat's head with a thousand shimmering eyes and five-hundred hungry mouths.

Snapshot

In Bernard's hands, a camera was powerful. More so than any gun, any sword, any painter's brush, his camera captured the world for what it was. Painters, though talented, were not true artists to him so much as they were professional liars, able to cover imperfections, omit telling details, add sweetness and color to a cheek where none sat. True, they could create an image that might seem to leap off the page, but those images weren't *truth*. They were still just the artist's interpretation of what they saw, no matter how skilled or detailed the painter's hand. But in his hands, oh in his hands, a camera brought forth life, captured every minute detail, recorded every glint of light, every blister, every darkened wrinkle for all the world to see. A camera never lied, never sheltered, never pandered. It only saw and recorded the truth, no matter how beautiful or ugly it might be.

In the park, his favorite place to sit, Bernard set up his tripod and felt in his bag for his camera, his most prized possession. Let the others keep their high-tech, high-speed digital marvels of the modern age. Digital was not for him. The images were too easy corruptible, too easily edited. For him, the images had to be captured in a special way. For his art, only a single camera would do.

The flat box he pulled from his bag was an anachronism, pulled from a museum or maybe found in some long-forgotten corner of an attic.

Droplets

It was luck that he found it in the old curio shop, but it was almost as if the thing called to him, drew him to the glass cabinet and pulled his eyes to the corner where it sat open and covered in dust. The last time a camera of its kind was sold new, FDR was president and gasoline was considered expensive at eighteen cents a gallon. Still, when he asked to see it, the old man behind the counter smiled and brought it out. It was still in working order, he said, and he would gladly sell it to Bernard for a token price. It took him the space of two breaths to make up his mind, and moments later he carried his prize home and began searching for film. As it turned out, Kodak still made film for their Vest Pocket series camera, though requests for it were few and far between, and it only came in black and white. Fine, he decided. Truth was determined in black and white and shades of gray. Color distracted from the truth anyway.

Delighted, Bernard set to work cleaning and oiling hinges, adjusted springs, and loved the camera back to life. Then he waited with all the patience of a narcotic-addicted squirrel for his film to arrive. When it did, he wasted no time and loaded his camera and went out in search of faces to capture, truths to be revealed by his art.

His first subject was a young woman and a man, he assumed her lover, who sat on a bench beneath a tree in the park. Through his eyes she was beautiful, he was handsome, and they were in love. But when he arrived home and rushed to his darkroom, the image in the photograph revealed more than he could have expected. The man was truly in love with her, that much anyone could see. But the woman. In the stark black and white and shades of gray, the truth showed in the lines on her face, the cut of her clothes, the far-away expression in her eyes. She did not look at him, but rather watched another man passing by. The bleached-white band on her finger showed where a ring should have been, and the cut of her skirt was just a bit too high. In the photograph, it became clear to Bernard that she didn't love the man. Her hair, light gray in the image darkened near her scalp. It wasn't real. What he took for beauty at first glance revealed itself in the photograph to be shallow, a mask of loveliness beneath which lurked an ugly person. Fascinated, he tacked the photo to the wall and went in search of other hidden truths he could expose with his camera.

For weeks he haunted the park, snapping photos with his ancient eye, capturing children, animals, adults. Any who crossed in front of him found themselves unwitting subjects of his need to reveal the truth. Puppies that seemed cute and friendly came clear with muddy paws and disease-ridden mouths. Children that looked playful and happy betrayed greed as they wolfed down ice-cream, and self-centered abandon as they soiled their clothing and smiled at children less fortunate than they. A photo of a homeless man, dirty and avoided by anyone else, revealed kind eyes and a genuine smile, despite his situation. So much ugliness, so much beauty, so much hidden, he felt a perverse joy at his discovery.

On a Sunday, he took his camera to the park as usual, eager to capture more truths and to unmask the world. He though about a display, a showing at a gallery, where he could unveil his vision and confront the world with its own pretentions. No filters, no airbrushes, no digital pen to slim the fat or erase the blemishes. Just truth in black and white.

As he walked down the path, he paused at random intervals, snapping photos of people whom he thought looked interesting, wondering what secrets his lens would reveal about them in his darkroom. Boulders here, trees there, the occasional animal, but mostly he photographed people, took them unawares as they went about their business. What would they be, he wondered, when he managed to get a good, close look at them frozen in time.

When he arrived home that evening, he felt satisfied. His cartridge was full, and the smell of developer and fixer beckoned him from his darkroom in the basement. It took him nearly an hour in total darkness to apply the chemicals to the film properly, a process he'd practiced and perfected over many nights and several canisters ruined. When he at last turned on the amber work-lights, he felt as if the day's shoot would reveal more to him than any other. He loaded the film into the enlarger and set to work pulling the images onto paper. The first few were nothing special, images of people who wore their disguised selves like a sheer pelts, opaque in the sun but transparent to his camera's lens. In one a mother looked at her child with despair in her eyes and a false smile on her lips. In another, a man spoke to a young lady while his eyes followed another woman down the path. One after another showed lie after lie until he was certain that there wasn't an honest person left in the city.

But the last photo in the spool caught his attention. The subject matter was not very different than the others, but there was something odd about the image. Beside the young man, in the periphery, stood a tree. In truth, there were trees all around him, but one in particular caught Bernard's attention. It wasn't the focus of the picture, but it was clear enough in focus that he noticed something strange about it. He adjusted his enlarger to its highest setting and focused it on a small section of the bark. There was something there, he was sure of it.

He slid another sheet of photo-paper into the holder and pressed the button to expose the image, then held his breath as he submerged the sheet into developer. As the image grew more clear, he stared. The whole page was filled with the rough lines and texture of bark except in one small area where there appeared what seemed to be fingers. A hand, even, reached around the trunk, its clawed fingers dug into the bark. He slid the photo into a tray of fixer then hung it to dry, then clicked on the main lights.

It could have been a blemish on the tree, perhaps a tear in the negative, but damned if it didn't look like a small clawed hand reaching around the base of the tree.

He snatched the other photos from where they hung and took them to his living room where the light would allow him to see more. Once there, he took a magnifying glass from his desk drawer and sat down to re-examine each print. There, in each, were tiny signs, imperceptible details of whatever the little things were, and he'd never noticed them before. In several, what he mistook for a leaf might very well have been a tail or an ear, in others small dots of light might have been eyes reflecting the sun. But the last photograph stole his breath away for the second time that day. Now that he'd seen them, whatever they were, they were obvious. Tiny black-taloned hands reached around the back of the bench, glistening eyes peered from between the slats, reached into the boy's knapsack, touched his shoes, and he never noticed.

Bernard went back to his darkroom with his negatives and stayed up the whole night re-developing images, refocusing on the backgrounds, and marveled as he saw signs of strange creatures that passed among the normal people unnoticed.

The next day, he gathered the best of his prints and took them to a gallery. The owner huffed his skepticism over the legitimacy of the photos, but as Bernard explained how he'd gotten the shots, his brow creased with interest. At the end of the day, he agreed to have a showing in his gallery. But there would need to be more photographs, more images of the strange creatures that existed in the periphery to fill the walls. Bernard assured him that there would be no problem, and set off toward the park, his camera loaded and ready, to capture the true nature of the world.

The sun beat a warm glare against the treetops as Bernard made his way to his favorite spot, where he'd first captured the unknown little beasts. He decided to forego shooting at the passers-by and target the areas where he knew the creatures lay. Trees, bushes, beneath benches and around lampposts, wherever there was an ignored patch of darkness, wherever people normally didn't look, that's where he trained his lens. When he'd captured more than a dozen images, he put his camera away and hurried home, eager to see what new animals his safari'd yielded.

But in his darkroom, he saw none of them. No glancing eyes from beneath the benches, no tiny clawed hands reaching around trees. As each image came into view, his heart sank by degrees. Were they gone? Had he lost the knack? Maybe they were never really there to begin with. Maybe he'd imagined them all, and managed to convince the gallery owner to follow him in his lunacy. As the last photo came into focus, he felt his breath hitch. The image was a mistake, a shot taken as he pulled the camera off the tripod in haste. Distinct in the photo were his own shoes on the grass. And between them stood one of the creatures, no longer hidden behind a tree or glimpsed in shadow, staring up into the lens with raw surprise in its eyes. It looked for the life of him like a small dog, except that it stood on two legs and its front paws were clawed hands. Great ears like the wings of a bat protruded from the sides of its head, each tufted with coarse black hair. Its black eyes shone against the sunlight, and its snubbed nose dripped with what he took to be drool. The creature's mouth hung open, revealing rows of wickedly pointed teeth. It at once repelled and fascinated him.

And then the thought hit him: The creature was standing between his feet, so close it could have taken a bite out of his leg with its saw-like teeth. And he never saw it, nor would he have, had it not been for an accident. Were they around people all the time? Were they to blame for missing pens and spilled drinks? Perhaps they were malevolent, little pranksters playing practical jokes on the world, or worse.

He returned to the park the next day, determined to capture more of them, but this time he knew the trick. Never head-on, never on purpose, the only way to see them was at the edges, to take them unawares. Otherwise, they'd hide again and his photographs would be of a false world.

He stayed until the sun dipped below the horizon and the light was too shallow for his camera. Throughout the day, he shot image after image of this and that, him and her, she and he, sitting, standing, walking, talking, but without much interest. It didn't matter though, so long as the little beasts didn't think he was looking for them. As he carefully placed his camera back into his satchel, his stomach fluttered with hopeful anticipation. He'd been so careful during the day, aside from a few nervous glances.

When he returned to his house, he headed to the darkroom straightaway, without any thought of food or sleep. He had to see them. He had to know if he'd been successful.

An hour in total pitch gave him time to think about the images from before, in which hidden creatures stalked mankind unseen. One image in particular, in which the creature stood in naked glory between his feet, chilled him as he imagined it standing with him, alone in the dark, and he unaware of its presence. By the time he was done, he had a first-rate case of the chills started, but could not make himself stop. The gallery aside, he just had to see. He had to know.

One by one, with painstaking care, he enlarged the images to normal sizes, then took them into the light where, with a magnifying glass, he sought out traces of the little beasts.

The first few images revealed nothing. Women, children, dogs, businessmen, normal lies from average liars. By the time he developed his fifth photograph, his mood was sour. Maybe he'd spoiled it by catching them before. Maybe the one he caught between his feet told the others to hide from him. Maybe he'd seen the last of them for the rest of his life.

When the sixth photo came from out of the fixer, he gave it a half-hearted glance. Two women, each regarding the other with patient disdain, sat on a bench. No doubt, they were "best friends," but in their eyes he saw jealousy and hatred for one another. But there, just behind the thinner of the two, there was a dark spot, so small, but it made his heart hammer. He took the stairs two at a time until he reached the light of his living room and snatched the magnifying glass from the table.

It was one of them, he was sure of it. The dark blob had shape and form, ones he recognized. He scanned the rest of the photo, but found no other sign of the creatures. But it didn't matter. He'd caught one. Even one was worth the hours spent. He headed back down to his darkroom to enlarge the image.

When the antique clock in his living room chimed, Bernard looked up from his enlarger with a start. Two chimes. Could it really be that late? Not that it mattered. His photographs absorbed him. Since the sixth, every image contained something wondrous. The seventh held three of the beasts, the eighth captured four. By the time he developed his twentieth image, it was easy for him to pick them out. A shadow here, a blur there, why, the park grounds teamed with them. It wasn't until his last image sat in his enlarger that he noticed something odd. Perhaps it was a trick of the light, but it appeared...

He exposed the paper and took it to the developer tray. As the image gained focus, he felt his mouth go dry. In the dim amber light, he couldn't be certain, but it seemed...

He thrust the picture into the fixer, shook it dry, then raced up the stairs to the bright lights of his living room. There, he didn't need his magnifier to see them. The hairs on his arms prickled at the image he held.

There were so many. Dozens of them crowded the photo, surrounded the pudgy boy on his tricycle. But they weren't playing pranks or pulling at his wheels. All of the creatures stood rock still. They stared into the lens of the camera. They knew his purpose was to capture them on film, and to that end, they'd given him one amazing shot. But the sight of it chilled his bones. They were staring at him, all of them with deep-set eyes and drooling mouths.

If his experience in photography had taught Bernard anything, it was how to read body language to reveal the truth. Now he wished he didn't know so much. Each of them held their arms away from their bodies a bit, flexed their clawed fingers wide. Their heads were slightly down and their butterfly-like ears laid back against their scalps. There was anger in their postures, but more than that. Every eye held a vicious gleam, every tooth a cruel curve. Their claws looked sharp enough to rend steel, and their hands fairly twitched to prove it. They knew he'd seen them.

He didn't sleep that night. Not for lack of trying, but every time he closed his eyes, hundreds of angry little faces stared back at him. Every creek or scuttle brought him up from his bed with terror in his heart. By the time the sun peeked over the horizon, he was exhausted. But with his fatigue came a sense of accomplishment. The gallery owner would love the new photos, he was sure of it.

A shower and breakfast later, Bernard still felt tired, but satisfied. He strolled down the street toward the gallery, certain that the pictures in his valise, particularly the one which he referred to as the "group photo," would make a fine focal point to his show. But as he showed the images to the gallery owner, he was met with ambivalence. Sure, there were pictures of monsters in the park, but only in the park. Weren't there other places that the little beasts lived? The group photo was interesting, but it looked staged. Couldn't Bernard find these creatures in some other setting? From the way they looked, it seemed they were around people all the time.

The thought hadn't occurred to Bernard before. The park couldn't be the only place they lived, could it? Things happened to people every day that were the obvious influence of the...whatever they were. Surely these creatures must live in other places, like churches and office buildings. And homes.

Were they in his home? And how many of them could there be? And did they know that he'd seen them? How could they not? Surely they'd seen the photos themselves. Perhaps the scuttling noises he heard at night weren't raccoons or rats in the attic. Maybe, when he stood in the pitch of his darkroom, he was never really alone. Perhaps, in the inky blackness, there were tiny eyes and hungry mouths waiting to commit evil upon him.

He opened the door to his house with caution. The living room looked the same, still smelled of dust and fixer. But he could not shake the feeling of being watched. Ridiculous paranoia or not, every step he took past his threshold gave him the sensation of a hundred eyes crawling across his flesh. They were here, he was sure of it.

His camera sat on the table where he'd left it, untouched. Maybe the creatures were here, and maybe they weren't. But he needed to find out. He loaded a new film magazine and went from room to room, snapping photos in each at random intervals. A photo of the toilet, one of the stove. He shuddered when he snapped a picture of his bed, dreading what the image might show him. As he made his way down the hall, the feeling of being followed was overwhelming, so much so that he spun once or twice and snapped a picture of the empty hallway behind him. When he finished, he opened the door to the basement, his work area, and made his way down.

When he flipped the light switch, the whole space seemed to shrink away. For almost six years, the only lights allowed were the dim amber bulbs of his darkroom. With the main overhead white lights on, he was amazed at how many nooks and crannies he didn't remember. He was also amazed to realize just how small the space really was.

He snapped a few photos, then made his way back up the stairs to his living room. He put his camera down on the coffee table and stared at it. For the first time, he looked at the flat box as something other than an extension of himself, more than a tool for exposing the truth. Though it sat quietly, he regarded it as though it radiated menace. Photos of others, exposing the truth of their lives and falsehood, he could handle. But he'd never taken photos of his own living space, never turned the all-seeing eye of the lens on himself. In the past, he'd told himself that he just wasn't that interesting, but the truth was he wasn't sure he wanted to know what his lens would reveal. Now, more than ever, with the prospect of strange creatures in his house, he was certain he didn't want to know. But he had to. The thought gnawed at him as he stared at the damned piece of machinery. If they were here, he wanted to know.

He snatched the camera up and made his way back downstairs to his darkroom. As he turned out the lights, his heart fluttered. If they were here, he'd be alone with them. In the dark. Would they let him develop the photos? How would they react at being discovered? True, the ones in the park knew he'd seen them, but here, in his own house, where he couldn't just walk away, would there be consequences?

He set his mind to the task at hand, removed the cartridge from the camera, and set to work developing the film. It was difficult to manage the task, though he'd done it a hundred times before. But his hands shook, and every stray sound echoed in the tiny space, now grown cavernous by the darkness. By the time he was done, he almost couldn't bear to put the film on paper. But his need to know grew, changed into morbid curiosity, not just about the creatures, but about the photos themselves.

With each image he developed, more than a dozen total, his curiosity grew, so much so that he did not follow his usual custom of looking at each image as it developed. He developed them all, hung them to dry, and stood watching droplets of fixer and water slide off the glossy paper. When he could no longer resist, he pulled them down and hurried up the stairs to the light of his living room. Once there, he spread the photos out on his coffee table and stared.

There was his home, his life, his personality in honest black and white. From the creases on his bed that revealed his poor social life to the spotless kitchen that showed him to be obsessive, he was there. A single note hung from the refrigerator, which made the thing look lonely and pathetic in the camera's eye. The image of the living room was, at first glance, tidy. Further inspection, however, revealed dust on the shelves and scuffs on the couch. The room was more-or-less unused, another testament to his lonely lifestyle.

When his eyes rested on the photo of the hall, the one taken behind him, he felt his stomach drop. Where he'd only seen carpet and bare walls before, there were eyes, teeth, claws and ears, tufts of hair and angry expressions. He counted more than twenty before he gave up and sat back on the couch. They were here.

He glanced back across the mosaic on his coffee table. In every photo, they were there. Little blobs, tiny shadows, glints that another person might take for light coming through the window, every picture had them. They were here.

The photos of his dark room startled him to tears. In the room where he developed the film, the room of pitch midnight black, they crawled on the walls and stood on shelves, balanced on the drying line and sat on his canisters. He was so afraid of being alone in the dark with them, and they were there all along. In the other section, where he enlarged and developed the prints, they clung to his enlarger and peeked from under the shelves.

His eyes came to rest on the photos of his bathroom. The creatures peered from behind the shower curtain and hugged his shampoo bottle. One lounged against his razor while another appeared to be scratching its backside on his toothbrush. As he counted, he noticed something in the photo that terrified him beyond reason. In the bathroom mirror, he'd managed to catch his own reflection, camera held in front of his face like a strange cycloptic monster. And in his reflection, he could also see them. They perched on each shoulder, climbed from around his back. On his head sat one that he was sure was the same beast he'd captured between his feet only days before.

They were here. They'd always been here, he figured. Always darting between his feet as he walked, always staying just out of sight, always watching. How many times, he wondered were misplaced keys their doing, or broken glasses, or missed telephone calls? How many times had his chemicals gone bad or his light-safe leaked? Were they to blame? Did they eat breakfast with him? Watch him in the shower? Touch him while he slept? The thought made his skin crawl, but more, it intrigued him.

So long he'd sought out the truth in the world, to capture the raw essence of what was real beneath the fantasy of perception, and now he had it. Proof that what people thought was the real world was only a thin veil.

He sat back on his couch and looked around the room. They were watching him. Every glittering eye burned into his skin like a cigarette. But they never came out where he could see them.

"I know you're here," he said.

At the sound of his voice, the room twittered. Chatters and growls came from every corner.

"I know you're here," he said again, louder this time. "And I'm showing the world what you are!"

The growls grew louder and more chattering voices joined them. They sounded just as he thought they would, like rats or tiny dogs. The voices came from everywhere. Down the hallway, behind the sofa on which he sat, above in the light fixture. They heard him. More unsettling was the notion that they'd understood, and they were angry.

He snatched his camera from the table and ran to the basement door. He knew they were down there, but so was his film. He needed another magazine. He needed more photos for the gallery. If that pompous ass of an owner wanted dramatic, he'd show him dramatic. The creatures were too small to do any real damage, and when it was all over with, he'd take the money he was sure to get from the gallery and move to another home. A quiet home in the countryside, where nasty little beasts didn't live.

At the base of the stairs he paused and listened. The growls and chatters came from up above, but the darkness of the basement was quiet. He hurried to the cabinet where he kept his extra film stock, tore off the wrapper, and loaded his camera. When he turned back toward the stairs, he froze.

So many eyes, so many rows of hungry teeth, so many angry little monsters stared at him with hatred in their eyes. No longer content to hide in the periphery, they stood before him, bold as brass. On the walls and ceiling were more, all staring, all silent. He was trapped and he knew it.

Bernard saw the sea of angry creatures surge and did the only thing he could think to do. He began snapping pictures.

* * *

Lights around the entrance of the Concept Art Gallery burned bright against twilight as silk shoes and faux-fox wraps strolled up the red carpet. The new exhibit was a smashing success, and Gary Mitchell reveled in the success of his gallery. He knew he had something special in the new photography exhibit from the first moment that odd little man appeared with his photos in tow. But until a week ago, he wasn't sure the showing would be a success. Until the man's mangled body was found in his basement darkroom. It took a large amount of money to convince the judge that the final images in Bernard's camera were his rightful property, but in the end, they were worth the expense. Dead artists, after all, made more money than live ones.

The procession of more than three-hundred people passed from one carefully matted print to the next, each one eliciting more gasps and nervous conversation than the last. A few of the attendees shrieked when they saw themselves in the portraits, unwitting participants in the artist's vision. Still more scoffed at the odd little creatures, calling them obvious hoaxes or careful bits of fakery.

The procession made their way through the six main galleries until they came to the last door. The seventh was left bare, with no frames or images on the white walls. In the center of the room, hanging from wires, where the final three photos taken from Bernard's camera. In the first, the sea of little beasts were visible, a few in the front moving so fast that they appeared to be blurs in the grainy black and white print. In the second, the room beyond them was obscured by all their course little bodies, their glittering eyes, wicked claws and razor-like teeth. The last image, one that haunted even Gary to the point that he didn't like to look at it, showed only one of the little monsters, his mouth covering most of the lens, his eyes visible, and in the reflection of his black eye, the photographer screamed.

Stalker

He'd watched her from across the street for weeks, keeping track of her every move and habit, knowing full well who and what she was, and the task that was at hand. Demons were often found in the city, particularly one the size of Austin. They arrived in every walk of life, their purpose the same. They corrupted even the kindliest of men and women, claiming their souls for their own. This one was a temptress, David knew. She used her body and soft touch to pull men from their good senses, to pull the righteous from their seats in the capital, and ensure that vile corruption continued to thrive.

It was raining, not that he cared anymore. Where he would normally flee to the shelter of a discarded box or a dumpster, he felt the water wash over him, a cleansing, a baptism. It was the will of God to wash away his sins so he could meet her pure, to erase any taint of human weakness for the task at hand. She would cry, beg for her life, he knew. But the bracing downpour anointed him, made him strong against her wicked temptations.

Like all of her kind, she led two lives. In the daytime, he watched as she left her modest apartment dressed smartly in a skirt and blazer, her luxurious red hair tied back in her best impression of professional repose. He followed her, making certain to stay hidden from her senses, all the way to the capital building. When she flashed her laminate and made her way inside, he waited, ignoring the pain of hunger in his belly, until he was certain she was there for a fair amount of time. Then he wandered the streets, moving as far as sixth or even ninth, looking for the discarded remains of gluttony that filled the dumpsters. God was good to him. He always provided, and David always gave thanks for whatever he found.

He tried his best to avoid the other demons of the city, for his target was already chosen by divine right, and no hunter could dispatch more than was granted him. When, at times, another found him, he ran. Their blue clothing and silver badges were supposed to give comfort, to lend an air of safety to those that could not see them for what they truly were. But he saw them. Their numbers grew by the day until it seemed to David that he was the last of the faithful in a city of sin.

Today, God told him, was the day. As he dug through the dumpster behind the old Italian restaurant, he found the sign he'd been waiting for. To any other, it might seem like a discarded newspaper, torn and stained. To David, however, it was a message. No man could be so vain as to think himself worthy enough to hear the voice of God. He spoke to all men, if only they were wise enough to look for the messages. It was only spaghetti sauce on newsprint, smeared like the blood of the lamb over the words "Act Today!" that let him know his sacred task was at hand.

As he made his way back toward the capitol, he gave thanks and praise, ignoring the passers by who called him crazy or looked at him with blind sympathy in their eyes. Let them, he thought. His work would soon be done, and the city would have the stink of one less demon.

He waited across the street from giant building. It always reminded him of a church, he mused. Such a great dome atop, claiming to work for freedom and order for all men, was that not what a church was as well? But corruption and avarice had already taken firm root here as well, as the Texas leaders worshiped their own power, keeping blasphemous sanctity over their own presidings. How David begged his master to let him topple the walls, to bring it down around their ears, a modern Jhericho. But, he knew, he'd not yet earned that right. God granted him but a handful of kills, and only when he'd proven himself worthy would God allow him to fully become his sword.

He settled behind a dumpster in an alley across from the capital where he could still see, yet was hidden from all but the rats. David felt the rain beat down upon his body, but did not care. He was impervious to the cold that came with wet clothing and the ache of pruning at his feet, so long as God willed him onward. As he watched the building, he felt his Lord, kind in all respects, grant him sleep until his task was closer at hand.

The morning ended with the rain, bringing David to consciousness and the wicked from their den to find food. As the sun beat down, bringing the fallen puddles to humid shafts of air, he scrambled to his feet and watched, knowing full well that she would emerge. They were clever, the demons. The vast majority of them dressed alike, in the same dark suits with the same professional hairstyles. It made finding one specific being difficult to the untrained eye, but David knew his business. He watched the tide spill forth from the capital taking special note of every dash of color until, at last, his eyes rested on the fiery red hair of his prey. She walked quickly, flanked by two others, who, David guessed, were unfortunates, soon to be corrupted by her vile nature. She laughed and smiled at them seductively, adding fuel to the holy rage that burned deep within him. He followed, never taking his eyes off the burning mane that struggled to free itself from the rubberband that held it prisoner.

The three stopped at a Chinese restaurant, shades of her second life in which she would seduce men into forsaking their sacred vows. David stood across the street, staring in the large window at them as she flirted and laughed, all the while feeling the insatiable need to end her immoral spree. He watched every move of her slender hand as she gently caressed the chopsticks, teasing her two male companions with thoughts of those fingers in other places. They fairly drooled as she sensuously placed each dumpling into her mouth. He was loath to admit it, but David could feel her power even across the street. It was no wonder she was so good at her chosen path, and no wonder the Lord wanted David to take her.

The three finished their meal and left the restaurant, David close behind. He knew that her charms had already worked on the two men, as they fawned over her like hungry dogs. They'd actually argued over who would pay for their meal. It made David sick to think of her, spreading her foul stink among these men who, no doubt, were once virtuous men.

He dare not claim her, as God willed, before the two who were so blinded by her that they would decry his actions as evil. They would never understand while her hold was strong, but, after time had passed, they would see that it was the will of God and for the best. He followed them back to weathered dome of the capital, resuming his watching place from the alley across the street. Not long now, he thought, as he felt his heart quicken with the impending task.

As the hours ticked by, he prayed for guidance, strength, anything that would help him attain his goal of becoming the sword of God. Twice a demon in blue had found him and rousted him from his blind, but they were stupid. They could not see what he was. He'd fooled them easily enough into thinking he was simply another of the homeless that littered the Austin streets. He'd gone just far enough to escape their watchful eyes, but where he could still see the capital and, should she exit, his prey.

When at last they spilled forth like a malignant tide, he was ready. He trained his eye on her and followed, keeping an even pace so as not to arouse her suspicion. This one would try to seduce him, too, to save her own miserable life. How often he'd dreamed of it, her begging, her offering to gratify him with pleasures of the flesh. He'd thought about letting her do her best, to cover his body in filthy kisses and plunge himself into her in defiance. He wanted to show her that, despite the power she had over the weak willed, his reserve was strong. God had fortified him against everything, even her carnal pleasures. He wanted to anoint her with his righteous seed before he took her life, one last spit in the eye of her kind, before proving he could emerge untainted.

As she approached her door he quickened his pace. In his haste, he'd tipped her off and she whirled, a perfectly feigned look of fear on her pretty mask.

"Seth?" she asked. "Is that you?"

How he hated being called by that name, that blasphemous moniker with which his parents saddled him. He didn't recall much of his life before his awakening to the call of God, but the name still rang a hated toll in his ears.

"Hello Wendy," he said.

"Oh my god, Seth! Look at you! You look like you've been sleeping outside."

"I know. I have."

"Come inside," she said. "We'll get you cleaned up."

Dear Wendy. She thought she could fool him with her feigned concern. But he knew what she really wanted. To trap another innocent with her body was her only concern. He smiled to himself as he thought of her realizing that he was no such lamb. He followed her up the stairs to the loft above the city streets where she thought she belonged. He would show her, however, that she belonged in hell with the rest of her kind.

"Jesus, Seth," she said, taking the Son's name in vain, a thing which David took note of. "It's been almost a year since you dropped out of site. Where've you been? What happened to you?"

"I had a bad day," he said coolly.

She removed her blazer and shoes and pulled the band from her hair, letting it spill in fiery glory over her shoulders. The seduction, he thought, had begun. The tight-fitting skirt came to just above her knee, showing the great curve of her legs and the fullness of her hips. He felt his resolve weaken a fraction as he saw her white blouse was cut low, showing the valley where her breasts came together. It weakened him enough that it made him doubt, made him remember. It made him see her as he did when they worked together, how she would flirt with him, how she embraced him fondly at the end of working days. He didn't know then what she was. He'd not yet been awakened. He thought he loved her then, giving her every whim his attention, collecting photos of her. He longed for her to love him in return, to be with him.

But that was before he glimpsed her other life, the way she teased almost every other man in the same way. She'd made him feel special, but he found that he was still nothing to her. She would speak kindly to him, then tempt other men with her body as well. He'd blinded himself to her fornications for a while, but reality sank in one night when he and some other interns had seen her, dancing nearly naked at a bar.

At first he felt pity for her, as if she were another lost soul, but when he saw the way she smiled and laughed as she took money from the same sweating politicians for whom she worked during the day, he knew otherwise. They could tell no one of her second life, or theirs would be ruined. More times than he cared to imagine, she'd convinced them to wallow in their indiscrescions. It was, as she told him, just the way the game was played.

He'd quit his job soon after that, and spiraled into disillusionment that eventually cost him his apartment. His possessions, life, everything, was gone from him. That was when he was awakened to the plan of God.

God, it seemed, had a purpose for Seth. He gave him a new name, a disciple's name, the name of he who slew the giant, and lifted the scales from his eyes so he could see. When he looked around, he was sickened to find them, demons, everywhere in the city. The spread like a plague of rats, unchecked save for a few who, like David, could see. He'd started out small, realizing that if he confronted the demon called Wendy, he'd be weak against her charms. But now, with the power of the righteous and the purity that comes from being God's chosen to gird him, he was ready for her.

"Sinner!" he cried as he leaped off the couch at her. "You filthy whore!"

Wendy screamed, a joyful noise unto the Lord.

"Seth please!" she begged as he wrestled her to the floor and sat on top of her. "Why? Don't do this!"

"The Lord sayeth, 'If thine eye offend thee, pluck it out!" he raved.

"Seth…!"

"My name, as given to me by God almighty, is David!" He rained down upon her with blows of heavenly force, shattering her jaw and swelling her eyes until she resembled her true form, all the while reveling in her screams, until, at last, she simply lay whimpering beneath him, bloody and bruised.

"I'm so sorry," she managed.

"Long and hard is the road out of hell," he said coldly as he covered her mouth and nose with his hands. She struggled. She lost.

When at last her body was still, he gave thanks to God for the strength to overcome the demon. He was still shouting his praise when the blue-and-silver-clad demons burst through the door, finding him standing and rejoicing over their fallen comrade.

Droplets

The Wrong House

No bars on the windows, no locks...They ought to be arrested for incitement.

Trevor slid the window up and climbed through. Not even screens on the windows. Whatever he got away with, it was their own damned fault for not securing their belongings. Most houses on the block had electronic alarms, spiky plants below the windows. A dog even. But the owners of this one, the biggest house on the block no less, didn't even have the common sense to lock the windows. Sure, the doors, but the windows slid open like butter.

He slid window closed behind him, careful to adjust the blinds and curtains. Just because this family didn't seem to care didn't mean their busybody neighbors wouldn't call the police. Not that it mattered. He'd been pinched before, and almost preferred life on the inside. At least there, a man knew where he stood. Inside, there were no friends, only uneasy alliances. Out here, without the protective bars, everyone smiled to his face and said they thought it was good of him to try to build a better life for himself. But they never came through with jobs, did they? Good for him and all, but when it came right down to it, no one wanted to hire a convicted thief. So, in order to survive, he did what he knew how to do.

The neighborhood reeked of money. From the fancy foreign cars to the landscapers they hired, everyone who lived in the neighborhood was better than well-off, snug and safe inside their alarmed homes, smug in the knowledge that the riff-raff, meaning him, didn't dare show their lower-middle-class faces on this side of town.

He drove the plumbing truck around the neighborhood for a month while he cased the neighborhood, watched as liposuctioned and bleach-blond wives came home to their fat impotent husbands, woke up each day to send their spoiled-brat children off to some posh private school while they jazzercized or had affairs with their pool boys. The problem was, they never left their houses unattended. He'd almost given up when he came across the big house on Hartson Street.

It was easily the biggest house in the neighborhood, with a wide circular driveway flanked by turrets on either side and tall Gothic peaks. It seemed like the sort of house a movie star would have, and that meant money. He watched the house for days after, noted every movement of the family who lived inside.

Weekday mornings, the children, a boy and a girl, left the house before seven-thirty with their mother, a shapely brunette who always wore black. Her husband left soon afterward in a car that was ostentatious, even for this neighborhood. The wife returned in a half-hour, went back in, then came out with an older woman with frizzy white hair. They got back into the car and drove away, and left the house empty until about four in the afternoon. Every day. Like clockwork.

Weekends, the family disappeared. He never saw them leave, exactly, but by the time he drove through the neighborhood on Saturday mornings, the cars were gone. No matter how early he arrived, they were already gone. And to make things even better, no matter how late he passed by, the cars weren't there again until Monday morning, when the whole strange ritual began again. Saturday night, he decided, would be the best time to hit the place.

Still, he hadn't expected it to be this easy.

Trevor clicked on his flashlight and surveyed the room. It was the living room, and every stick of furniture, he was certain, cost more than his last car had. The scrollwork on the couch and matching loveseat stole his breath away, as did the stained glass shades on the lamps. This house didn't just reek of money, it *dripped* with it.

Over the mantle stood an old-fashioned family portrait. The father stood with a jaunty grin while his wife looked cold and serene. The children, one on either side of their mother, stared out of the portrait with such an impassive gaze that for a moment he could've sworn the eyes followed him. Behind them all stood the old woman, a crazed look of dementia on her face. No wonder she lived with them. She was probably too far gone to live on her own, and a family with this kind of money wouldn't suffer the indignity of putting a woman in a retirement home.

He crossed the room to the next, the dining room. On the table, five place-settings sat waiting for dinner. The plates glinted around the edges. When he took a closer look, he realized they were edged in gold leaf with lacework in the glaze. The glasses, two at each plate, appeared to be crystal instead of glass. The only things that seemed out of place were the silverware, which was "silver" in name only. Instead of what he expected, rough steel flatware sat beside each plate.

"Weird."

The rest of the downstairs was as beautifully overdone. Elegant curtains over every window, tapestries on every wall, it seemed less a home than a museum. A set of French doors opened up to reveal the study, every shelf lined with books so old he could smell them. On the desk, carved figurines of marble sat beside an obsidian long box of fine cigars. He took one and stuck it in his mouth, and made a mental note to return before he left for the rest. Cigars he could sell, but they were too fine for that. They'd be his gift to himself for a good night's work. Yessir, whoever these people were, they were filthy, stinking rich. And if the downstairs held such apparent wealth, he could only imagine what riches awaited upstairs in the bedrooms.

His feet made little noise on the thick carpet of the stairs as he made his way up. On the wall, antique pictures showed what appeared to be generations of the family, color then black and white, then faded sepia. Old money. It meant that whatever lay upstairs in jewelry boxes had to be old, passed down for generations, and would be worth a bundle.

At the top of the stairs, he saw six doors, four on the left, two on the right. He figured the one at the end of the hall, on the right, had to be the master suite. One door was probably a linen closet, another a bathroom. But he didn't feel rushed. After all, the family disappeared for days on the weekends. He could take his time.

He opened the first door and shined the light in. There was a desk and a few toy trucks. It was the boy's room. There probably wouldn't be much in the way of jewelry, but maybe there was a computer or game system, something he could fence quick. It was worth a look.

Trevor slipped inside as if he were afraid of waking someone and shined the light around. No, nothing obvious. In fact, the room was remarkably clean to belong to a young boy. The pool of light scanned the floor and walls until it landed on something peculiar. A cage stood against the wall. No, not a cage, he realized, but an enormous kennel. The thing was built for enormous dogs.

Or fat, ill-behaved kids.

The thought echoed in his head and he chuckled until he realized something was missing from the room. A bed. A dresser stood against a wall with baseball cards and a few other knick-knacks on top, a bookshelf overflowed with books, and the desk sat with what he took to be homework. But there was no bed in the room. Only the cage with a blanket in the bottom. Did they make the boy sleep in the cage? It gave him a sick feeling in his stomach. Petty larceny he could deal with, but abuse of a child? That was just plain wrong. He backed out of the room and moved to the second door.

It had to be the girl's room. She would have jewelry, he'd bet money on it. Little girls always like their shiny pretties, and he just bet her room would be made up like a princess suite. She was probably the favored child over her brother. Stealing from her would serve her right.

But the room beyond the second door was not what he expected. Instead of pinks and ribbons, the flashlight revealed a room painted in drab shades of grey. Her bed was large, sure, with four posts and a canopy, but the curtains that hung down...Were they black, or was it a trick of the light? Her room looked almost like a mausoleum. He shrugged. What was it his father always said?

The difference between weird and eccentric is money.

True enough. Judging from the looks of the place, these people had enough money to be called eccentric.

He made his way into the room to her dresser, black lacquered wood, and found the jewelry box on top. Just as he thought, inside were delicate chains of gold and a couple of rings that looked ancient. In one, a red stone that was either garnet or ruby, he didn't care which, sparkled. He pulled a small black sack from his backpack and upended the jewelry box into it.

A quick glance around the room revealed nothing more of interest. A good thing too, as the room gave him a first-class case of the creeps. It was too much like digging through someone's death chamber. He closed the door on the way out. Four doors left.

The first door on the right turned out to be the linen closet, as he thought, and the third door on the left turned out to be a bathroom. Both of them looked normal, except that the sheets were the expensive kind, even for this neighborhood, and the bathroom was spotless.

The fourth door on the left, he figured, belonged to Granny, or whoever the old woman was. For some reason he couldn't identify, it bothered him as he pushed the door open. He was a thief, after all. Why should the thought of rummaging through an old lady's unmentionables bother him? The smell from inside the room made him choke. It was the scent of roses and lavender, heavy over the scent of age and urine. It couldn't cover the stench, so they tried to overpower it. What billowed out was far worse than any of its singular parts, so strong it made his eyes sting and his stomach roll. He closed the door without going in. Whatever was in there, he'd get it later, after his eyes stopped watering. Besides, the master bedroom awaited, and if experience had taught him anything, that's where all the good stuff would be.

He took a deep breath. The door looked just like the others in the hall, but this one made him nervous. Behind the other doors, his flashlight showed him weird things. Cages and death-beds and unholy stenches. Behind this one, he had no idea what to expect.

The door creaked as it opened, not horror-movie style, but just enough to make a noise. He shined his flashlight into the room and stood, frozen in the doorway. Cops and nosey neighbors be damned, he needed the overhead light. He reached out and flicked the switch.

Gold. Not inlay, not filigree, not leaf, but honest to Fort-God-Damned-Knox gold lay scattered all over the room. In one corner, a pile of gold coins at least as big around as a beach ball and as tall as his shin glistened. Atop the dresser, gold chains lay like yarn. The jewelry box overflowed, and offered more. Loose stones of every color and shape glinted. Jackpot.

He shoveled as much as he could into his bag and turned to see what other interesting belongings were in the room. On the walls hung strange items that looked almost like medieval weapons. Almost, but that they looked new. Still, they might fetch a good price to the right dealers. No telling what sort of sick crap some people were into.

He glanced down at the foot of the bed and blanched. Something peaked from beneath the comforter, a strip of leather or a suitcase handle. Of course they'd hide it under the bed. Where else? They left the windows open and piles of, well, treasure laying around. Why wouldn't they keep a suitcase full of cash under the bed?

He pulled the comforter away with a jerk and stared for a moment. The suitcase handle was there, but attached to the bedframe were chains. Not the kind kinky people got from S&M shops, but the real deal. The leather cuffs attached to them looked well worn. He looked at the artifacts on the wall, then back to the cuffs. Eccentric in deed, he snorted. Kid in a cage, another in a crypt, stinky old Granny down the hall, it made sense. He felt bad for the children, wondered how warped they'd grow up to be, especially the boy. But it wasn't his problem. His was trying to figure out how much of their stuff he could get out with. Greed would get him caught, but, damn, there was just so much of it.

When he pulled the suitcase from under the bed, it brought with it an odor. At first, he thought it was left over from the stink of Granny's room. But it was missing the scent of flowers. The smell that came out from under the bed with it smelled like a bad pot-roast. He unzipped the case and lifted the lid. It took the space of one heartbeat for his muscles to jerk, his breath to freeze. It was full, alright, but not with money.

That can't be...

Hands.

The door slammed below him.

Oh shit.

"Darling," purred a woman's voice. "I do believe we have a guest."

"Go get 'em, boy!" shouted a man.

An animal howl rose up from downstairs, unlike any dog Trevor'd ever heard. It sounded bigger, meaner, like it was starved and angry.

Heavy footsteps hit the stairs fast, accompanied by growls that made his knees weak. He slammed the bedroom door and put his weight against it as the...*whatever it was*...hit it hard. The impact rattled his teeth and bounced him off the door. He tipped the dresser on its side in front of the door and hoped it would hold until he found a way out.

Right. These people have a suitcase full of freakin' hands, for Chrissake!

The creature hit the door again. Wood splintered. The dresser edged forward. The beast outside snarled and growled. Trevor made a frantic scan of the room. The window seemed his best hope. He ran to the curtains and threw them aside.

And stared into a blank wall of cinderblock. It was almost as if they'd set a...

"Is he in there, boy?" asked the man's gleeful voice. "Which one is it?"

"Oh, I do hope it's the one in the plumber truck," cooed the woman.

That's me!

"Who are you people?" he shouted. "What do you want?"

Laughter from the other side of the door.

The snarling monster howled and hit the door hard, sending the dresser across the floor and leaving Trevor face to face with the monster.

It was the boy. He crouched like a feral beast and growled as his glistening eyes locked with Trevor's. Behind him stood his family, his father's jaunty look now a mask of crazed mania. His mother wore the same chilly serene smile. His sister wore neither, but a look of intense disdain. Behind them, Granny showed a gap-toothed grin and cackled.

"Sic 'em," said the father.

Trevor didn't have time to raise his hands before the boy leaped and drove him to the ground, his knees planted in Trevor's chest. When he hit, he felt his sternum pop. The boy's face was only an inch away from his own. His breath smelled like ice-cream.

Then the boy raised one meaty paw and drove it down hard against Trevor's temple, and the room went dark.

He woke up cold and wet. His head throbbed. There were voices. He opened his eyes, but all he saw were the dark joists in the ceiling above him. He tried to sit up, but could not. His arms and legs were tied down to a large table. And he was naked.

"You win, my love," said the man's voice behind him. "It was the one in the plumber truck. I was sure it would be the electrician."

"You should always listen to me, darling," she said. Something about the way she said it made his insides crawl.

"Doesn't matter," said a new voice, cracked and old. He bet it was Granny. "Long as his hand's good. Did anyone bother to look at it?"

"Not yet," said the man. "Patience, Mother."

Metal and wood squeaked as the table lurched until he lay at an angle and could see the rest of the room. It was a basement, like he figured, but the walls were covered in foam egg-crate, the windows in heavy velvet cloth. Sound-proof. The children sat in front of him. The boy no longer resembled a rabid dog, but sat stone-faced on a wooden bench next to his sister, who may as well have been made of wax.

Their mother came from behind him, still in the long black dress she always wore.

"Please," he croaked. "Let me go. I won't tell anyone. I swear. I'll never steal again."

"That's a fact!" said her husband as he joined his wife. He wore an apron that said *Kiss the Cook* over his dress shirt and tie. "Sorry, old man, no can do. We've got plans for you!"

"Don't talk to it," spit the old woman as she shuffled into view. "You know how they get."

"There's no reason to be impolite, Grandmama," said his wife. The old woman grunted as she grabbed the head of the table and turned him to face the opposite wall. In front of him, a large iron pot sat on a raging hearth. The lid clanked and bumped as its contents boiled. The heat warmed him for a few seconds, then sweat beaded on his skin.

"Oh shit...no...Don't...You're going to eat me?!"

"Language," chided the woman in black. "Of course not. We're not cannibals. Well, not all of us anyway."

"Speak for yourself," chuffed the older woman. "He looks damned tasty."

"What're you going to do with me?"

"Good question!" shouted the man. "A smart man always asks good questions, and I think I'm right in thinking you are a smart man! Tell me, smart man. Have you ever heard of a hand of glory?"

Trevor shook his head.

"The hand of an unrepentant thief," came a small voice from behind him, the daughter. "Severed just above the wrist, dipped in tallow made from the boiled fat of other thieves. His hair is used to make wicks on each finger. It opens locks and doors."

"Excelent!" beamed the man. "Isn't she a doll? Smart as a whip, that one."

"You're fucking kidding! You can't be serious! Please! Don't take my hands!"

"Just one," said his wife. "And watch your language in front of my children."

"You're crazy!" he shouted. "You're all psycho! You can't do this! Help! Help!"

"Now, now," said the man. "You broke into our house, didn't you? You went through our private things. How many other houses have you broken into? Tell me, when you saw that big pile of gold in the master bedroom, did you feel bad? Or did you feel like you'd finally struck it rich?"

Trevor couldn't think of what to say. He was certain they wouldn't believe him if he lied. The truth damned him. Hell, he was damned anyway. His hot cheeks stung as tears rolled down them.

"Told you not to talk to it," said the old woman. "I hate hearing them snivel like that. Boy!"

He heard the boy's heavy frame stand behind him.

"Time to get started."

Metal scraped against stone as the boy's heavy footsteps approached. When he came into view, Trevor saw a large two-handed cleaver. The boy's piggish eyes twinkled as he smiled and hefted the blade. The little girl wrapped a chord around his left arm just below the elbow and pulled it tight, then took another and tied it around the wrist.

"I imagine this'll hurt," beamed the man.

"Not really," said the little girl, her voice an eerie monotone. "The trauma will deaden the nerves, and it won't start to hurt until you start to bleed out."

"Smart as a whip!" beamed her father.

"Please," he begged the child. "Please help me. Don't do this. I'm so sorry..."

"Did you go into my room?"

"Wha..?"

"No one goes into my room."

The cleaver fell and Trevor screamed. Not from pain, though, the little girl was right about that, but the sight of his ruined arm, the spastic twitch of his fingers as the little girl held it aloft like a trophy, was too much for him.

"Bravo, my boy!" said the father as he clapped his son on the back.

"Your turn, my dear," said the mother.

The little girl carried the twitching hand to the pot as the old woman removed the lid.

"Dip it in," said the old woman. "Say the words."

"Hand of thief," said the girl in her strange, awful monotone. "Open locks and doors. Slip like shadows between the cracks. Light our way to glory."

"Don't forget the wicks!" chimed the father in a sing-song voice.

Trevor winced as his wife's hand clamped under his chin and cold steel pressed against his scalp.

"Scissors do a ragged job," she purred. "The old ways are best, if messy."

She scraped upward. Trevor yelped as the straight-razor blade bit

---

into his scalp. Moments later, he was effectively bald. His scalp hung in ragged chunks off his skull.

"Please," he sobbed. His voice cracked through his dry throat. The fire felt more like it cooked than warmed him.

"Yes?" said the man. His eyes bulged as he leaned down close to hear Trevor's whisper.

"Call the police," he cried. "Let them lock me up. Just don't let me die."

"Sorry, old man," he said. "We went though a lot of thieves to find you. They all had tragic reasons to steal like starving families or desperation, some such thing. But you..." He slapped Trevor on the shoulder. "You steal because you enjoy it! You're good at it, and it's just what you do! Unrepentant to the bone, aren't you?"

It wasn't supposed to end like this. He was supposed to get caught, maybe, but end up back in jail, or shot by some NRA homeowner. Not this. Not used in some bizarre ritual and slowly bled to death.

"Tell me something," said the man, his maniacal grin widening. "Why us? What made you pick our house?"

"Looked rich," he croaked. He couldn't feel the fire anymore. He shivered against cold that built from inside him. "Thought you wouldn't be back."

"You were right!" he shouted to his wife. "As always!"

"Of course I was," she said.

The child drew the thing that used to be his hand out of the pot. Beneath the tallow, it looked shriveled, almost claw-like. So strange, he thought, that it once was attached to his arm, the arm he could no longer feel.

"Wicks," said the girl.

The piggish boy brought Trevor's hair, now rolled in tiny bundles, to his sister, and she pressed them into place atop each finger.

"Your plan worked perfectly, my darling," said the man as he drew

---

his wife close to. They kissed as the old woman by the fire cackled, and the little girl hung what used to be his hand up to dry.